Dead Men Don't Decorate

Also available by Cordy Abbott
writing as Lane Stone

Tiara Investigations Mysteries

Domestic Affairs
Current Affairs

Pet Palace Mysteries

Changing of the Guard Dog
Support Your Local Pug
Stay Calm and Collie On

Dead Men Don't Decorate

AN OLD TOWN ANTIQUE MYSTERY

Cordy Abbott

NEW YORK

Copyright © 2022 by Lane Stone

Published in the United States by Crooked Lane Books, an imprint of The Quick Brown Fox & Company LLC.

Crooked Lane Books and its logo are trademarks of The Quick Brown Fox & Company LLC.

Library of Congress Catalog-in-Publication data available upon request.

ISBN (hardcover): 978-1-63910-125-2
ISBN (ebook): 978-1-63910-126-9

Cover design by Rob Fiore

Printed in the United States.

www.crookedlanebooks.com

Crooked Lane Books
34 West 27th St., 10th Floor
New York, NY 10001

First Edition: November 2022

10 9 8 7 6 5 4 3 2 1

This book is dedicated to Alexandria, Virginia, USA, and all who sail in her. Especially, *Camille* and *Paul.* You know who you are.

Chapter One

"*Extra* virgin? Would you please explain that to me?" I returned the bottle of olive oil to the pantry. My kitchen and family room looked like a war zone. Lipstick-smudged glasses, crumpled napkins, and mostly empty plates covered every surface.

Opal Wells, my wing woman, was my last remaining guest. "All I know is I'm not one," she answered with a laugh, flashing her dimples as she reached over for a toast with her wineglass. "Camille, your glass is empty. Chardonnay?" She was already turning to the fridge. "That was some luncheon! I thought I knew everyone in Marthasville, but I guess I was wrong. Thank goodness most of those people can walk or roll home."

I laughed. "That's another advantage to living in north Marthasville. Almost anyplace you need to be is in walking distance. Do you think any of them will go to work now?"

"If they even remember it's Wednesday, some of them might try. Too bad your son couldn't be here to celebrate his own election. I was hoping to congratulate him in person. I still can't believe he's going to be our next mayor."

"I didn't really expect him to come today. He needed to thank his big-ticket donors. This party was for everyone who got *me* through these last few months. Like you!"

"My pleasure."

I picked up my phone and swiped the screen. "Is David coming to get you?"

"He'll be here soon, but he can wait." She swatted the air. Her husband was as long-suffering as he was good-natured. "So can cleaning up. My housework *always* waits."

I found the perfect song for the occasion on my music app. "Nope, it's *urgent*!" I tapped my phone, and Foreigner belted out the lyrics. We raced around the room picking up the dirty dishes, singing at the top of our lungs like we were teenagers in the eighties again. "When Doves Cry" came next on my playlist, which we pantomimed and sang while we loaded the dishwasher.

Suddenly Opal froze, looking at something over my shoulder. "Uh-oh."

I turned to see my son, Paul, at the kitchen door. He had his hands behind his back and a judgmental look on his face. He raised an eyebrow at my untouched wineglass. "How many of those have you had?"

"No idea." Why had I, one of the few sober people at the party, said that? Maybe because I had been the old me for the length of those two songs, and I wanted to keep that up. It felt good. Now I was back to the literal *old* me.

He grinned and pulled his arms from behind his back, inch by inch. "These are for you!" He handed me two dozen roses, half yellow and the rest white, dotted with baby's breath and greenery.

I hugged him. "Aww, thank you. They're beautiful."

"Just like you," he said, as any good son would. "You worked as hard as I did on the mayoral campaign, and this is to thank you. I wanted you to know that I did notice all you did."

"It was my pleasure!" He had no idea how true that was. It was *too* true. I had enjoyed every single day of it, more than I had anything in years.

I stood the bouquet up in the corner sink I used for food prep and flower arranging, then reached for a vase from an overhead cabinet.

"Mom, be careful. Are you sure you can reach that? Can I help?"

I placed the crystal vase, inherited from my maternal grandparents, on the butcher-block countertop. Because of the sterling silver base, it *was* heavy, but I didn't let on. I quickly filled the vase with warm water, arranged the flowers, and turned back to the conversation.

Opal patted Paul's back. "I remember the day you were born, and now here you are, mayor of Marthasville! I am so proud of you!"

She and I had been friends for all but the first five of our fifty-five years, so I got her meaning as clearly as if there had been a bubble over her head written for my son: *If you're going to let us know how feeble you think we are, I'm going to show you how green we think you are.*

"Well, I still have to be sworn in. Thanks to people like Mom and you, I was elected mayor of Marthasville's fifteen square miles and eleven neighborhoods. I want to do a good job for every part of the city." Paul was truly handsome, even if I did say so myself. His dark-brown hair had a habit of falling in his eyes in the cutest way. And he kept himself in great shape by running.

My doorbell chirped. "Who can that be?"

"I'll get it," Opal offered, running a hand through her short, brown hair.

She was back in seconds with David. "My ride's here." David Wells taught American literature at Marthasville High School. He had a PhD in American lit, and his area of specialization was nautical literature. Two of his books on the subgenre were used as college textbooks, but he chose to teach at the high school level.

The two men shook hands, and he congratulated my son.

Paul kissed my cheek. "Gotta run. I want to personally thank as many people today as I can. Tomorrow I'll be back in my nine-to-five job."

I thanked him again for the flowers and walked him to the townhouse door. "When does Common Good start?"

"In about a week and a half, the weekend before Thanksgiving." In every election year, the last two weeks of November were known as Common Good for the Commonwealth. Every single candidate who had run for office worked with all the others on civic projects. Election losers went out with a positive image and good publicity, and the winners started their terms with goodwill and unity. Businesses used the two weeks of celebrations to kick-start the holiday season. Events were held throughout the commonwealth. Virginia and three other states were commonwealths, a term interchangeable today with the word *state*.

When I came back to the kitchen, David was helping Opal with her coat.

She looked at me. "I have to work later, but I am definitely going to need a nap, since we stayed up so late last night. Are you okay?"

I nodded. "Do you have a moonlight monument cruise?"

Opal was the only woman cruise boat captain on the Potomac River. The job was made for her. Her twenty-year career in the Coast Guard, plus her innate intelligence, qualified her for the position, and her charisma and confidence endeared her to passengers on the *Admiral Joshua Barry*, a double-decker boat that could hold up to fifty guests.

She shook her head. "Those start Thanksgiving week. This afternoon I have a canine cruise. Your guys love those. Too bad they're boarded." She lowered her voice. "You sure you're okay? And I don't mean this mess." She motioned to the stacked dishes.

David took the hint and ambled off to the door.

I took Opal's arm, and we shuffled behind him. "I keep thinking, what do I *do* now? I mean, now that the election is over? What do I do with the rest of my life? Do you ever find yourself thinking about that?" She was my best friend, and the only person I could ask such a personal question.

"I'm good. I love what I do. And as for you, when the next semester begins, you'll go back to teaching art history at NOVA."

Northern Virginia Community College, one of the largest in the country, had been my employer for what seemed like the last hundred years, though it was probably less.

"That's just it. I don't know if I can make myself go back. It was beginning to seem like a life sentence."

"You need some rest." She patted my arm. "Before I go, I'll tell you a compliment someone paid you. I think it'll cheer you up. You know the couple that owns Olde Town School for Dogs?"

"The Mejiases? Of course."

"They asked me who your decorator was. I told them you did all this yourself and that some of your furniture was from your parents' antique store, but you added just the right number of contemporary pieces. They were quite impressed."

"I've bored all of you for years with my strong opinions on houses with too many antiques lined up around the walls, and now you're preaching that theory too. Good girl."

David cleared his throat. Only a little obvious.

"Hold your horses," Opal said to her husband playfully. He opened the door for her and she walked out, only to turn on her heel and come back in. "And speaking of your parents' store, I have some news on that front too. Waited4You might be up for sale."

"My parents' old store?" My heart pounded so hard I imagined it showed through my sweater. They had owned the antique store on King Street until my dad's death. "Did that old, cantankerous guy die? Because that's the only way Marthasville's going to get rid of Roberto Fratelli."

"No, but he wants to retire and move someplace." Her laugh was a tiny bit off.

"Why are you telling me this?"

"Hmm, no reason."

Right.

After they left, I fiddled with the flowers and smiled at Paul's thoughtfulness. Roses drank a lot of water through their stems and warmer water was better, even though the higher temp made the blooms open up faster and shortened their life. How boring. There had to be more to life than this.

* * *

The first phone call came in at three o'clock. "Camille, is it true you might buy Waited4You?" Deb Burfoot, owner of the children's clothing consignment shop on South Royal Street, wanted to know.

I was at the Princess Street Paw Palace, paying the bill Stickley and Morris, my two standard schnauzers, had run up during their overnight stay. The attendant on duty had just explained to me that when she'd asked the guys if they wanted to go swimming last night, they had both answered in the affirmative. Right.

Whoa, had I heard Deb right? "Huh? No!"

Water lapped against a boat and happy dogs barked in the background.

I didn't ask her where she had heard that rumor, since I could guess the answer. "Are you on the canine cruise?"

"Yeah, can't you tell? Wait." I held on as someone else on the boat spoke to her. "The Margalits are here with Lucky." He was their Yorkshire terrier. "They're thrilled. I'm giving Noah my phone."

Noah and Helen owned Margalit Gallery and Framing, just two doors up from Waited4You. They were both in their eighties and had been friends of my parents.

"You should have done this years ago! It's in your blood," Noah said, on speakerphone.

"And we wouldn't have to worry all the time about one of those incidents happening again," Helen said.

"What kind of incident?" I asked.

Noah faltered. "It's nothing. Just talk."

Was there a single local merchant Roberto Fratelli hadn't offended at one time or another? He charmed his clients, or at least enough of them, but was oddly ill-mannered toward his neighbors and anyone not in the market for an antique. Shocking stories of his rudeness regularly made the rounds, and this, I was sure, was just another example. Such as when two Marthasville High students had gone in to apply for jobs in the stock room or maybe making deliveries during the summer and Roberto had yelled at them in the store and followed them out to the sidewalk, shaking his fist. "What are you saying? Do I look like I need help? I don't need help! You need help!"

"Your parents would be so very proud!" Noah said.

Then Deb was back on the line. "Camille, please save us from that man!"

"What do I know about running a business?" The question was to myself as well as to Deb, a successful small business owner.

"How hard would running a tiny little shop like that be?" she asked. I hadn't been inside Waited4You since we'd sold it, but I didn't think of it as small. "You would do fine. All the other small businesses would benefit if we didn't have to worry about him offending tourists."

Marthasville was considered a suburb of Washington, DC, and many visitors added our town to their itinerary, but in the last few years it had become a destination of its own. The seaport town had been founded in 1749. It was a modern city steeped in history.

"Dad's been gone for ten years and Mom five. Everything's different from when they had their gallery." I walked the dogs out of the pet spa and along the sidewalk. As I waited for the light at the intersection of North Washington and Princess to change, I thought back to my mother's smile as she glided across the sales floor to talk to a customer. Her graciousness created an ambience that was irresistible. A piece of antique furniture actually looked better when she stood next to it.

"Promise us you'll think about it," Deb pleaded.

"Okay, I promise to think about it. Tell Opal I said hi."

Promise? I had thought about little else since the luncheon. I thought about the financial risk. Then about how much I dreaded going back to the classroom in January. How could I make a profit knowing so little about trends and prices? There would definitely be a learning curve.

Four round brown eyes stared up at me. The dogs looked at each other and then back to me. They wanted to know why we were still standing in the same spot. All I had to do was turn right, and we'd head home. Except I turned left.

Chapter Two

The dogs and I walked to King Street and turned to head east. Waited4You sat midway down the hill. I had dressed in layers, but we were getting closer to the Potomac River waterfront, and the November late-afternoon air was nippy.

Storefront signage along King Street was minimal and functional. Drivers and walkers could easily read the white wooden rectangles, since they were suspended over the sidewalk from rod-iron brackets and a post. Each had the same dimensions and was raised to the same height, but they weren't required to match otherwise. Subsequent owners had kept the wooden board, bordered in copper, and glossy black lettering my parents had chosen for Waited4You.

I peered in the storefront window, trying to seem casual. Why hadn't I crossed to the other side of the street? Then I could have looked at the shop in a nonloitering kind of way. I toyed with the dogs' leashes and then checked the watch I wasn't even wearing, doing anything to stay there until I answered the question going around and around in my head. Could I see myself there? The wooden door had been painted boring brown at some point by someone, then left to fade. I shut my eyes and envisioned it once again painted glossy forest green. It was closed and its four windows were dark rectangles. I imagined it propped open, with a topiary on each side and a special water bowl for dogs. I went back to looking in the window. What if the store was light filled and bright? Between the large storefront display window and those in the door, there was no shortage of natural light. Maybe there could be classical music or jazz playing? The location was prime, halfway between city hall and the Torpedo Factory Art Center on the Potomac. "Yeesss," I said out loud. I *could* see myself there!

I pushed my oversized sunglasses onto my head and took a good look at my reflection in the glass. I was dressed in winter white from my sweater and wool coat to my wide-leg wool pants and suede boots. Then I looked at my face. I wasn't happy—hadn't been in a while—but I thought as long as I didn't admit it, I could snap out of it. I hadn't been able to shake the feeling I was less alive every day. And then the campaign had come along and energized me in a way I hadn't felt in so long. Yes! Waited4You, the antique store that had been like home for me growing up, could be a future for me that I would look forward to and not dread.

Suddenly, I saw a man staring at my face from over my shoulder. *He could be my future?*

"Can I help you?" he asked.

Startled, I jumped back, before I realized the image was his reflection in the glass and slammed into him. The back of my head hit his chest. He took my shoulders in both his hands and steadied me.

"I'm so sorry!" I said.

He shook his head, like he wanted nothing to do with my apology.

"The heels of my boots were definitely on your toes, yet not a single curse word was heard. I'm impressed."

"Can I help you?" He still hadn't cracked a smile.

When he didn't laugh at my joke, I involuntarily lowered my gaze for a second. Then I looked back at him. "You're standing on my dog's leash, so other than moving, nope. I'm good."

"Oh!" He looked at his feet and picked up the one on Morris's leash, stammering, "Sorry about the little . . . uh, guy?"

I nodded at that and walked away.

He caught up with me next door in front of Suits to a Tea!, a café famous for their sweet potato flan.

"I'm sorry, I wanted to introduce myself. I'm Brennan Adler."

"Thanks. It's good to meet you."

"I own the building Waited4You is in." I was five ten and he had to be over six feet, about Paul's height.

With what I knew of Roberto Fratelli, I wasn't sure if he was bragging or complaining. Maybe this humorless man and his cranky tenant deserved one another. "My condolences."

"The old guy isn't so bad once you get to know him."

"Really?" I was skeptical.

Finally, he laughed. "Just kidding. He's actually worse."

We began walking together, according to some unspoken plan. With one smooth step behind me, he was on the curb side of the brick sidewalk. Something inside me thawed at this all-but-forgotten gesture of chivalry.

After the first block, he asked, "So, are you really considering buying the business from him?"

I jerked to a stop, startling the dogs. "Where did you hear that?"

"I was out of cigars and my tobacconist told me. His wife took their dog on some boat trip, and people were talking about it. A cruise for dogs. Can you believe it?"

"Mmm." I pulled Stickley's and Morris's leashes tighter and stopped to let a young man with a big mixed-breed dog walk past us. The dogs would have loved a flash playdate, but I was enjoying my own conversation. "It's a big decision, especially since I've never owned a business, and I only learned it was for sale today."

"I just wanted you to know I'd be happy to let him out of his lease and transfer it to you."

"Your tenant is known as the meanest man in Marthasville. How do I know you're not just trying to get rid of him?"

"I have no idea what you're talking about," he said. He looked all around and pretended to be absolutely baffled.

"Don't play dumb with me. I'm as dumb as they come and I'll see right through it."

He laughed so loud that the dogs stepped behind my legs for shelter. "Ah, you found me out." He was still grinning. "Honestly, I have thick skin and I've gotten used to him. And since I rarely run into him, I'm not on the receiving end of his eruptions."

Brennan Adler, Stickley, Morris, and I walked on again. On the next block we passed the Claw Foot Tub, a home goods store, and King Street Souvenirs. Both had been there for decades, but for some reason I felt like I was seeing them for the first time.

Whenever I could, I stole a look at Brennan's face. All I could see was his profile, but that was enough. When he smiled, he was dangerously handsome, but when he wasn't smiling, he just looked dangerous. I guessed he was in his sixties, but even with his wavy silver hair, he had the vigor of a man half that.

Finally, I said, "I would need an attorney."

"I'm an attorney, but that'd be a conflict of interest."

"Who is his commercial sales agent?"

"He's doing it himself."

I rolled my eyes. "How many did he go through?"

Brennan laughed again. "Two that I know of."

I would definitely use an attorney. That is, *if* I bought it.

"I think he hopes to sell quickly. Once he decided to retire, he was ready to move on."

"I can't imagine living anywhere but Marthasville," I said. "Where's he moving to?"

"He didn't say. He never has offered much personal information. I moved here from Richmond a year ago after I inherited the building, and I have to say, I feel the same way about the town as you." He looked at people milling around the shops and restaurants.

"Roberto has owned that antique store for at least five years. It's a shame he never put down roots," I said. Since it was November, the sun was already setting, backlighting us as we headed east.

"He has only himself to blame for that," Brennan said.

We had walked to the end of King Street. I pointed up North Union. "I'm going this way."

We shook hands through our gloves and laughed, though I wasn't sure what was funny.

"I hope I haven't scared you off," he said. "It would be a fairly simple transaction. You'd buy his inventory and fixtures, and you'd take over his lease."

I knew better. What if Roberto's affairs weren't aboveboard? What if there were liens or unpaid taxes? And then there was so much involved in the running of a business. The gallery had been like a third parent to me, always there in the background. I'd seen firsthand how hard small business owners worked to make a profit. There would be insurance, retaining or hiring employees, sales tax, and who knew what else. What about incorporation? How did that work?

The dogs and I walked away from Brennan, but after less than half a block, I peeled off one glove and took my phone out of my pocket to call my favorite attorney.

"Paul, it's Mom. I'm going to buy a business, and I need an attorney."

Barring any bad surprises, I was going to buy Waited4You.

Chapter Three

Saturday

I was dressed for another day of hard physical work inventorying the store, but also ready in case I needed to introduce myself to customers. I wore black jeans, a black sweater with a scarf around my neck, and ballet flats. By late morning I knew I'd worried needlessly about being too dressed down to greet customers. There were none in the store—still. Opal was there to help me and give me emotional support.

Roberto came out to the sales floor from time to time, only to scowl at us and then the front door, which I had propped open without asking. Since the store wasn't mine yet, that was a bold move, but I craved fresh air when he was around.

During one appearance I asked what he had told his employees about the transfer of ownership. I didn't know how many people I would need, but the current employees would be considered first. So far Roberto was the only staff I'd seen.

"No one to tell," he barked.

"No sales help?" I asked.

Behind him Opal shook her head side to side. She mouthed, *Stop*. How could this be an off-limits topic?

"No!" he barked.

"No assistant manager?"

Opal held up two stop-sign hands, an exaggerated pleading look on her face.

"No!"

"You were in the store all the time?" I asked.

Opal made a last-ditch effort to get me to stop before Roberto went off on me. She clasped her hands in prayer. *Pleeeease*, she mouthed.

"If I'm here, the store is open. If I'm not, it's closed. Simple. You! You hire a hundred people if you want. Here, I'll help!" he yelled. He went to the door and stepped out to the sidewalk. "Anybody want a job?" he yelled in one direction. "She's hiring a hundred people." Then in the other direction, "Come on in."

I pulled him inside, apologized to people walking by and staring wide-eyed, and closed the door. He glared at me before he stomped back to the stock room.

"Whew," I said. "That was fun."

Opal came close enough to whisper. "He's crazy. We'll finish, and he'll be gone."

*   *   *

Each time I looked at the sales floor, I saw what it could be. And would be. Lighter, brighter, and if not modern, then with more of the ambience of the past, an homage to the merchandise.

I had so many ideas, but I didn't want to talk about them in front of Roberto. Not after that performance. For instance, the sales floor was one main room flanked by two alcoves, and I planned to use one side niche as an interior design center, where I would give free consultations to help clients find the right antique, or antiques, for their home.

"Opal, thanks again for giving up your Saturday to help me. You're the best."

She shrugged off my thanks. "One plant stand." She tapped the item into the computer tablet she was holding, using an app that allowed us to collaborate on Waited4You's inventory using different devices. Later, I would correct her latest entry to read *jardiniere*.

I tried to make conversation with Roberto again later in the day, complimenting him on the copper-colored, oval stickers with an embossed *W4Y*. They'd been placed discreetly on each item, not at all taking away from the beauty of any of the pieces. Price tag strings dangled from some of them. The font was charming. This was a change he'd made that I liked. He looked at me, and for a split second I thought he was going to soften, but he grunted and walked away.

Paul and I had spent Thursday with my new accountant, speaking their language. I'd learned that intangible assets, like the business's reputation and customer lists, were called goodwill. When I requested quotes for insurance, I was pleasantly surprised to find myself reeling off terms like general liability insurance, professional liability insurance, property insurance, and casualty insurance plus workers' compensation. I felt my father's love all around me any time I remembered these bits of information I'd grown up half hearing. *Thank you.*

I knew what due diligence was, and because of who I was buying Waited4You from, I inventoried every item in the store. This was my world. It wasn't the world of attorneys, brokers, or bookkeepers. I enlisted Opal, and we worked all day Friday. Now, on our second day of inventory taking, we were close to having the information I needed to determine a fair price to offer Roberto. She listed the furniture, leather-bound books, and accessories, and I examined every tabletop, cushion, and knob.

"I really do appreciate this," I said to Opal.

"Are you kidding? Think of all the times you've crewed, cleaned, and helped me with reservations."

I ran my hand over the top of a Victorian side table. "Hmm." The square of marble was surrounded by burr walnut. It was tasteful and sturdy, but something about the piece wasn't quite right. I opened the delicate drawer and looked inside, then I pulled it all the way out to see the dovetail joints.

"Mid-nineteenth century," Roberto said. He stood behind me. Actually, he slumped behind me with rounded shoulders and his head thrust forward.

"It's lovely." I replaced the drawer, picked up the computer tablet I was using, and moved on to the next item.

"What's that supposed to mean?" My tone had not been lost on him. I tried to hide my skepticism because I didn't want another explosion.

I smiled and walked away.

"No! What did you mean by that?" If he was going to insist I answer, then that's what I would do.

Before I did, though, I looked around to be sure a customer hadn't come in. We'd had a whopping two customers, and I'd made it a point to introduce myself to each and get their names and contact information for an email list. Now the store was empty except for the three of us.

I took the drawer under the tabletop out again and pointed to the interlocking wood pieces in the corners. "It's the tails and pins. They're too perfect to be handmade. They appear machine-made. Like they were cut with a router." I took a deep breath and pointed at the signage, which took his side of the argument, and the font suddenly looked like it had been chosen to deceive. "I doubt this was made in the mid-nineteenth century." I waited to see what I had unleashed.

"What? That's here on consignment! The dealer misrepresented it to me!"

*　*　*

"The *Casablanca* defense! I guess some antique sellers still use that one." I raised my wineglass to Opal and Paul. Roberto wasn't the first irreputable antiques seller to plead ignorance and indignation, like in my favorite classic movie, nor would he be the last.

Opal laughed and grabbed her side. "Shocked! He was shocked!"

After our grueling day at what was now *my* antiques gallery, we were celebrating making it to Saturday night. We polished off a well-earned dinner in Vicissitudes' upstairs dining room overlooking King Street, and then we moved to the bar.

Paul grinned from ear to ear and addressed the line of patrons. "To the new owner of Waited4You!" We clinked glasses. The contract had been signed and funds transferred that afternoon, and now it was time to celebrate.

"I have so much work ahead of me to be ready for the holiday season," I said. "Please tell me I'll have lots of customers!"

Opal laughed. "I can think of one you won't have."

"The man with the puppy?" I asked.

"Ha! No way he's coming back!"

She summarized the story for Paul. In the late afternoon, a young man, who looked like a former football player, had come in holding a collie puppy. When he put the dog down on the floor to take a book from the rare-books shelf, the pup took off and ran into the stock room at top puppy speed. We heard Roberto explode in rage. He ran out in hot pursuit of the terrified fluff ball. I guarded the open door so he couldn't run out onto King Street, and his owner kneeled and called to him. The dog skidded to a stop, like in a cartoon. He ran to the voice and jumped up into the man's arms.

"What was it Roberto yelled?" I asked, over the growing volume of talk and laughter at the bar. "Oh, now I remember. It was something like, 'What are you looking for?' What was that about? He thought the puppy was a shoplifter?"

Paul laughed. "Or involved in corporate espionage?"

"I don't blame the customer for getting mad at him. He didn't have to yell at the puppy!"

Opal shook her head at the memory and took a drink of her wine. "It took both of us to calm the man down. He held the dog in one arm and reached for Roberto's scrawny neck with the other." Opal imitated how the man had done that. As she and I had talked the guy down, I'd patted his arm and felt a rock-hard bicep.

"Did Roberto appreciate us saving his life?" I asked, though everyone knew the answer to that.

"Hell no!" Opal yelled, lifting her drink above her head. "That question is about as funny as when you asked if he had a list of customer email addresses that he would leave with you. Hardy-har-har."

"Or when I asked if he sent out a newsletter!" I turned to Paul. "He said, 'People don't need to know my news. It's none of their business.'"

"Is he paranoid? Is that his problem?"

I shrugged. "Who knows?"

"And with the way he acts, who cares?" Opal added.

"Mom, with no customer list, sounds like you're starting from scratch. Are you sure this was wise?"

I thought I had shielded myself from any negativity from my supercautious son, but those words got through. Maybe because he had named my worst fear and put it out there in the atmosphere. I'd sunk a good bit of my savings into buying Waited4You. Could I make a go of it? I didn't know, but I didn't want to wonder *what if?* for the rest of my life.

"I'm not really starting with nothing. I have his sales records, and I can add those names to my own contacts. And I have ideas for increasing walk-ins. There's a lot of foot traffic because of the location. I want to change the mix of furniture and accessories to get tourists to come in. If I can do that in time for the holidays, I'll be fine."

My son was about the kindest man I knew. One morning at Starbucks, some random guy had walked in, picked up someone's food order from the counter, and walked out with it. The man who had paid for the meal was shocked speechless. Paul handed the barista some money to pay for the food and walked out. Low-key. Not wanting to call attention to the generous act or get credit for it. That was him. I just wished he had a girlfriend to worry over instead of me. That was what we both deserved.

"Mr. Mayor?" The bartender leaned closer to get my son's attention. "The next round is on that gentleman." He pointed to the far end of the bar, and we craned our necks to see Brennan Adler, his martini glass raised to us. His cheeks were flushed, I guessed from the winter air.

"He has the best eyebrows," Opal whispered over my shoulder. "Seriously." Then she waved to him. "Come on over here. Join us!"

Paul turned and mouthed, *Cut her off.*

"Too late," was my response.

"Camille, why was a leather case taped to the bottom of a chair?" Opal tilted her head as if to say *I'm all ears* and waited for my answer.

"What case? What chair?"

Brennan was making his way to us, but the bar was packed with Saturday night partyers, so it was slow going.

"Didn't I tell you? When I moved a chair out of the way, I felt something under the seat"—what Opal actually said was more like *the sheat*—"so I looked."

"Which chair? Where was it?"

"It was against the left wall, just past the uh . . . uh . . ." She drew a half circle on the bar with her finger.

"Alcove?"

"Yeah, that's the word."

"It was probably the paperwork with a description of the piece. You know, it's country of origin, whatever," I explained.

"I don't think so. Looked like it'd been around a long time, really old, and it schmelled like really old leather." She covered her mouth and laughed. "Have you ever met a man that didn't like duct tape?"

"A leather case? What was in it?" I asked, hoping she would tell me before my handsome new landlord got there. She hadn't heard me and I wanted to let it go until later, but the fact that it had been hidden concerned me. "Opal, what was in it?" I asked, louder this time.

"A letter. The tape was in the middle, not over the top, so I could open it. I think it was a love letter in there. Ahhh." She put her hand on her heart and feigned a romantic swoon. "It looked brittle and fragile. It was in plastic, inside the, uh, the leather thingie." She made a motion like she was opening something. A box? A folio? A document bag? I couldn't say. "I didn't open the plastic inside thing. Promise." Here she straightened and gave the Girl Scout salute. "It was addressed to someone named George, in seventeen something."

Brennan was almost to us.

"It was dated 2017?"

"No, silly. Like seventeen fifty-something. I couldn't read it all."

A letter from the mid-eighteenth century? I could hardly breathe. "Opal, you should have told me."

She straightened the lapel of my tapestry jacket. "So glad you wore this tonight. Now talk to him. Remember, bring your A game." She giggled again.

Paul and Brennan shook hands and started a conversation. The amount I'd paid Roberto for the business was fair, or so I'd thought, but if Opal was right and there was a letter from over two centuries ago, was it? Could she be right? I needed to see it for myself. There was nothing to be done about it until Monday morning. Tonight I would enjoy myself.

"Welcome to King Street Merchants!" Brennan had a beautiful smile. Not scary white or aggressive, which always made me think of dentures—just nice to look at.

"Thank you!" I finally remembered my manners.

Opal pulled my sleeve to get my attention. I turned my back to him and faced her in case she wanted to talk about the love letter, or duct tape, or eyebrows. "I'll show you," she said.

"I'll look at it on Monday," I whispered.

"No, let's go look for it now."

"Are you kidding? It's almost midnight." I turned back to Brennan.

He was gone.

"I think she needs to call it a night." Paul looked at his watch. "I know I do. Want a ride?"

"Thanks, but we'll Uber," I said.

He hugged us both and paid the check. Opal and I stood there watching until he left, though with all the talk and laughter going on around us, there was no way he could hear us after he was as much as a foot away.

"I won't sleep until I see that latter," I admitted. Going to Waited4You in the middle of the night was a crazy idea. Maybe Opal wasn't the only person who had celebrated a little too much.

"You have the keys, and we're practically across the street," she reminded me.

"Let's wait until we're sure he's driven away." I motioned to Paul's back.

"Shhh." She put a forefinger to her lips and snickered.

We retrieved our coats from the coat check and went outside. The cold air, plus Opal walking into the street, cleared up my thinking fast, and I ran to catch up with her and took her arm. "Let's cross at the light."

"Better idea—let's jaywalk." She crossed King Street, and I let myself be swept along with her.

The handful of keys to the building were still in my handbag, and I took out one and unlocked the door to Waited4You. "This is the first time I've let myself in." The thought made me smile with pride and faith in my future. I couldn't wait to get started.

Opal swept an arm in a wide arc. "Just think, this is all yours." Her voice was already clearer.

"Even that?" I pointed to the body on the floor.

Chapter Four

Ve took halting, uncertain steps, with a *step, step together, step* cadence, like two of the world's worst bridesmaids ever.

"Opal, call 911."

"Maybe it's a rug. I'll turn on a light," she whispered. The glow from the streetlamp was bright enough for us to see the body and not trip over furniture but not much more than that.

"No, don't touch anything. Don't you watch TV? How can you not know that?" She hadn't made a move to call the police. "I'll call the police if you don't want to."

"I'll do it." She let go of my arm and rummaged in her handbag. "Maybe he's asleep."

"I don't think so." My eyes had adjusted to the semidarkness, and I looked at the body again. I couldn't see his face, since he was turned to the back of the store, but I could still tell who it was. "It's Roberto Fratelli."

He lay on his side, and his legs were tangled together. Behind me, Opal told the 911 operator who we were and where we were. "There's someone lying on the floor." She listened. "Just a sec. Camille, she wants to know if we need an ambulance. Is that what we need if the person is, well, you know, dead?" She motioned to Fratelli to avoid any confusion at all on who she was referring to.

"We don't know for sure that he's dead. Say yes to the ambulance in case he's just unconscious."

She took my arm, and we inched closer. We walked around him and leaned over to see him better. We looked at each other and shook our heads.

"He's so dead," I whispered. He was too still to be otherwise. What was that smell? Rust?

"Could you just send everything you've got?" That seemed like the best idea.

After she hung up, I asked, "What was he doing here? He gave me all the keys. Or at least he said he did."

"He must have kept one." She looked back at the door. "Doesn't look like he broke in. It's just like him to have a heart attack in your store. I never trusted that guy."

"Shine the flashlight from your phone on him."

She ran the light the length of his body. When it shone on his head, we could see more than those staring eyes. Blood from his mouth, nose, and right ear ran over his face and puddled on the floor under him. That was it for us! We screamed and ran.

Opal looked at something at the side of the room and almost tripped me. When we finally made it to the door, we learned the hard way it wasn't wide enough for both of us to go through at the same time, and it took what seemed like forever to free ourselves.

"I hope no one saw that," I said. "Oh no. We cannot start laughing. Not now."

"Let's think about something else—like how cold it is out here." She stamped her feet to keep warm.

I wrapped my coat tighter. "This is better. I didn't trust myself in there. I might start cleaning."

"I could tell you were about to crack and pick up a towel. What do you think he banged his head on?"

I shrugged. "He's not lying near anything, is he? Maybe the bleeding is from hitting the floor? Could he have hit his head in some other part of the store?"

"Nah, there would have been a trail of blood if he had," she answered.

"Did you notice how neat everything was?"

"You mean, except for the bleeding corpse?" Opal walked a few steps along the sidewalk. "Maybe this is what happened. See, his hand held back the blood." She put one hand over her ear and the other over of her nose, then mouthed, *Ow*. Then she staggered toward me. "Good-bye, cruel world."

"Somehow I can't believe Roberto Fratelli's last words were the title of a Pink Floyd song. I wish the ambulance or police or someone would get here." I rubbed my forehead. "I need to call Paul, don't I? I mean, as the incoming mayor, he would want to be told about this."

"He'll want to know because of you being involved, but do you have to? He's going to be so mad at us."

"He won't be mad. Annoyed. That's what he'll be." As I heard myself, I knew it was illogical but oh so true. "I would hate for him to hear about this from someone else."

"I don't guess there's any way he might not find out? Wait, I need to tell you about something else —"

She was cut off by the sound of sirens from two City of Marthasville police cars and an ambulance. Lights bounced off every storefront window on the block. They were soon joined by a few more police cars and an unmarked car that didn't fool anyone. When they double-parked on King Street, they turned it into a one-lane road. Several officers donned yellow vests and took positions on either end of the block. They stopped cars from the nearest through streets—North and South (depending on the direction) Fayette and Henry Streets—from turning onto King in our direction and directed those inside the cordoned-off area so everyone could exit via the one available traffic lane. It looked professional and logical to me, but the scowls on the drivers' faces suggested they were less than pleased at having their tax dollars used to inconvenience them in this manner.

"Dr. Benson?"

I turned to see a fresh-faced young man in a City of Marthasville police uniform. He looked familiar.

"I'm Mark Zhou. I took two of your classes. Are you all right?"

I smiled and shook his hand, remembering a smart young man always prepared for class. "Just a little shocked and confused." I pointed to the door to Waited4You and was about to say more when two women police officers approached.

Opal and I were separated from one another to give our accounts of what we'd seen. I was vaguely aware that someone turned on the lights in Waited4You behind us. I told the officer assigned to me that we had walked in, seen Roberto Fratelli's body on the floor, tried not to touch anything, called the police, then walked out. She took notes and went off to her next job in the process.

In the few minutes it took to tell my brief story, there had been a lot of purposeful and organized commotion. The police cars had left room on the street for the ambulance to pull up close to the store's door. Three paramedics went in, leaving another one outside with a stretcher. Within minutes, they returned and made eye contact with someone I hadn't noticed with us before. The first paramedic in line gave a quick shake—actually more of a jerk—of his head to Marthasville police chief Ralph Harrod, who stood near Opal and the officer assigned to her.

The meanest man in Marthasville was dead.

I looked at Opal to see if she realized it too, but she seemed engrossed in telling . . . what was she saying? A lot of people used their hands when they talked. Opal used her entire body. Had she not sobered up? She seemed to be mimicking lifting something, being surprised by it, then leaning over for a closer look. Ooooh, yes. Finding the leather folio—if that's what it was—was what she was pantomiming. Chief Harrod twisted to glance at me and then trudged over to the officer who had taken my statement.

They talked, the chief scanning the area every minute or so, and then he came and stood in front of me. "Looks like you failed to mention a treasure hidden underneath a chair. I understand it might be quite valuable." Though he was in his midseventies, he'd looked the same for decades. Same moustache, same drawl. Thankfully Paul had been a good kid, so I'd been spared meeting him during my son's teen years. These days I occasionally ran into him at a fund raiser or a city meeting.

"I haven't seen it, so I'm not ready to call it a *treasure*. I forgot about it. That's all."

"And now it's missing."

"It is?" I asked. I might have sounded blasé, but actually I was keeping some perspective. First, a life had been lost. Next, since I hadn't seen whatever it was, I was hardly attached to it or upset that it was missing.

"According to Mrs. Wells, it is."

I moved around him to look inside. A dining chair sat in the alcove against the wall. It was 1940s, mahogany, with a split back and a square opening in the center and a contoured seat typical of midcentury.

Two strips of silver duct tape hung down from below the seat. Was this what Opal had been trying to tell me when we ran to get away from the dead body?

"So this was a robbery," I said. There was no need to phrase it as a question.

"Yeah, Mr. Fratelli could have come in on a robbery in progress. But, Ms. Benson, have you *forgotten* anything else?" Chief Harrod asked. "Because if you have, this is the time to tell me what it is."

I shook my head. "Nope." His attempt to bully me was laughably transparent. Only . . . wasn't there something I was supposed to do?

"How are you and your friend getting home? She shouldn't be behind the wheel of a car."

Opal stood with two young Marthasville police officers. She laughed out loud at something one of them said.

No, she should be under the wheel of a car.

"Would you like to call your son?" Chief Harrod asked.

I looked straight up at the night sky. "I forgot that too."

He bellowed out a laugh. "You seem to be forgetting a lot. We can help you get home." He motioned for Mark to come over. While he walked around his squad car, he motioned to Opal. "Mrs. Wells, you can go too."

A coverall-clad crime scene tech came out of Waited4You and interrupted him. "Chief, there's something you should see in here."

"Yeah, Frenchie?"

The tech looked at me. "You're the store owner?" I heard something in his voice. His tone wasn't unbelieving, as in "*You're* the store owner?" There was an apology hidden somewhere in his words.

"Yes, I'm Camille Benson."

"That back room was tossed good," he said. "Or maybe I should say it was tossed funny."

Chief Harrod turned and went inside, the man he'd referred to as Frenchie and me following close on his heels. Twice, maybe three times, the chief turned to looked at the front door.

Beyond the sales floor were a number of small rooms. There was a desk in a large stock room, but there was also a coat closet, a small, sparsely outfitted kitchenette, and two other small windowless spaces. All had nice flooring and beautiful wood trim. Maybe one of those was where I had napped and done my homework assignments as a child. When I had time, maybe after the holidays, I planned to find out which were retaining walls and which could be eliminated to enlarge the gallery. I looked straight ahead as we walked by Roberto Fratelli's body. I didn't want to see that staring look on his face, or the trails of blood coming from his nose, mouth, and ears, every time I thought of him in the future. *If* I ever did. Would anyone care that he was dead? For days, all I'd heard was how happy people were that he was selling out and moving away. Could we fast-forward to forgetting the things we'd said about him and start describing him as eccentric, or "a real character"?

When we got to the door of the back area that Roberto had used as a stock room, the chief scanned the room, then stepped to one side so I could see in.

The wood floorboards and floor-to-ceiling industrial metal shelves had been covered with dust when I first saw the room. As Opal and I listed and counted the merchandise, we'd tried to bring at least a little order. We'd closed the box tops by tucking the flaps under and over. That was all undone now. Every box gaped open. The boxes sat in the middle of the room in an odd configuration. Had the unboxed items been left alone?

Walking was tricky, so I turned to my right. According to the dust ring, the Stiffel lamp on the middle shelf had been moved. Before, the room had looked neglected. Now it looked battered.

"We ought to be able to get prints in here," Frenchie said.

"Do you have an estimate for the time of death?" the chief asked.

"All I'm seeing is very early signs of lividity, so my initial call is an hour, if even that." He emphasized the word *initial*.

Chief Harrod put up his hand, palm out and almost touching the man's chest. "Are you saying he just died?" He looked at *me* when he finished the sentence. I didn't like what he was implying.

"No, at least half an hour. That's just preliminary. We still need to—"

"Uh, Frenchie, is it?" He nodded, so I went on. "Let me make it easy for you. I don't want to see you using your rectal thermometer on Mr. Fratelli any more than you want me to."

"That's not really how we—"

"I'm pretty sure I would faint. I just want to call it a night."
I started to walk off but stopped. "And in case you're wonder-
ing, that's not rigor mortis in his face. That's how he looks.
Well, looked."

Chief Harrod's gazed out at the body. Without moving his
head, he said, "You can go now. Maybe tomorrow you can let
me know what all is missing."

At that point their voices became background noise. I was
busy trying to understand the state of the room. Nothing
was right about it. First, how had the intruder, the murderer,
gotten out? It didn't look like the cardboard boxes had been
hopscotched over. Had he or she walked out the front door?
Frenchie's word for this, like on TV crime shows, was *tossed*;
this looked anything but. Sure, the boxes had been ripped
open, and some had been slashed, but it looked as if they were
positioned on the floor. Something about it seemed, well,
intentional. The boxes made an obstacle course because they
were no longer lined up against a wall. Those in the center of
the room were turned forty-five degrees, like floor tiles in a
diamond pattern.

"I didn't leave the boxes like that," I said.

Two boxes were stacked in front of my desk, and next to
that was a tower three boxes high. I looked up at the ugly
acoustic ceiling tiles. Those would have to be replaced with
something better looking, but this wasn't the time to think
about that. One had been moved to the side. I could see into
the attic through the gaping square opening.

"I think she's upset," Chief Harrod said. Maybe because
I had been studying the room rather than talking to them.
Or because he didn't think the fact that the boxes had been
moved to the center of the room was as odd as I did.

"I'm standing right here," I said, annoyed at his use of third person. I pointed up. "Could that be how he got out? Or in? Or both?"

The men looked up at the ceiling, then at one another.

Frenchie whistled. "Damn," he said, and walked by us to join the others on the sales floor. "Good catch."

"Let's not overcomplicate this," Chief Harrod said to his back. Frenchie turned around to hear the rest of what he had to say. "He could have come in the back door." As he spoke, he pointed to a door on the far wall, which led to an alleyway and our assigned parking spaces. "Or been let in." He ran his hand over his head. "Frenchie, I have someone posted out there with your guys, but so far it doesn't look tampered with, does it?"

Frenchie shook his head no.

"Then I'll pull him and use him on traffic."

On his way to join the others, Frenchie called back over his shoulder, "I assume you want the ceiling and whatever is upstairs processed?"

"Yeah," Chief Harrod answered, not even trying to hide how exasperated he was. He begrudgingly added a thank-you while craning his neck to see the front door. Under his breath, he said, "Where is he?" Hmm. He was waiting for someone who hadn't shown up. It was the middle of the night. A Saturday night at that. He should cut whoever it was some slack. Then to me, he said, "Maybe someone should give you a ride home, Ms. Benson. I'm happy to arrange that." He flipped the light switch by the door on his way out. I was as in the dark as the stock room was. If he hadn't been the chief of police, would he have had the nerve to touch a light switch at the scene of a murder?

Frenchie gave instructions on where he wanted lights placed and how he wanted the stock room processed. I looked at the roomful of men and women hard at work in the gallery, inspecting every inch. As they did their jobs, they handled the dead man gently and respectfully. What was Chief Harrod doing, other than keeping a constant eye on the door, his phone, and his wristwatch? The sudden and fake solicitude toward me was disgusting, but I did want to be home with my dogs and to let the professionals find Roberto's killer.

I walked back through the store, but this time the chief was on my heels.

"Do you have an alarm?" he asked.

I nodded.

"Maybe next time you'll use it."

"I activated it, but I guess Roberto turned it off. I haven't changed the password yet." I hated to admit that to him, but it was the truth.

I looked around for Opal, and he went to speak to Mark Zhou. It was decided that his patrol car would be our ride home. Mark opened the rear door for me and said, "I'm afraid you'll have to ride in the back seat because of my laptop. Sorry." Then he went to the other side of the car and opened that door for Opal, before getting behind the wheel.

"Okeydokey." Before she got in, she yelled over the car, "I think I know who did it."

"Just a sec," Chief Harrod snapped. "Who?"

"A guy with a collie puppy. They got in a fight in the store today."

The angry look Chief Harrod lasered her with froze the moment. Time started again when he shook his head and waved his hand dismissively. "Don't know what you're talking about," he grumbled.

Then a man yelled, "Mrs. Benson!"

I was getting in the car but turned when I heard my name. He raised the crime scene tape and scooted under. Three officers ran to stop him, but a second later, the flash of a camera was all I could see.

Chapter Five

Sunday

Yellow crime scene tape crisscrossed the front door of Wait-ed4You, and more stretched between the two trees in the hell strip, the strip of land between the sidewalk and King Street. I thought about the garden I planned for spring and immediately wondered if that or any of my other ideas for the store would happen. A dark cloud hung over my future.

Opal and I were to meet Chief Harrod at eleven o'clock to tell him more about the missing letter—if that's what it was. I had yet to see it. And to find out what else, if anything, had been stolen.

I looked up King Street to the west for Opal, then down toward the Potomac River. A couple—she was very blonde and very made-up, and he had an oversized head bobbing on a short body—walked up the sidewalk. I probably wouldn't have noticed them if they hadn't started when they saw me. Same reaction from both of them. He put his arm around her waist and led her across the street. She looked over his shoulder back at the taped door and then at me before she scurried away.

The two sections of yellow police tape that had blocked the sidewalk last night had been removed at some point. While they'd been up, pedestrians had been compelled to walk on the pavement to continue along King Street. Because of the street parking, that could be dangerous. The tape was gone now, and I was thankful for small favors. I didn't need any more ill will. I wondered why the couple had crossed the street, but realization soon set in.

They were acting like murder might be contagious.

That was the final straw. I wanted to cry. I hadn't broken down when I saw the online edition of the *Marthasville Daily News*. Paul had called to warn me, but there's no way to prepare for seeing yourself in a photo looking like that. It was right there on the paper's landing page. A kind assessment would be that I appeared disheveled and confused, whereas a less-than-generous description would say I looked old and drunk as a skunk. I liked to think my white hair made me look chic and confident in my choices. Not in that photo. From what I'd been able to see before the flash blinded me, the photographer had taken several shots. The newspaper had to choose that one?

"Camille!" Opal came out of Suits to a Tea! holding one of their bags. "I brought you sweet potato flan."

I hugged her for her thoughtfulness. There was a plastic fork in the bag, and I took a bite of the flan right there. "Mmm."

"Did you get me one of those?" a familiar voice called out. A white BMW 5 Series sedan parked at the curb and Marthasville's commonwealth's attorney, Janie Fairfax, lowered the passenger-side window. Her position was like that of a district attorney. There were 120 of them in Virginia, one in each county and city.

I held the flan out for her, but she shook her head. "I need caffeine."

Opal said, "Here, take my latte."

"Bless you. Let's split it." Janie gratefully took a sip and handed it back to Opal. "What the hell? Camille, you bought your parents' old antique store from that crotchety old guy, and that very night you found him murdered?"

Opal threw her head back and laughed. "You do know how to condense a story to its essence."

"Yeah, Janie, that was a little too on the nose," I said.

"Well, I have to be that way because I'm playing catch-up. Someone from my office should have been on the scene last night, but I didn't get the call. It doesn't look good for me not to be here."

"On TV, you people don't have to do anything until the police have someone they want to charge," Opal said. She took a drink of the latte and handed it back to Janie.

"Is that right? I guess I've been doing it wrong," Janie kidded. "I like to come to the scene to get the case started on the right foot and get a file started. They're supposed to call one of my assistants when I'm off or if they can't reach me." Her raised right eyebrow said there was a story there and it wasn't pretty, though I was sure we'd never hear it. We three had known each other a long time, but I wouldn't say Opal and I knew her well. Fran, her mother, had been in our group of friends until that damn breast cancer beast came for her. We tried to keep an eye out for our young friend, but she didn't make it easy. Janie was as reserved as Opal was gregarious.

"But no one thought to make that call." She looked down, and her glossy, black, blunt-cut bob fell into her face.

"Ladies." The volume of Chief Harrod's booming voice was the last sound I wanted to hear after too little sleep and too much to drink. I jumped and Opal winced. "Ms. Fairfax, better late than never. Let's go in, shall we?"

Got it. He wasn't happy she hadn't been here last night, but did he have to speak to her like that in front of civilians?

"Good morning, Chief," Janie said, looking down.

I ate the last bite of the sweet potato flan to calm my nerves and walked to the nearest trash can. It was covered, but when I tossed my wrapping in, it looked empty. Opal came up behind me and threw away the latte cup.

I had left keys with the police chief last night, and he unlocked the door. He pulled away the tape on one side and left it hanging.

Opal took Janie's arm before she could follow him in. "Did the police take the trash to look for DNA?" she whispered.

"Are you kidding? In Marthasville?" I asked.

Janie exhaled. "It probably means the trash truck has already been around."

We went inside, and once again I realized how odd it was that the sales floor looked the same as it had before we'd found Roberto's body—when we'd finished the inventory. The fake Victorian side table was now in the back, but everything else looked to be in place. Shouldn't the very spot where someone had taken his last breath feel different? Be different?

"The medical examiner's preliminary finding for Mr. Fratelli's cause of death is injury," Chief Harrod said, after we were all inside.

Opal and I looked at each other. What was he saying? That this was an accident? Now I exhaled. I could handle this. I was going to be all right. Then I saw Janie's hair swing with an almost imperceptible side-to-side motion of her head. What about the state of the storeroom? What about the missing letter?

"What did he hit his head on? The floor?" I asked.

"His death has been classified as a homicide."

My eyes widened, but that had been Chief Harrod's intention all along. He wanted everyone to know he was the boss.

"So it *wasn't* an accident?" Opal asked. "When you said injury, I thought you meant . . . Well, you know what I thought." Her voice trailed off.

Harrod rocked on his heels. The smarmy grin on his face told me we had walked into the trap he'd childishly laid. "You're confusing cause of death with manner of death. This is now a medical examiner case . . ." How fragile was his ego that he felt he had to play word games like that?

His mouth was still moving, but I was walking to the chair in the alcove. "Opal, what did the case that was taped under here look like?"

"It was brown leather," she said.

I wore gloves, and I picked the chair up and turned it over. It was substantial, despite the cutout in the back, and I had to use both hands and hold it by two legs. There was nothing to see but the bottom of the seat of a chair. "The police took the duct tape?" I asked Chief Harrod. Last night it had hung down from beneath the seat. That was how Opal had first seen the letter was gone.

Chief Harrod grunted, while I looked closer.

Opal came and looked over my shoulder. "You can tell where the tape was."

Harrod ran his hand over his head. "Ms. Fairfax, it appears the victim interrupted a robbery. Ladies, is anything else missing?"

If the letter, or whatever it was, was in fact from the 1750s, it might be quite a find, depending on the author and its condition.

That alone should have been enough for a thief, but if Chief Harrod wanted a full accounting, that's what he would get.

"It should be easy to tell, since we just inventoried the store. Let us look around and I'll let you know," I said.

"Take your time. Say, by the end of the week?"

"No worries. We'll be done in an hour or so," I said.

Opal had placed herself slightly behind him, where she could take advantage of being out of his line of vision to share her real opinion with me, using exaggeratedly raised eyebrows and eyes enlarged to the diameter of a Norman Rockwell plate. Next, she pointed to the floor with one finger, then another, pausing a beat between each. Ahh! He was slow-walking the investigation.

Janie stood near the door, writing away in a notebook. Her brows were knitted in concentration over her eyeglasses. What a striking contrast there was between her energy level and Chief Harrod's languid pace—just like last night, when I'd compared him to the crime scene techs and uniformed officers.

"Have you reached his family?" I asked.

"I have someone working on it."

"How was he killed? What was the murder weapon?" I asked. "Last night I didn't see anything lying around his body."

"He was struck on the side of the head with a large and heavy object, but we haven't identified it, nor have we found it."

"Who should I speak with after we find out if anything else was stolen? You've assigned a homicide detective to the case?" *Please don't say you're going to handle this.* I felt quite the diplomat for phrasing it like that.

Janie's pen stopped moving, but this time she didn't look up.

As reprehensible as Roberto Fratelli had been, he deserved justice. I was losing faith that he would get it in this century from Chief Ralph Harrod.

"For now, I'm taking the lead on it. It'll reassure the media, the merchants, and citizens to see me involved."

Right.

Chapter Six

I walked Chief Harrod to the door. Foot traffic had picked up, and everyone who passed by stared at the yellow crime scene tape. CRIME SCENE DO NOT CROSS, it shouted in black uppercase lettering.

"How long does that have to stay here?"

He looked out like he was seeing the tape for the first time. "You can take it down." He stopped and turned around. "When did you plan to open?"

I wasn't wild about his use of past tense, implying as it did that I needed to make new plans. "Black Friday."

"Hmm. Maybe. We'll see." With that, he walked toward his car, which he'd more or less parallel parked. Was he moving in slow motion, or was it just my eagerness to get started checking for missing merch? For each step, he gingerly picked up one foot and then the other. He stooped as he walked and looked down at the brick sidewalk. Should I go to him and offer my arm? Or would that embarrass him? I was still arguing with myself when he made it to his car. I slipped back inside as quietly as I could.

"What happened?" Opal asked when she saw the look on my face.

"He doesn't know if I can open for the start of the holiday season. I'll be sunk if I can't."

"Don't borrow trouble." It was one of her favorite expressions. "The police will find out who's responsible, and everything will be fine."

The three of us looked out the window at the chief's shiny white Ford Taurus police cruiser. By tradition, the police chief's car was white. He sat behind the wheel but hadn't driven away.

"What do you think happened to all those old Crown Vics that used to terrify us back in the day?" Opal asked.

"They were taken to a farm where they play outside all day long," I said.

She and Janie gave a laugh, and Opal said, "Time to get to work. Do you have your computer tablet with you?" For both of us, getting busy was the go-to cure for any problem, and that's what we would do now.

"Yeah, it's in my handbag. And I have another on the shelf beside the counter." I walked to the back of the showroom and handed one of the tablets to her.

"If this started out as a break-in, wouldn't this have been taken?" Opal asked. "It was right out in the open."

I nodded. "That is odd."

"Maybe his killer knew he could be tracked when he turned it on?" Janie offered.

"He would be? Hmm, who knew?" I looked around. My accountant had surprised me with a lavish floral arrangement when I signed the papers. The only table in the room large enough for it sat against the back wall. The bouquet featured comforting orange zinnias, roses in a warm, yellow-toned red that was perfect for fall, and sunflowers. Not so much as a petal had fallen. "There's something wrong with this, uh, well, all of this. If there was a robbery for Roberto to interrupt, wouldn't something, anything, out here be disturbed?"

Janie shook her head. "Not if the robber wanted one particular item and knew where to find it."

"That's just it. If the letter was what he was after, I don't think he did know where it was. Let me show you the stock room."

Janie gasped when she saw the boxes in the middle of the floor, all with their top flaps open.

"Wait, these boxes were moved," I said. "This isn't the way they were arranged when I saw them last night." The diamond pattern was gone. The boxes were separated so that a path to the back door was apparent. I told Janie and Opal about the previous placement of the boxes, relaying how some of them had been stacked, and mentioned the separation in the ceiling tiles. "I guess the police needed to move them to get a ladder in here."

Janie pointed with her pen to the back door. "Did the crime scene team look at that?"

I nodded. "They were dusting for fingerprints on the outside when I left. I don't know if they found anything. And they said it was still locked."

"Maybe the burglar did get in through the ceiling, but wouldn't that be hard to do?" Janie wrote something in her notebook.

Opal whistled. "Yeah, it'd be hard to get in that way. And then how did he get out? That would be even harder."

"If he had a key, he could let himself out the back door and lock it back," Janie said. "Hopefully, some security cameras along the street will give us the answer to that." She reached out and ran her fingers along the folded edge of a quilt on a shelf. "Hmm. This is like two crime scenes. In this room, he had to move everything around, looking for something to steal." She led us back to the sales floor. "But in here, he went straight to the chair. He couldn't have found it under there without moving a few things around, unless he already knew where it was. But if he did, why toss the storeroom?"

"He must have wanted more than the letter," I said.

"Or maybe he just threatened Roberto and he told him where it was!" Opal said, with her usual fervor.

"But if he got what he came for, why did he kill him?" I asked.

"We can't dismiss anything yet," Janie said. "When you know if anything from back there was stolen, you'll know if it was just the letter the killer was after. Or if he wanted anything of value he could get his hands on." She shook her head. "I wish the other Harrod was the detective assigned to this."

"What other Harrod?"

"I'm going to my office to start the file on this." She was already walking to the door.

* * *

Opal powered on the tablet and tapped away. "I have an easy way to walk back through our inventory document. See, I've reverted the spreadsheet back to the order we inputted the items. Now we can retrace our steps to check for anything missing."

On the recovered older version, I saw her *one plant stand* entry and smiled. "Can you add a column that we can use now to check off each piece as we account for it?"

We made quick work of reinventorying and went to the storeroom.

"I was surprised at how little back stock he had, weren't you?" I asked.

"If you say so. I don't know what a reasonable amount of stock looks like. Remember, my business is on a boat. Has to be sparse." She hesitated. "Do you think Roberto Fratelli took the high-dollar pieces with him?"

"Could have, but he was only paid for what was here."

"Yes, but since he kept a key, he could have taken anything he wanted after he got his money from you."

I had to agree. "I'm glad you're less trusting than I am, but so far, the letter is all that's missing. And there are many really nice things here. Like this." I picked up a nineteenth-century carved pedestal and lugged it to the alcove. I put the flower arrangement from my accountant on it and rotated it until I was satisfied I had the best side forward. "These crystal and bronze lamps are from the 1950s. And in the back is a Louis XVI demilune chest from the 1920s. I'll probably bring that out here. Don't you think it's sneaky that those are mixed in with the fake Victorian table we found? That's another way to try to trick customers."

"It is, uh, sly! That's what it is. Aren't you afraid anything he had might be a fake?"

"I am, a little. I plan to spend time with each piece between now and opening day. I've just started, but so far everything else is true to what he labeled them."

We counted two shelves of books in the stock room. There were more on the sales floor, and the signage out there labeled them *rare*. "Now, these, I'm not so sure about. Some don't seem used at all." I'd spend time on them later.

"At least the amount is the same as yesterday," she said.

"Let's get that crime scene tape down."

There was a knock on the door, and then it opened. "Hello? Camille? Anybody here?" It was Brennan Adler.

"Shh. Maybe he doesn't know we're back here," I whispered.

"What the hell?" Opal shot back. "Go talk to that man."

"Can't you go?"

"No!" She grabbed my arm and pulled me out to the sales floor.

"Hi." Brennan seemed confused when he saw Opal tugging my sleeve. "I was worried. I saw the article in the paper, and now this." He turned to point outside.

Some tenant I'd turned out to be. "Well, we were just about to take that down. Chief Harrod said we could."

"No, I meant . . . nothing." He wasn't a good liar; he had been about to say more. Finally he did. "I was asking if *you* were all right."

The truth was, I had no idea. Someone had been murdered—in Marthasville. Looking at the situation from a purely business point of view, I didn't know if Waited4You could survive the bad publicity. But how could I have the nerve to complain? Roberto Fratelli had lost his life. He'd been alone when he was alive, and it looked like he was still alone in death. That was sad. Was I all right? Good question, but I'd have to get back to him on it. "Thanks for asking." Not much of an answer, but it was all I had.

I walked around him and opened the door. There was a line of people waiting to get into Vicissitudes for brunch. Every single person stared at Waited4You.

Opal and Brennan joined me to help. She huffed. "Like they've never seen anyone taking down crime scene tape the day after a murder."

We got to work pulling it down from the door and then from where it was strung between the trees. The quicker, the better.

"That's where the murder happened," I heard a man say.

"Yeah, last night."

Like a game of telegraph, the message went down the line.

"Brennan, I didn't have the heart to read the article. Did it say he was murdered?" I whispered. No need to mention the nose-dive I'd had from seeing that photo of me getting into a squad car. Tenant-wise, he had gone from the frying pan to the fire. "Chief Harrod confirmed it to us, but is that part public?"

"It said apparent homicide, so yeah."

We went inside to toss the tape in the trash.

"I need to get going." Opal put on her coat. "Brennan, would you be a doll and help her change the passcode for the alarm? She's clueless with machinery. Just helpless."

Helpless? Machinery? What happened? Are we all of a sudden in the 1950s?

I thanked her for everything—seemed like I had been doing that a lot recently—and walked to the door. "I'll email Chief Harrod to tell him nothing else is missing."

Brennan stood to the side and waited for her to leave. "Nice flowers. From an admirer?"

"From my accountant."

"Good. I mean . . . we can change the alarm code on the box by the door, but maybe some other time." He accidently nudged my computer tablet, which I'd left on a table, and it lit up. He leaned over and read aloud the title of the blog post I was writing. *"Context Is Queen."*

"Yeah, especially with banjo music," I said.

He laughed out loud. It was the kind of sound someone made when they really needed a good laugh. He wiped his eyes and asked, "Exactly what does 'context is queen' mean, anyway?"

"It means don't try to decorate in a vacuum. Consider what makes your home special. If it's an older home, it might be a design feature. If it's a condo overlooking the Potomac, you could take that view into account."

"Are you one of those influencers I hear about?" he asked.

"I wish! I would be happy just to get a few newsletter subscribers. Roberto didn't have a customer list to leave me."

"No surprise there," Brennan said.

"Remember when you were cool if you were an early adopter? Not anymore! Now you have to be an *influencer*. Want to sign up for my newsletter?"

"If I subscribe, will you have dinner with me Tuesday night?" he asked.

Now I laughed at the condition he'd put on my request. Going out with him was a bad idea for so many reasons. He was my landlord, and my business might not make it. I was asked out on my share of dates, but I didn't go on very many. Did I even know how to date? He hadn't said it was a date. Maybe it was a business dinner. Had I almost made a fool of myself? It was settled: I would tell him no.

"Yes, you have a deal."

Chapter Seven

Monday

O pal and I walked outside, and I locked the door to Waited4You behind us. "Look! Another page of people signed up for the newsletter!" I took the top sheet off the clipboard and proudly showed it to her before I pocketed it.

Opal brushed a leaf off the forest-green aluminum bistro table. "I'm not surprised. People are anxious for you to open. Then they feel guilty about being so happy to have you here instead of you-know-who because of what happened." She shook her head. "It's not like you buying the store had anything to do with him getting killed."

"I am worried about people making that mental association, though. I'm holding my promotions until closer to the opening out of respect, but maybe I'm making a mistake. It's like I'm silent, so when people talk about Waited4You, all they have to talk about is the murder."

"Gotcha, but to come out all *This is what you do to make your home beautiful* and yada yada seems, I don't know, tone-deaf. Kind of insensitive. Even though he was the meanest man in town."

"Yeah, like I didn't read the room," I agreed, and took her arm to start the walk up King Street. I trusted her business sense. "I'm writing articles so I'll have them ready to use for blog posts or to go in the newsletter when the time is right."

Yesterday I'd taken three quilts home for a DIY photo shoot. Stickley and Morris had modeled and been paid in treats. The title of the article was "Ditch the Display." Rather than trying to make your bedroom look like a display in the home store, I'd offered, choose pieces that hold meaning for you. I wrote that I was as guilty as anyone else of falling in love with a look in a store or online and buying up everything from shams to throw pillows to the duvet cover so I could duplicate it once I got home. That was then, and this is now, I wrote. I tied the advice to my running theme of something I called *modern antiques*. My suggestions included concealing a matchy-matchy throw pillow with a pillow cover from a crazy vacation spot or swapping the blanket from the bottom of the kid's bed with yours. Of course, I finished by saying that Waited4You had a selection of quilts and accessories guaranteed to help your bedroom detox from the display.

At the intersection with Royal Street, Opal took off, yelling, "Let's cross here," over her shoulder. She ignored the *Don't Walk* hand, but at least we weren't jaywalking, so maybe there was hope for us. I forgot all about my business plans and ran to catch up with her.

"Janie's like our secret weapon," I said when we were safely on the same side of King Street as the courthouse. I was relieved when Opal said she had time for the three of us to have lunch so we could hear the latest on the investigation.

"What did she say when you told her we don't trust the chief?" Opal asked.

"I told her our theory that he was dragging his feet because he was near retirement, and she thinks it might be just the opposite." We stopped at the intersection with North Pitt Street to cross. "She thinks he wants to go out with a big win."

"He hasn't announced his retirement, has he?" Opal asked.

"That's just it. He hasn't," I said. "Both scenarios, retirement or not, leave a killer on the loose. I asked her about footage from security cameras along King Street and behind the buildings. That's when she suggested lunch. They reviewed it this morning."

"This is Monday! You would think the police would have looked at it the night of the murder!" Opal flailed her arms.

"Well, at least they have now, and it sounds like they found something juicy. Paul didn't know what that might be."

She cast me a sideways glance. "How did *that* talk go? You didn't mention it yesterday, and I didn't want to ask."

"I wish he could find someone to date. Soon!"

"Mayoring should keep him busy, right? So what did he say?"

"Ugh. I wish he hadn't seen the online edition of the *Marthasville Daily News* with that photo and article before I talked to him, but he did. It was so late when I got home, I decided to call him Sunday morning. He wants me to get out of the contract to buy Waited4You since I'm within the three-day grace period. I told him I was going to keep it. And I hope I can." I exhaled and shook my head.

"What do you mean?"

"If I can't open for the Christmas season, I don't see how I can stay in business."

"The police chief didn't say you couldn't open for business, did he?"

"He implied I couldn't. I didn't think he could stop me, and Paul confirmed that for me. After all, they're finished with the crime scene. I'm still worried that if Waited4You is known as the place where the murder happened, no one will want to shop there. Not exactly the vibe I was going for. I planned to have jazz playing in the background. Now, because of the murder, that seems out of place. Okay, that's enough moaning from me."

Opal rubbed my arm. "I understand your apprehension, but remember, don't borrow trouble. That's solid advice."

"There's no fool like an old fool. That's true too. I wonder if it's too late to get my old job back at the community college."

"Don't think like that! Your business plan for selling quality antiques, along with free decorating instruction, is sound. You'll be fine." We stopped before climbing the steps that would take us to the archway and into the courthouse building. "Wait. There's more to this than you're saying, isn't there? What else are you worried about?"

I exhaled. "I'm afraid the murder will overshadow Paul's participation in Common Good for the Commonwealth. I never want to cause him any embarrassment or hurt his political career."

"Aha. I thought there was more."

"Let's talk about something else. Remember the guy with the puppy that Roberto got into an argument with? I've been thinking of how to better arrange the store so dogs will be welcome."

*   *   *

Janie met us when we got off the elevator. "I feel naked without my cell phone," I said as I gave her an air kiss.

"I know, but the rules are the rules," she said, opening the glass door and leading us down another hallway. As commonwealth's attorney, she was exempt from the no-cell-phones-in-the-courthouse-building part of the Virginia Code, but Opal and I were not.

We walked past her staff and pretended to be serious women on serious business, but when we got to her office, with the door closed, we could be ourselves. She sat in her leather chair and dropped a folder onto her massive desk, which took up most of the office.

I sat in one of the two leather guest chairs and shrugged off my coat. "Chief Harrod doesn't seem at all curious about some questions that are bothering me, and I know nothing about law enforcement or investigations."

"Like?" Janie asked.

"Why did Roberto Fratelli keep a key? Obviously, he knew he was going to sneak back in. Was the key on him when he was found?"

Opal took the other chair. "Yeah! Or is the killer out there walking around with it?"

Janie opened the folder and thumbed through pages. "Here it says a couple of keys were in his possession. Someone will come by and see if one fits your door."

"Do you think he kept a key so he could meet someone there?" I asked.

She took her glasses off. "Whether he intended to meet his killer or was surprised by him, we know it had something to do with something he left in that store."

"I was about to get to that. We only know of one item missing from the inventory we took, but it might be very valuable. Dealers in the area should be alerted."

Now Janie was taking notes. "You're talking about the letter? The letter was all that was taken? I'll let the detective know."

"You mean Chief Harrod?" I asked.

"You'll be happy to know he handed the case off to a detective." She concentrated on the folder and said, "Nick. Uh, that's his name."

"Tell her about *Casablanca*," Opal said.

"About what?"

"We—"

"*You*," Opal interjected. "Camille, you were the one who spotted it."

"There's a table he was passing off as Victorian, and it's not. It's newly made."

"Are you thinking maybe he ripped off the wrong customer?" She was still writing, with one raised eyebrow and several nods.

I thought about that possibility. "Could be. I don't think there's any such thing as an unscrupulous dealer that cheats *once*, so I spent this morning going over old records. He sold these same marble tables with burr walnut trim over and over. I kept going because I wanted to see if I could learn who bought the others and who was supplying them." I reached into my handbag and pulled out my notepad. "The supplier's name is Ritchie Potts. I've never met him, but I know his work. He makes custom furniture and other woodwork projects, like built-ins. He made a doghouse for a friend of mine."

She took down the name. "Good. The one lead the police had fizzled out." She placed her perfectly manicured hand on the folder and drummed her fingers. "They tracked the victim's movements on Saturday night using security cameras on King Street and the location on his cell phone. At around midnight, Mr. Fratelli and Ella Coleman, his ex-wife, were seen *and heard*, according to a waitress, arguing at the bar at Mykonos Taverna. You know the place?"

Opal and I nodded. It was a good lunch spot that you could almost see from Janie's window. Now that I was working in Old Town, I could go there more often.

Janie continued, "Fratelli walked out, but she followed him back to Waited4You, where the argument continued. He went inside Waited4You, but she didn't." The hope I'd started to feel for a quick resolution faded with that last sentence.

"Have the police questioned her?" I asked.

"They probably will later. But I wouldn't count on a lot coming out of that."

Opal pointed at Janie and then me. "I know what happened. She went inside later!"

"I'm afraid not. We have her car, with her behind the wheel, turning left in front of the George Washington Masonic Temple half an hour later."

The nine-story neoclassical landmark was an active masonic lodge as well as a museum, but mostly it was a love letter to George Washington and his memory from his brother Freemasons. It regally presided high over Marthasville's Old Town neighborhood on land between Duke Street and King Street, following a tradition of building temples on a hill or mountain. A left turn meant Ms. Coleman had been headed to Duke Street.

"Are you sure she didn't turn around in the Amtrak parking lot? Or that lot where the police are selling Christmas trees for summer camp, next to the train station?" I asked.

"She went to Duke Street and turned right," Janie answered. "When she left him, he was still alive. Ladies, not every bit of information is a clue."

Since I'd never even known anyone who was murdered, all evidence seemed important and felt like truth.

"Too bad," Opal said. "If she had gone the other way onto Duke, it would have been an easy drive back to Waited4You." Duke, King, Queen, and Princess Streets run parallel to one another, east toward the Potomac River or west toward other parts of Marthasville. If Ella had taken the first street back to King Street, she would have driven by the King Street Metro station. Marthasville has three stations for commuters to go to DC for their government or federal government contractor jobs, or maybe to work at one of the twenty museums and galleries of the Smithsonian Institution. "So much for the stalking-ex-wife-who's-still-in-love-with-him theory."

"Can you really see Roberto Fratelli in a lover's spat gone wrong?" I asked. I surely couldn't.

"She remarried, so that's not likely." Janie stood and straightened her skirt. "I need to take care of something, and then I can go to lunch."

"A new husband? Well, in that case, we're looking for a green-eyed monster—"

I held my hands up, palms out. "Opal, nice try, but there was no burning caldron of passion and jealousy beneath Roberto's exterior nastiness."

Janie shook her head at us and left. "Be right back."

"Yes!" Opal said with a fist pump after she left. "See, now that a detective has been assigned to the case, this murder is on its way to getting solved. Pronto. ASAP. Stat. Customers will forget all about it." She stood and reached for the folder Janie had laid down, scanned the label scribbled on the tab, and opened it. "Hmm, this is very interesting."

"Opal, what are you doing? Are you supposed to be reading that?"

"I read whatever I want. Sometimes I don't understand it. Like now." She flipped a few pages over and then returned to the beginning. "This is harder than reading my medical files when the doctor leaves the room, but I can give it a try."

"Then what does it say?"

"I don't know. I can't read it. Did you know she wrote shorthand?" She turned several pages over. "Oh, good. Finally, a typed report. Listen to this: *Ella Coleman, of 301 South Ranger Street, Marthasville—*'"

"Say that address again," I asked her.

She repeated it. "Why?"

"That's where Ritchie Potts lives."

Chapter Eight

We returned our laminated menus to the waitress at Gadsby's Tavern and ordered our lunches as soon as we had a table. As regulars, we didn't need to consult them. Ordinarily the downhill walk toward the river would have been pleasant, but Janie was in a huge hurry to get back to the office, so we drove the seven or eight blocks to get there.

Europeans had first settled in Marthasville in 1695, and the area had grown into an important colonial seaport. Around 1748, business interests petitioned the House of Burgesses to create a city along the Potomac River. An aspiring surveyor named George Washington sketched the shoreline for the legislative body, and the petition was later approved. The House of Burgesses was now the House of Delegates, the lower house of Virginia's General Assembly.

There had been one tavern or another at the intersection of North Royal and Cameron Streets since 1746, because travelers needed food, drink, rest, and news. Actually, they still did. The current Gadsby's Tavern was two buildings and listed on the National Register of Historic Places. The tavern, 1785, was now a museum, and the City Hotel, 1792, was where we were about to eat. George Washington had visited several times, including twice for the Birthnight Ball, which is still held annually to celebrate his birthday. Now it was Opal, Janie, and me there for a quick lunch.

"Roberto's filing system is a little odd, but he did leave me some records. From the files I've been through so far, there's no old letter of any kind mentioned. Opal, you're the only one who's seen it. Can you remember anything else about what it looked like? Anything at all?" It sounded like I was bringing a meeting to order.

Janie took her computer tablet out of her handbag. "I want to know everything about it too, and the leather case."

Opal laughed. "As you both know, my memory from that night is a little fuzzy."

"I assume the clear covering was an acid-free polyester sleeve." The waitress was back with our drinks, and I waited before I spoke again. "What did the outside case it was in look like?"

"I researched document cases on the internet and found one similar to the one I think I saw. It was a leather folio. I saw near the top of the sheet that it had a date of 1-7-5-something, and I saw *Dear George* in squiggly handwriting."

"Black ink?" Janie asked.

"I guess it was black when it was new. Just looked faded."

"Did you see a watermark on the paper?" I asked.

"What's that?"

"I'll take that as a no."

"Honestly, I didn't touch it, so I only saw the top part of it."

"Are you saying it was folded? And inside the clear covering?"

"Yeah," Opal answered.

"It *so* is not from the eighteenth century." I exhaled.

"If it turns out to be real, won't that be cool for Marthasville?" Opal asked the table.

"Yeah, it'll be amazing," I agreed before I turned to Janie. "Have they had any luck finding anyone from Roberto's family?"

"Unfortunately, no. Ella said he had a brother and that she'd look for his phone number. They were married for such a short time and have been divorced about ten years, so who knows if the brother is still alive, or if any phone number she finds will be any good. Whatever. It's a thread to pull."

"Hopefully, you'll find someone. Especially since there's money to inherit," I said.

"How do you know that?" Janie asked suspiciously and quickly.

"There's at least the money I transferred to him on Saturday afternoon to buy the business."

"Oh, sorry. For a minute I thought you'd been trying to investigate the murder, the way the women do on TV and in books."

I held up both hands. "Not me. I'm way too busy."

"The police are going to Mr. Fratelli's residence this afternoon. They might find something they can use. Like maybe papers that will let us know where he was moving to. He may have been moving to be closer to a family member."

"That would be nice, but I just don't see it," I said. How lovely it would have been to think he had a big family waiting to welcome him back and take care of him in his dotage, but no, that image was as off as a dishwasher at Mount Vernon. "Can I look in his home?" I asked. I sounded tentative because

I didn't really want to intrude on his private life, nor did I feel I had a right to ask if I could tag along.

"Why?" Janie asked, surprised at the request.

"Yeah, why would you want to do that?" Opal repeated. I gave her an *Excuse me?* look, since she had given me the idea. "Oh, I just remembered. We want to know if he was killed over something other than the letter."

"Opal and I wondered if he could have taken some of the more valuable pieces of merchandise home with him. If he did, then he would have taken them home before we inventoried the store, since only the letter was missing when we reinventoried. Maybe there's something at his home that's so valuable someone would kill him to get it."

"Uh, I don't know. It's not typically—"

"The police think the letter might be there, don't they?" I asked.

"That is one thing they're looking for," Janie agreed.

Opal snapped her fingers. "Ask Mark Zhou! He's so nice." She was suggesting I go around Janie to get what I wanted. I liked the way she was thinking.

"Mom!" Paul, with two of the partners in his law firm, came in. I waved, and they came over to our table. He introduced Opal to his colleagues, and they already knew Janie. Their firm was the only one in Marthasville that specialized in litigation.

Janie pointed to the table next to ours. "Ask if you can sit there."

"Sure thing," the waitress said from behind the drinks counter.

The three men moved the heavy, dark, wooden table closer to ours and ordered their sandwiches.

"So how are things at Dewey, Cheatem & Howe?" Opal teased, as they arranged the spindle-back chairs. It was an old joke, but she told it with such mock seriousness that they loved it.

"You're behind the times. Didn't you hear we changed the name of the firm?" Paul said.

"To what?" Opal was happy to play along.

"Sue, Grabbit & Run."

"Oh, that's much better for business," Janie said with a laugh. "Did you guys walk from your office?"

"Sure," one of the guys answered.

"Won't that make it hard to chase an ambulance?" We cracked up at the way Janie had led them right into a trap.

"Paul, did you hear your mom has a date tomorrow night?" Opal asked between bites of her Love Me Tenders chicken fillets.

"What's this? A date?" Paul asked. "Who are you going out with?"

"Brennan Adler," Opal answered for me.

"Two names, huh? So he's a football kind of guy?" Paul teased.

Opal and the other men laughed at our ongoing joke.

"Janie, I happened to point out that fans use NASCAR drivers' first names—" I explained.

"Like Dale, Kurt, Kyle, Austin," Opal interrupted.

"—and professional basketball players are also called their first names," I went on.

Paul joined in. "Michael, Magic, Kevin, Charles."

"But for football players like Patrick Mahomes, Jalen Hurts, Tom Brady, Lamar Jackson, you use both first and last names." I pointed to the rest of the table. "They don't want to admit it, but they were all impressed with my brilliant insight. Even though they couldn't explain this phenomenon . . ."

The first wadded-up napkin came from Opal's end of the table. The next was lobbed—surprisingly—by Janie.

"I ran into Chief Harrod on the way over," Paul said, while the waitress doled out the guys' food orders. "I told him about the customer with the puppy that got into it with Fratelli the day he was murdered."

"Good! Opal tried to tell him about that on Saturday night, and he ignored her. Anyway, that guy didn't look like a killer to me. He looked like a nice man."

"Mrs. Benson, do you know what a murderer looks like?" the lawyer sitting next to Paul asked.

We all laughed, and I admitted I'd only seen them on TV.

"She's sticking up for him because of the puppy," Opal said. "He was a cutie-pie collie."

At some point, Janie's usual guarded demeanor returned. She didn't look bored or distracted; she had just reverted to her quiet self. Opal and I could only hope that if she needed us, she would reach out, and not mistake our minding our own business for not caring.

I told Paul the locksmith was coming in the morning to rekey the locks and that I'd changed the passcode for the alarm system to something unknowable. An unbreakable code.

"You used my birth date, didn't you?"

I had.

* * *

The mention of a dog in the store had me wondering how to make Waited4You dog friendly without risking damage to the valuable merchandise. I felt an infusion of hope thinking about something other than the murder.

After lunch, when I went home to walk Morris and Stickley, I decided to bring them back with me and see how they acted in the gallery. Would they get lost among the boxes? Would fringe on a sofa be too hard for them to resist? That might be asking too much, especially of Stickley.

To save time, I drove rather than walked back to the gallery. My latest favorite toy was my Range Rover hybrid electric SUV. The exterior paint color was something called Santorini Black, and the seats were in almond leather. The music I chose for the short trip was "Another Brick in the Wall" by Pink Floyd.

* * *

After ten minutes of sniffing every corner in every room of the shop except those I'd closed the doors to, both dogs curled up on a stack of rugs. Granted, they weren't puppies. My boys were three-year-old littermates. Completely different from the young pup the young man had brought in. Stickley and Morris had fully formed bladders, and their energy level was much lower than the collie's. The customer had shown consideration and care. I didn't blame him for not tying the puppy up outside. It might have been too cold for the little guy, and besides, it wasn't safe. He had held his dog in his arms, and when he'd seen a book he wanted to take off a shelf, he'd put him down near his feet. You couldn't ask for more than that. Running into the stock room wasn't the worse thing a dog could do; it was Roberto's overreaction that had made the incident unpleasant.

I had put a water bowl by the door, like so many of the King Street stores did. Most restaurants welcomed dogs in their outdoor dining areas. Several had special dog menus. There was even a dog bar park, Barkhaus, on East Howell. If they found a way to make it work, I could too.

Both Stickley and Morris stood up on the stack of rugs by the front window, wagging their tails so happily their bodies swung side to side. A woman with a toddler by the hand and a newborn in a baby sling stopped outside the window. The little boy waved at the dogs with his free hand. Then he blew Stickley and Morris kisses as they walked on. Maybe, just maybe, Marthasville was warming up to us and Waited4You wouldn't forever be known as "the place where that murder happened."

I gave each dog a behind-the-ear scratch and then called the police station to leave a message for Mark Zhou. He returned the call within minutes. I hoped Janie wouldn't mind that I was making an end run around her, but I felt like shaking things up.

"Mrs. Benson, I got your message. I was coming to your store this afternoon to see if the keys found on the victim from Saturday night fit the doors to Waited4You. Is that okay? Is that what you were going to ask me?"

I asked him if I could see Roberto's home and gave him my reasoning.

"Let me ask the detective, and I'll let you know."

Next, I took my laptop to the desk in the stock room. I had another idea for a blog post, which would also be a newsletter article. Now that I had a customer list started, I needed to write more content.

"Uh, no," I said to the dogs. "It's way too dark to work in here. And it sends the wrong message. My desk should be out there." I pointed back to the sales floor, and the dogs' tilted heads told me they agreed completely.

I tossed my shoes to a corner and started moving furniture. A late-nineteenth-century oak refectory table had been shoved against a back wall. It was late Victorian, from England, and beautiful. It would be my new public-face desk after a little overdue TLC.

I went over the piece with the brush attachment of a hand-held vacuum cleaner. The finish was in excellent condition, but until I had it completely free of dust, I wouldn't be able to tell if I needed my conservation-grade furniture detergent. I dipped a cotton swab in denatured alcohol and tested a discreet spot on a table leg. I cheered when the finish didn't budge, because that meant it was something like lacquer or varnish. Oil soap and warm water should do the trick.

I lovingly cleaned the thick barrel-turned legs with a soft brush and the top of the table with a cloth. The haze that had discolored the three planks that made up the top disappeared and the red cast of the legs was restored. The piece was maybe six feet long, and the width was about a third of that. Beautifully proportioned. If someone wanted to buy it, I would sell, but until then I would enjoy using it as my desk in the gallery.

I put my shoes back on and went to the storeroom. What else deserved a spot front and center? I chose a plum-velvet-upholstered dining room chair and put it behind the table.

The title of the blog post was "Collecting Antiques Versus Decorating With Antiques." I included a self-test so readers could tell where they fell on the spectrum but concluded that the two types of antique buyers overlapped as often as not. A beginning collector might be someone buying an antique to decorate a home. I heard my father's matter-of-fact voice alternating with my mother's silvery manner of speaking in my head, and my fingers flew over the keys of my laptop. My personal style was to mix old and new, but some people were soothed by old things and loved being embraced by history. The questions were designed to help readers get clear on what they liked and what fit their lifestyle.

My next job was to call Ritchie Potts. The fake marble-top table needed to go. I sat at the stock room desk and found his number in an old phone book. Roberto had left me two landline phones: a desk phone in here and a white wall phone in the kitchenette. Thanks, but no thanks. I preferred my very own cell phone.

As I waited for Ritchie to answer, I examined the table that was his creation more closely. The workmanship was truly excellent. I ran my hand over and under the top. It was perfect. But wasn't it too perfect? Maybe that had been my first tip-off on Saturday, and it hadn't registered at the time. Still, the table was handmade. It just hadn't been made when Roberto's sign said it had. It hadn't had a life. Who was this guy?

Ritchie hadn't answered, so after I hung up, I Googled him. Richland Potts—that's who he was. His unusual name was one I'd heard before, but a long time ago. The name of Ritchie's custom handmade furniture business was Custom Quality, and I had heard of it from friends, the way a good contractor's name gets passed around in a small town. After a few more clicks I learned that a decade ago, Richland, known in Virginia as Ritchie, had won the prestigious German Emerging Furniture Designer of the Year Award. His category was tables. It was his design for a computer desk that had wowed the judges. I stared at the two photos of his winning entry. He had designed a one-piece computer desk and chair. The first photo was shot from behind the chair back but a little higher—the view of the desk for the user.

I'd never seen anything like it. Its use was obvious, but it didn't look utilitarian. The aesthetics were just that good. And it was ergonomic, yet still pleasing to the eye. Ergonomics focused on the interaction between the human and the "thing," an idea that had always been a little off-putting. It could make you feel as if the thing had some power or agency, and this canceled out any benefit or comfort. It made people like me run back to antiques as fast as we could. Not so with Richland's chair.

Most computer desks had two levels: one for a monitor and one a few inches lower for a keyboard. His had one. The keyboard was at the user's fingertips, and the monitor was sunk into a cutout in the center of the desktop. The image on the screen was projected onto a white glossy surface in front of the user's face. The seat, with a supportive back, was all of one piece.

The second photo was a bird's-eye view. We looked down on Ritchie's creation. There wasn't a single right angle, just undulating curves. It was organic and sculptural—suggesting Elsa Peretti's bean jewelry or her home goods. The version on the website was in glistening white wood. It wasn't different just to be different. It was brilliant. Imaginative.

I tried Ritchie's number again, and when he answered, I introduced myself. "I have a table here on consignment that I would like to return to you."

"Okay." Thankfully, he didn't ask why. If he was surprised, it didn't show in his deep, pleasant voice.

"Would you like me to bring it to you?" What I really wanted was the chance to see one of his computer desks. Fingers crossed.

"No. I'm on my way to Old Town. I'll come to Waited4You."

We hung up, and I went to his company website. Lots and lots of built-in shelving with an occasional custom cutting board. Garage shelves. Laundry room shelving. Window seats. Wainscoting. I ran my mouse over some examples of his work. He was definitely a skilled carpenter. I saw an eye for detail. But did any of this show his chops as an artist? No. I looked at the table I was about to return to him, then back at the web page for the design award he'd won.

"Mr. Potts," I asked the computer screen, "what happened to you?"

Chapter Nine

"Stickley, what are you doing?" Maybe dogs in an antique store wasn't such a good idea after all. Stickley pawed at the baseboard molding under my desk in the stock room while his partner in crime, Morris, watched over his shoulder. I pulled him out from under the desk. I was about to lead both schnauzers back to the sales floor when they took off and ran around me. A second later there was a knock on the door.

The man standing there was tall and muscular. His khakis had a knife-edge crease, possibly heavily starched. Definitely precision ironed. The cuffs of his flannel shirt were rolled up. I unlocked the door, and he good-naturedly petted the heads of the welcome committee.

"I'm Ritchie Potts," he said with a smile. His handshake was firm, and his palms were calloused.

"I'm Camille Benson, and this is Stickley and Morris."

"Nice to meet you, Gustav and William. I'm a big fan of your work—that goes for both of you. Maybe more so for Mr. Stickley's mission furniture," he said with a laugh.

I thanked him and said, "I have mission end tables at home, and whenever one of them goes under it, they look like they're in dog jail." I turned to go back to the stock room. "I'll bring the table out."

"I'll get it." He walked by me at a quick pace, so he obviously knew his way around Waited4You. A large mirror I hadn't found a spot for leaned against the back wall. From where I stood, I was able to watch as Ritchie checked himself out when he walked by. He wasn't displeased with what he saw.

"Uh, okay." *I* was the one who had put the table back there, so why did he think he knew where it was? Maybe since the stock room wasn't all that big, he'd figured he would see it if it was there—but there was more than that one room beyond the gallery floor. The others were empty, but he wouldn't know that.

His phone rang, but he made no move to answer it, and it sounded again.

"I think that's your phone," he said over his shoulder.

I laughed when I realized where the sound was coming from. "It must be the landline. This is the first call I've gotten on it." I remembered there was a wall phone in the kitchenette and answered it in there.

"Is this the new owner of Waited4You?" a woman's voice asked. I told her I was, and she gave me her name and said she was with Makers and Movers, a co-op of northern Virginia craftspeople.

She talked about something she called "our collective artisanal past." I was interested personally, but professionally, not so much. I hadn't heard much mention lately of the maker movement per se, but the industry was booming. Between Etsy, Amazon, and other platforms, these craftspeople had a virtual storefront in a global marketplace. They no longer lived in campers as they traveled across the country from one craft fair to another.

Ritchie was coming out of the stock room.

I thanked her for the call. "For now, I'm not going to carry crafts. Can we talk again after I'm up and running?" She wished me a successful opening. I said, "Happy holidays, and bye for now." I hung up and followed Ritchie and his table to the sales floor.

* * *

Both dogs scampered under my new desk when Ritchie Potts came back. The table he carried was big enough for them to be wary of it but not so big he couldn't carry it without breaking a sweat. He put it down in the middle of the showroom. "I see you've made a few changes." He pointed down at his creation. "Was this not to your liking?"

The question surprised me. I didn't want to read too much into it. It hadn't sounded like a challenge, but didn't he know the table was being misrepresented to buyers? Only one way to find out. "I didn't like how Roberto labeled it. Did you know he was claiming it was mid-nineteenth century?"

"Nothing the guy did surprised me." It sounded like he had Roberto's number, all right, but that answer didn't tell me whether or not he was in on the scam. He was still standing there, so maybe he was about to say more. After an awkward beat, he looked out the front window. "I dropped my wife off, and she's going to walk down here when she's done." That explained why he was hanging around.

"Have a seat. We have plenty of chairs," I joked.

Instead, he walked around the periphery of the gallery.

"I know Roberto Fratelli rubbed a lot of people the wrong way, but still, it's a shame what happened to him," I said.

"Yeah," he said, all but ignoring my attempt to start a conversation. He circled the room again, this time stopping to check out the rare books on the shelf on the left wall.

"Did you know him well?" I asked.

"Not really." My phrasing made the question easy to evade, but I couldn't exactly ask him if he knew whether or not Roberto Fratelli had sold one of his fakes to a mobster, terrorist, or gangbanger who had become violent when he learned the table wasn't really Victorian.

There it was again. Several times since Saturday night, I'd known something was *off*. I felt it. Like I did now. I couldn't describe it, but this sense was different from instinct. People always said I had a good eye, and I liked to think I'd inherited that from my parents. Now I stood in awkward silence with this strange man. When he was younger, maybe in his twenties, he'd designed a work of genius. Now he built what other people designed. Built to plan. He was the one who had made an attractive table that would later become a forgery. I wondered why he was still hanging around here. Why not load up the table and wait for Ella wherever she was? Maybe I should make another attempt at conversation?

"Do you use a 3-D printer to make furniture?" I asked. Surely this topic would interest him.

"No!" he said. Was that an offensive question? Maybe it was. If he considered himself an artist rather than a maker or a craftsperson, he might feel technology would soil his work. I hated to break it to him, but the lines between those things had been smudged and finally erased a loooong time ago. Crafters and makers were artists. Besides, he had created a *computer* desk. I made a mental note to Google 3-D furniture making to see if it had been a thing ten years ago when he designed his winner. That would be one way he could have achieved the curves that looked like waves. If possible, I was even more curious about that computer desk.

"How long have you lived in Marthasville? Or are you from here?" I asked, hoping for more than a one-word answer.

"My wife is. Her mother was a librarian at Beatley Central Library. She wanted to move back. There's a lot of work here, so it was a good decision." For him, certainly, there was a lot of work. I'd heard rumors of waiting lists months long for him to start a home project.

The banging on the window made both of us, plus the dogs, jump. I put my hand on my pounding heart and then laughed at myself.

"That's my wife, Ella." There was a smile in his voice when he said her name. *Ella.*

This was Roberto Fratelli's ex-wife that Janie had talked about? I could not have imagined anyone less likely to be married to him—if I could have imagined anyone at all married to him. There was the obvious age difference, but more than that, Ella Coleman seemed a super-high-maintenance woman. She, in an earlier decade, would have been called a blonde bombshell or sweater girl. Would she ever be happy with someone like Roberto? Opal had once described him as a human pickle because he was unattractive and sour. They'd divorced, so at least one of them had agreed they were a mismatched pair, and not in a good way, like in table settings.

She had certainly traded up. With his flannel shirt and calloused hands, Ritchie Potts looked like the guy that gets the girl in Hallmark movies.

The next minute I was wondering where I'd seen her before, because I had. Oh, yes. She was the platinum blonde I'd seen yesterday morning. She and a gentleman, who was most definitely not Ritchie Potts, had crossed the street when they saw the crime scene tape. She looked like Marilyn Monroe and, like the icon, I thought, would have looked more beautiful wearing half as much makeup.

Ritchie picked up the table, and I walked to the door to hold it open it for him.

"The chief himself questioned me!" Ella declared. So that was where she had been. Why hadn't the newly assigned detective questioned her? That would be interesting to know. What was up with this Nick person? Was he lazy, or overworked, or both? Or maybe he'd had the misfortune of meeting Roberto Fratelli at some point? No police detective worth his salt would be so unprofessional that he wouldn't spend some of his precious time investigating even the most unlikable victim.

As we maneuvered to get the table out, Ritchie asked her, "What'd he want to know?"

"He asked if I knew of anyone who had a grudge against Roberto, and I said, 'Other than the whole town? No one.'" Her voice was breathy and smoky. What man wouldn't fall for a woman that mysterious? The look in Ritchie's eyes when he looked at her said he was completely devoted. "Then I asked him, 'Why don't you talk to your son?'"

Ritchie could easily handle the table by himself, but I wasn't going anywhere. With the pretense of holding the door open, I positioned myself to take up as much room as I possibly could. No need to speed this up.

"What'd he say to that?" Ritchie asked her, after giving me a look, which I chose to ignore.

"Not a word, but I think steam was coming out of his ears." She giggled. Even that wasn't high-pitched. She sounded like Kathleen Turner in *Body Heat* or Lauren Bacall in *To Have and Have Not*. "Then I said, 'He hated him.'" It took feistiness to challenge Chief Harrod to check out his own house first, and I admired that very much. I could see Ella married to Richland Potts, award-winning furniture designer, much more than to Ritchie Potts, woodworker.

"You did? You said that to him?"

Who'd said that? Oh no, it was me. I'd yelled it out before I could stop myself. They both looked at me in surprise, like I was the eavesdropping hired help. Which was exactly what I'd been caught doing. Chief Harrod's son hated Roberto Fratelli? Could he be a suspect? Was that the reason for the slow-walk on the investigation?

"Yeah," she said. "They got in a *horrible fight* the day Roberto was murdered."

"What was it about?" I asked. "Did you hear—"

"I'm parked right over there." Ritchie nodded at a nearby white Ford van and walked off with the table. *Custom Quality* was advertised on the passenger-side door. Some of the letters were formed with hand tools. The *T*s were a handsaw. The *C* was a vise. "Ella?"

"I understand you were once married to him," I told her. "I'm sorry for your loss." Lame, but if she was in a talkative mood, I was happy to listen. She only needed to ignore her husband, who was not-so-subtly exhaling a few yards away, and stay.

"Thanks. It was years ago . . ." She waved the memory away with pumpkin-colored acrylic nails.

"Ella? Ready?" Her husband was obviously trying to hurry her up, and I was out of chitchat to keep her where she was.

She gave her head a little shake. "He was never going to change, not really. He probably couldn't even if he wanted to." Before I could ask what she meant by that, she teetered off in her stilettos to where the van was parked and climbed in.

I should have had Ritchie sign something to confirm the piece was returned to him, but I'd never found the consignment agreement. Nor had I found any record of him being paid for the other tables Roberto had sold. Hmm. That's what I would use to keep them from driving away. "Ritchie, did he owe you any money for your consignment pieces?"

He looked down at the brick sidewalk. Thinking, but about what? Suddenly, he slammed the back door of the van shut, walked around, and opened the driver's side door. A cold wind blew down King Street, and he ran a hand through his longish hair to repair any damage. Then he took a pair of dark-black wraparound sunglasses off the dash and put them on. "Nah, we're square."

A black-and-white cruiser with Mark Zhou behind the wheel pulled into the parking space in front of the truck. Ritchie and Ella stared at the police car, mesmerized. Finally, the van pulled into King Street traffic.

Mark got out and came to the door.

"Why do people gawk at police cars like that?" I asked. "It's not like you just pulled them over."

"Now, Dr. Benson, would I do something like that?"

"You would, and I bet you have," I answered.

"I didn't this time. Besides, my lights weren't even on." He held up a baggie containing two keys, and I opened the door for him. "Here's the first key." He tried it in the lock, and the deadbolt shot out. "I'll try the second one too. It doesn't look the same, but since I'm here . . ." That one didn't fit, not even the tip. He put both keys back in the labeled plastic bag.

"Mark, thanks for coming today. The locksmith will be rekeying both doors tomorrow morning."

"Perfect timing. Now, hopefully, this other key is for his apartment door," he said.

"About Roberto's apartment . . . ?" I hinted.

"I asked about you going with me and taking a look at the victim's home, and the detective said that'd be fine. He said to tell you he might be late but for us to go ahead. I'll give you the address, but you can follow me over there. It's not far, just off Route 1."

* * *

Roberto Fratelli's condo was in the Potomac Yards area of Marthasville. The complex was new, just two or three years old, and pricey. When Mark had given me the address, I'd been so relieved I'd thought I would cry. Because of Roberto's reputation and personality, I'd pictured him living in a sad hovel. A gray shack. The problem with that image was that it would mean Waited4You hadn't made much of a profit. I felt better now looking at the luxurious building.

After I parked my Range Rover in a visitor's space near Mark's police car, I opened the sunroof for Stickley and Morris and joined him.

"The building manager is meeting us in the lobby," he said as he opened the glass door.

A young woman in a navy skirt and blazer saw us come in and walked up. She introduced herself and gave Mark the up-and-down before leading us back outside. "These are condo-townhouses," she explained. Roberto's unit was a two-story condo.

When we got to the door of unit 232, she unlocked it and stood aside for us to go in. "You have my cell phone in case you need anything," she said with a flirty smile at my young friend as she turned to leave.

"Excuse me," he called to her.

"Yeeees?" She turned back around.

"Someone else from the police department will be here soon. Would you mind showing him where we are?"

She gave him a big two-thumbs-up, bending her knees and making a *click-click* sound with her tongue before she walked away.

I stood at the open door and took in the spacious home with its newish furniture, built-ins lined with books, large television, and gourmet kitchen. Definitely not a sad hovel.

"Mark, I didn't expect him to live in a place like this. Did you?"

"No, I didn't. I only met him a couple of times, but I heard so many stories about him that I felt I knew him. This is so, uh, happy looking."

I laughed at the apt description.

"I mean, this looks like where a younger person would live," he elaborated. "And all the furniture looks comfortable and normal."

He was right. The lemon-yellow sofa and off-white over-stuff chairs begged to be sat on. The rooms were sunny. Pale paint colors and blond flooring bathed the living room in light. The kitchen was modern. I didn't see anything dated at all on the first floor. Had this been his attempt to change for Ella?

Mark checked the other key from the baggie in the lock in Roberto's entrance door. "It's a fit."

I walked around, looking, for what I didn't know. If I'd hoped to find a valuable antique or masterpiece, I was sorely disappointed. There was nothing from Waited4You or any other antique store here.

I tried to reconcile these surroundings, Roberto's private life, with his meanest-man-in-Marthasville reputation. Was there another side to him?

A minute later I saw it. One of Ritchie's Victorian side tables sat in the corner of the dining room, by the sliding glass door to the balcony, mocking my optimism and smacking me down for giving Roberto a chance.

The spot was a no-brainer for a plant, or a crystal vase, or a sculpture that would catch the sunlight, but the table sat empty. It was here because Roberto couldn't have two on the sales floor. That would make a customer question its history and therefore its value. And after Friday, he hadn't been able to keep the extra in the stock room, because I would have seen it. I had been included in the people in the universe he was willing to cheat.

He'd charged almost $800 for each of the tables, but I didn't know how much of that Ritchie got and how much was store profit, since I hadn't found records of Roberto paying him anything. And Ritchie had been no help there. I was happy I didn't owe Ritchie any money for the tables Roberto had sold, since that would have come out of my pocket.

I walked back to find Mark. "I don't see any furniture that might have been taken from Waited4You. Can I look in the cabinets and drawers for what might be more valuable?"

"The missing letter?" he asked. I nodded. "Sorry, Dr. Benson. That we better leave to the professionals."

Click-click. I imitated the young woman with the exaggerated thumbs-up. "I'll walk around, but I won't touch."

He laughed and went to the kitchen. I went upstairs.

Roberto's bedroom was as minimalist and clean looking as the downstairs rooms. The bed looked new, comfy, and expensive. I wanted to press down on the mattress but remembered my hands-off promise. A large armchair sat in a sunny corner of the bedroom. I tried to imagine Roberto kicking back in it.

"No," I said out loud. "It's what I don't see. Boxes." Why hadn't he started packing up? Why was there no for-sale sign? Of course, there could be a simple explanation, like how quickly the deal had gone through. Except his part of the process hadn't been all that speedy if he'd gone through two commercial sales agents.

"Whoa," Mark yelled. "Will ya look at this?"

I went downstairs to do exactly that.

Mark stood before the open door of a pantry. His mouth hung open, and he pointed to the contents. I prepared myself for the worst but didn't take a step until I sniffed the air. I didn't smell anything at all, so I walked over. Would I find more counterfeits? Maybe a second set of accounting books?

"Whoa," I echoed. I couldn't do better than Mark's word.

Store containers of processed food filled every shelf except the highest. Anything that didn't have to be cooked or even heated up was in here. Cups of pudding, canned fruit, applesauce. Packets of peanut butter crackers and cheese crackers. Cans of tuna. Bottles of fruit and vegetable juices.

"Does the power go out here a lot?" I asked.

"Not that I've heard about." His eyes stayed on the packaged foods.

"Mark, you're a bachelor, aren't you?"

"Yeah."

I looked at the shelves and raised my eyebrows. "And it looks strange even to you?"

"Uh, yeah! I mean, I can't cook, but I can use a microwave and I eat out a lot."

I hadn't seen any evidence of Roberto being a hoarder at Waited4You. Actually, the amount of stock was pretty low.

Mark shook his head. "This looks like some survivalist shit. Sorry."

Chapter Ten

"Camille? Camille?" Helen Margalit scurried up the sidewalk as I brought the bistro table inside. She handed me a large plant. "Welcome to King Street Merchants."

November temps gave a pink glow to the eighty-something-year-old's pretty face. She was dressed in wool slacks and a three-quarter-length wrap coat, in camel, along with sensible shoes. A beret that matched the coat was pulled over her silver hair.

"Thank you! Is this what I think it is?" It was an indoor version of a geranium, but not just any variety.

"It is! It's a Martha Washington geranium."

I hugged her with one arm and held the plant with the other. "This is beautiful! Come in."

I had just returned from Roberto's house an hour ago. Mark and I had talked about why there were no antiques in the home, valuable or otherwise—not so much as a candlestick. We'd concluded that since Roberto worked with antiques all day, he probably didn't want to look at them in the evening. Whatever the reason, there weren't any in his home.

I hadn't seen the letter, but maybe the police would find it. Or maybe not. The working theory was that his killer had taken it.

Helen walked up to the refectory table that was temporarily my desk. "Is this new?"

"Just newly cleaned." I pointed to the back of the room. "Roberto had it against that wall."

"It's stunning. I never noticed it before." The TLC I had administered had given the table new life.

I placed the plant on the end and smiled at it. "The purple blooms are perfect on this warm-toned wood, aren't they?"

"Un-huh." She looked at Stickley and Morris, who were back to sitting on the rugs. I was going to have to stop that. "It's safe for dogs too," she assured me.

"Maybe having a plant named for Martha will bring me luck." It occurred to me that she might not know what had happened to my predecessor. "Did you hear about Roberto? Maybe you saw it in the paper?"

"Yes! My, my. So upsetting." She looked away. "I just wonder."

"What?"

"Oh, nothing."

"Please tell me. You mentioned something last Wednesday when you were on the canine cruise with Lucky. Something about hoping one of those incidents wouldn't happen again. What was that about?"

"On Labor Day, your security alarm went off in the middle of the night. The thieves stole several, I think six, rare books."

My eyes darted to that shelf. "Did the police catch whoever did it?"

"No, and I don't know that Mr. Fratelli ever reported the break-in to them. He would never tell us anything." Her voice, always soft, now quavered.

"Six, huh?" I wondered if that was all a burglar could carry.

"They tossed the books in the alley." She pointed over her left shoulder to the back corner of the store. "The next morning I found five of the books myself. I knew they belonged here because they had the little copper sticker on the inside, so I brought them back to him. He was so very rude. More than usual, if you can imagine that. I guess because it was before opening hours. It had rained all night and was still pouring at the time, but he didn't even invite me in. First, he said, 'You keep 'em.' Just like that."

Speaking to a person of her age so rudely went well beyond eccentric, especially when she was doing him a favor. "I'm so sorry he talked to you like that," I said.

"Oh, it gets worse. After he said for me to keep them, he must have changed his mind, because he reached out and grabbed them out of my arms."

I stared in shock. "Would you like to sit down?" I asked.

"No, I'm fine, dear."

"Well, I think I need to. Would you like a cup of tea?" I had cleaned the kitchenette within an inch of its life and bought a Cuisinart electric kettle.

"No, thank you. I need to get back to Noah soon."

I pulled out the dining room chair that I used at the desk and sat down. "What you're telling me is crazy."

"Oh, it wasn't so bad. Really. I wasn't eager to carry the soggy mess home with me." She laughed. "The next day when it stopped raining, I found another book."

"What did you do with it?" Then I added, "I hope you kept it. He didn't deserve to have it back."

"I cleaned it up as well as I could, then I put it in the window to dry out. I was planning to donate it to the Marthasville Library, but I forgot about it until I heard you were thinking about buying Waited4You. Camille, I have to say, the thought of someone else being here gave me such hope that I could finally admit to myself how disturbing the matter had been. Since he didn't report it to the police, the robbers could come back anytime. And of course, the new owner being *you* made it even more special. Noah and I do miss your parents."

"So do I." I got up and hugged her thin shoulders. It was Noah who hadn't wanted her talking about this "incident" during the canine cruise. It had truly upset them. I pulled back to look at her. "Are you saying you still have the last book?"

"Yes. Would you like to have it? It is yours, you know."

"I would. I'd at least like to see it. May I walk back with you to get it?"

She said that would be lovely, and I pulled my cardigan on and buttoned it up for us to head out. "I wonder why anyone would go to the trouble of stealing something just to toss it. Were the police chasing him? Or her?"

"I never heard they were."

I tied on my scarf and pulled on my gloves, then hooked the dogs up to their leashes. Margalit Gallery and Framing was only two stores away, and we took our time on the brief walk.

We talked about her dog, Lucky, and how cold the weather had turned compared to just last week.

* * *

I carried the book back to the gallery in a Whole Foods cloth shopping bag, wondering exactly what was in it. Helen's account made the book very mysterious. Some of the books Roberto had left me were old, and all were used. His signage proclaimed them all rare. Was this one?

Rare-book thefts were, unfortunately, not rare at all. Sometimes collectors stole to add special volumes to their collections. Sometimes they paid thieves to do their dirty work.

I'd had a long day and looked forward to a night at home. After I double-checked the alarm (turned on) and both doors (locked), Stickley, Morris, and I got into the car.

* * *

Once I was cozy in yoga pants, a T-shirt, and UGG boots and had a fire going in the fireplace, I made a cup of tea and sat down with the book.

Considering all it had been through, I expected a bedraggled disaster. *Boys & Girls & Families* was a beautifully illustrated children's storybook from 1921. Other than the water stains on the cover and the binding and on the edge of the pages, the book seemed untouched. The pages of a children's book should be roughed up, at least a little.

The author's name wasn't on the cover, so it might have been created by various writers. It explained family relationships. A brother and sister grew up and married pleasant-looking—though maybe less attractive than they themselves were—spouses. On the next page, the brother and his wife became parents. On the facing page, the sister and her husband did the same. The next pages explained cousins, then aunts, uncles, nieces, and nephews. By the end, the boy and girl were grandparents. Got it.

I closed the book and studied the dust jacket. I had my pocket microscope on the coffee table in case I needed it later. The earliest dust jackets were blank and used to protect a book's ornate cover. Later on, titles were printed on the spine so customers could find a particular book without taking it off the shelf. Books with dust jackets from the nineteenth century were rare because so many people threw them away. That changed after World War I, when artists took corporate jobs and some were hired by publishing houses. Soon dust jackets had artwork, a short summary of the book, and maybe the author's biography and photograph. Artwork had changed through the years, but dust jackets hadn't changed much since the 1920s. The humble, once disposable, book jacket was now an important sales tool for a hardcover book.

Some dust jackets were printed digitally, which would leave uniform edges on the images. Of course, that wouldn't apply to this book, since the technology had been developed many years after 1921. Some were printed with offset lithography, in which the ink was pressed onto the paper, which resulted in the edges of each color field holding more ink than the rest of the image. I smiled, thinking maybe I hadn't forgotten everything my parents had taught me.

The dust jacket could provide clues on the book's origin. I started by examining the bottom edge. If the book was from 1921, it should have tiny tears or scuffed areas here and there. I *saw* several scratches, which was odd, because I didn't *feel* any. I ran my forefinger along the bottom edge of the dust jacket. It was smooth. Even after being left in the rain, it was perfect. I held the pocket microscope up to my eye and took a closer look. Aha. The dust jacket was a reproduction. A copy, scratches and all, had been made from another dust jacket.

Could the jacket be a facsimile but the book be authentic? That would be unlikely. Was I ready to say this book wasn't a century old? Why didn't I go ahead and call it?

I opened *Boys & Girls & Families* again and looked at the endpapers. The last was pasted to the inside of the cover. The other was the flyleaf, or the first free page. I went through the pages of the front matter, which included the title page and then the copyright page. A series of numbers near the bottom of that page gave the year of publication and the number of the printing. The first number was *1*, meaning this book was a first edition. Or at least it claimed to be.

There was a smudge on the title page, and I went back to it. The rain had smeared a few handwritten words. I moved to the end of the sofa and held the book under the lamp. *Merry Christmas! Aunt Minnie, 1922.* Was I holding a century-old book, or not? If it was new, that inscription showed the intent to deceive, and that was what made the book a fraud. Of course, if this wasn't a first edition, the copyright page had incorrect information on it also, but the average book buyer wouldn't know what the *1* meant. The inscription, however, was a clear signal designed to lure unsuspecting collectors.

My parents had made me look at, smell, and touch—with gloves, of course—hundreds of old books to learn the difference between what was real and what was a forgery. The passage of time gave pages a special scent and patina. My father had said for me to close my eyes and imagine a book that had spent one or two hundred years in a church or a library, then ask myself if the book I was holding gave me the same feeling. When I looked at and held *Boys & Girls & Families* in my hand, I felt nothing. Not a yes. Not a no. Nothing.

Thanks a lot, Roberto. What other surprises had he left for me? I leaned my head back on the sofa and stretched my neck. I was tired. I had worked hard moving furniture and organizing the stock room. If not for the murder, I would have called it a good tired. Now I was glad I'd decorated my own home for fall, preparing for Wednesday's post-election party. At least that was done. Hadn't my mother said something, during the lead-up to most holidays, about the cobbler's children having no shoes? Waited4You looked like a dream, but year after year, there was never any time to decorate our own house for the holidays. Or was that by design? Rather than a house packed with decorations, we had subtle touches like Christmas towels in the bath for the month of December, and red and green candles on the dining room table. Simple. Tasteful. Nothing overdone or looking like it was trying too hard. The most important place had been decorated. Maybe that was another reason Waited4You felt like home to me.

* * *

What seemed like a lifetime ago, I'd planted six red amaryllis bulbs and put a dozen paper-white bulbs in pebbles and water. The color of the amaryllis was Red Reality. It was almost burgundy. With any luck, all would be blooming in time for the holidays. I considered where in the store, besides the front window, they would look best. Hmm, I was already thinking of Waited4You as an extension of my home.

I ran my hand over the sofa cushion, upholstered in what was now called performance fabric. It was pet friendly, durable, and fade resistant, and it looked good but didn't have to be coddled.

I looked at *Boys & Girls & Families* again. Why was I giving the book one more chance and then another to prove it wasn't a pirated copy?

With that thought, I missed my parents more than I ever had. I had grieved when each died, but this was different. Now I felt like I needed them here. Even though, or maybe because, I wasn't doing anything the way they had. I was arranging the store very differently from how it had been set up when they owned it. For one thing, I had about half as much merchandise on the floor as they'd had. Where was it written that an antique store had to be cluttered? Or that a historic house had to look dated? The traditional jam-packed antique store didn't work with my business plan. Was my idea to give decorating advice—for customers wanting a clean, modern look that still exuded warmth—even viable? The store had been a success when my parents owned it. Even Roberto seemed to have made a go of it, if his pricey condo was any indication. I felt like I was sliding into failure with my crazy idea of a store that felt familiar but not stale.

I shook my head so those negative thoughts couldn't adhere to my brain.

The dogs' round, dark eyes looked up at me. If schnauzers could smile, that's what they would have been doing behind their salt-and-pepper beards. They were ready for one of their favorite games. Stickley jumped up on the sofa on my right side. Then Morris joined him, but on my other side.

That was my cue. I grabbed for Stickley, pretending to just miss him as he jumped down. Then I tried to put my arms around Morris, again just missing him. Then I looked away, completely uninterested. They jumped up one at a time, then back down. Again, I lunged for them and came up empty. After a few rounds, I gave them a sad face, and they jumped up to be loved on. The standard schnauzer breed was known for having a sense of humor, and life with these two was never boring.

"I'm not a rare-books expert, but I know that Marthasville has one," I said to them as I reached for my phone. The Barrett branch of the Marthasville Library had a collection of rare books and a librarian who specialized in their acquisition and care. I emailed the reference desk at the library and asked to meet with her, preferably tomorrow.

After I fed the dogs, I checked my phone. A response had come back that the local history librarian wasn't in on Tuesdays, but she could see me Wednesday.

Next, I called Janie. I reached her on her cell phone, and she was still at work. "Do you know anything about a robbery at Waited4You a couple of months ago? Some rare books, or books Roberto was claiming were valuable, were stolen."

"I don't remember hearing anything, but it's easy to check out. Hmm. Um . . . well, well," she said, punctuating her words with impressively fast key tapping. "I can't find anything on a theft. How did you hear about it?"

"Helen Margalit said the security alarm at Waited4You went off, and—"

"Let me search by alarm calls."

"They tossed the books in the ally. I have no idea why. Helen found six of them. Really just an armful. Maybe the thief stole something else too, something he wanted more, and couldn't carry everything."

"I see something interesting here. Someone walking along the sidewalk heard the alarm and called 911, but when the police telephoned Roberto, he said it was accidently set off and he didn't need an officer to come out."

"So he lied?" I asked. "I mean, *someone* threw those books in the alley."

"Are you, uh, thinking maybe the thieves returned on Saturday night and Roberto disturbed them? This time they wanted the letter?"

"I know better than to think anything." I laughed. "Seriously, who lies about a robbery that really happened?"

"You would be surprised. Victims sometimes do. Maybe out of fear or intimidation, any number of reasons. Since the thieves got away with it once, I wonder if they figured they could get away with it again." She was warming to the idea.

"To give credit where credit is due, on Saturday night and again on Sunday, Chief Harrod said Roberto might have interrupted a robbery and the thief killed him." Maybe I was wrong about him slow-walking the investigation.

"I'll tell Nick. He can get more information from Helen."

"He won't upset her, will he?"

"Him? Never. He's kind and he's old-fashioned in a good way."

Both dogs stood up at the family room bay window, then jumped onto the window seat and barked. It was snowing.

Chapter Eleven

Tuesday

After a good night's sleep and an early-morning spin class at the YMCA, I felt better about the future of my store. Before I'd had ideas for what Waited4You could be, but now I had clarity on the steps I needed to take to accomplish my vision for the store. Sure, Marthasville had a lot for visitors to enjoy, but I would focus on locals. When a store, restaurant, bar, or park was truly part of the local scene, tourists followed because they wanted to see what was special about the town.

Maybe it was just my imagination, but people had seemed distracted during the hard workout. Like, not as intense as they usually were. The East Monroe Avenue location had its usual bustling, high-energy vibe, but I felt something in the air. Something unsaid. That is, until the class ended.

Dr. Denise Goodman, my former boss and dean at the community college, came up to my bike before I dismounted. "You know it's not too late to change your mind," she started. "We don't have anyone to teach your classes next semester yet."

I wiped sweat from the back of my neck with a hand towel that proclaimed, *Nothing haunts us like the antique we didn't buy.* "Thanks, but I feel good about my decision." Feel good? That might have been an overstatement.

"You do?" Deb Burfoot joined her. "How can you say that?"

"Hi, Deb. Nice to see you. The last time we talked was when you were on Opal's canine cruise."

She held up a know-it-all finger. "That was less than a week ago! Do you think you may have rushed into buying that antique store?"

"Probably," I said. Where would we be without hindsight's twenty-twenty acuity?

She gave Denise a smug smile. "I didn't think you understood just how hard running a small business could be. Even without"—she lowered her voice to a whisper—"you-know-what happening, it's so demanding." Deb owned a successful children's clothing consignment shop in town and was in her midthirties. She was a walking, talking chamber of commerce.

"You're right. There is a lot involved. Some aspects you can control, and sometimes something no one can see coming crashes down on you. I appreciate your concern." She showed none, of course, but we lived in a small town and lied to each other like that from time to time. What I didn't appreciate was being made to feel that I needed to defend my decision.

Deb walked off, but Denise wasn't quite done with me. "Keep my number on your phone in case you need it in the future." Her tone, like Deb's, was *I told you so.* She followed the other woman out. I rehydrated as an excuse to keep from seeing them in the parking lot.

What was it Eleanor Roosevelt had said about no one making you feel inferior without your consent? With all due respect to one of my sheroes, I wasn't so sure about that. I hadn't given permission for that intervention, or whatever it was, and I felt gutted.

On Sunday, I'd mentioned getting my old job back to Opal. Now, two days later, I wouldn't take it if it was offered to me on the proverbial silver platter. Even an antique one that someone else had polished for me. I stood up straight and turned to look at—no, *see*—myself in the mirrored wall. It didn't matter if I thought I was good enough to make Waited4You a success, even after the murder. I was on a train and I couldn't get off. I might mix a metaphor from time to time, but in my mind, I'd burned my ships. There would be no turning back. Thanks, Deb and Denise, for that unintended gift.

Chapter Twelve

The warmth earlier in the day had melted a good bit of the snow, and now lower temps had frozen any water puddled on the brick sidewalks or cobblestone streets. Driving was safer, even potentially less embarrassing, than walking, but Paul and I ventured as far as Suits to a Tea! for a late-afternoon pick-me-up. We sat at a table by the window for a good view of the holiday lights strung along and over King Street. I had worked on displays, creating vignettes, all day. It felt good to sit down for a few minutes.

"Beautiful!" I said, looking out at the thousands of tiny white lights. It was only five o'clock, but it was dark outside.

"Wow, she *really* is."

I followed his gaze and saw who he meant just as the young woman slipped and fell on the ice. My son had faster reactions than any human had a right to, and he was out the café door in a second. He helped her up, and they stood looking at one another. She said something, and he picked up the three packages that had flown in as many directions. Oh, good. They were coming in to join me.

"Mom, this is Pepper. This is my mother, Camille Benson." She was petite, maybe five two, and had thick strawberry-blonde hair. Her cheeks were flushed, maybe from her fall or the cold.

"Nice to meet you," I said.

"And you're curious about my name?"

I laughed. "Yeah, since you mentioned it."

"My parents were Snoopy fans."

"Oh no, they didn't!" Paul said. The waitress brought another cup, and he picked up the teapot on the table and poured a cup for Pepper. He seemed mesmerized by her voice. As for Pepper, she looked like the comic strip *Brenda Starr, Reporter*, with stars in her eyes.

Grandchildren! I thought, before I could rein myself in.

"Yes, they did. My birth certificate reads Peppermint Patty. I used Patty for a while, but when they both died in a car accident when I was a teenager, I went back to what my dad called me. Sorry, but I'm a little defensive."

"Not at all," I assured her.

"I like it," Paul said. I liked her.

* * *

Forty-five minutes later, Paul and Pepper were still getting to know one another. I tried to interrupt to say I needed to leave, but I was invisible to the two of them.

This was going so well.

"Beethoven, Bach, Mozart, Brahms, all of them—they were creative geniuses, right?" Paul was saying. When had my son ever listened to classical music? Maybe while he jogged? Pepper played cello for the Marthasville Symphony Orchestra, so of course, she was a connoisseur.

The look on her face told me Paul was making an impression. She nodded and smiled, probably happy that this was something they had in common. A lot of men couldn't even name four composers. Sure, he'd listed the easy ones, but still. They seemed to be perfect for one another, and I grinned at both of them. He was handsome. She was lovely. He would fall in love and get his nose out of my business.

"Well, then what happened when it came to putting titles on their music? Symphony No. 2, Symphony No. 10, Symphony No. 5 in something major or minor? They couldn't come up with anything better than a number? Something catchy?" He was getting worked up.

"What?" Her smile sagged ever so slightly. *No, no, no. Oh, please stop.*

"I'm just saying they could have tried a little harder. After all, the most important and the hardest part of the job was done. Just needed a little more effort, that's all I'm saying." He raised both hands, signaling he rested his case.

She stood. "It's been so nice meeting both of you." He wasn't in the friend zone; he was in the acquaintance zone. My brilliant, athletic, handsome, good-man son had done it again. On his first date, when he was sixteen, he'd brought a girl he knew from Marthasville High back to our house to watch water boil. Really. She had quoted the adage, and he'd just had to prove to her that a watched pot did, in fact, boil. That had been his first and only date with her.

I shook her hand. "I own Waited4You Antiques. Please stop by when we open. I hope the soft opening will be soon." I wanted to tell her that this unwavering sense of the way things should be would make him a true husband and an amazing dad someday.

"A friend of mine told me about Waited4You. Cute name. Uh, you're not going to change it because, of, well, you know? That was horrible. Sure, *he* was horrible, but still."

I had better get used to people bringing up the murder. I would tackle it the way she handled curiosity about her name. Straightforward. "I agree, and I hope the police will solve it soon. I'm keeping the name."

"I heard you plan to give decorating advice when you open?"

I nodded and exhaled with relief. That was all it took. I had acknowledged what happened. Maybe that was all potential customers wanted. No denial of the tragedy. No glossing over it.

"Waited4You was the name my parents, Paul's grandparents, named the store. They said I wrote it like that when I was six years old and informed them it would be chic. I don't really remember. They married late in life and had me when they were older. They believed that when you find what you truly love, you'll know it because it will tell you, *I waited for you*. I believe that too." Suddenly the image of Brennan Adler popped into my head. Whoa, where had that come from?

Pepper sat down again. "I'm looking for a part-time job. Are you going to hire sales help? At least for the holidays?"

"Yes, I am. I put a help-wanted sign in the window this morning." I stole a glance at Paul and beamed. He looked smitten. I doubted he had any idea how close he had come to blowing it. She looked at him and smiled. This was salvageable.

"Hi!" Opal waved at us from outside. She pointed to the door. "I'll join you." She came in and gave Paul a hug, and he introduced her to Pepper.

I pushed my chair back. "Just leaving. I need to give Brennan a new key. He's my landlord," I explained to Pepper.

"Why can't you give it to him on your *daaaate*?" Opal teased.

Brennan and I were meeting at Vola's Dockside Grill. The restaurant was named for Marthasville's first female city manager. She was an animal lover, and Marthasville's animal shelter was also named after Vola Lawson.

Transferring the key at dinner was exactly what we'd agreed to do, but for now I needed an excuse to leave these two alone. "No! We texted, and he said I definitely should bring it to his office. He said he loses things all the time." My lying words tumbled out, and I hoped Opal would get that I had made up the story. I wasn't trying to lie to her, just everyone else at the table. I planned to set the record straight later.

"I'll go with you," Opal said. Good.

Pepper stood. "I'm parked up the street. I'll walk with you too." Not good.

Paul drained his teacup and got up. "Ready to go." Again, not good.

I walked out of Suits to a Tea!, and they followed in a line. Brennan's office was on the other side of Waited4You. That didn't give me much time to come up with a plan. I had one of the new keys on me. It was the copy I planned to give Opal if I ran into her when I was at the restaurant later. I thought it made sense for someone other than me to have access if it was ever needed.

If I couldn't shake Paul and Pepper, I guessed I *could* give it to him, but would he think I was senile? "We'll just leave it with his secretary," I said. Did he even have an administrative assistant? I hadn't seen anyone else in the office when I signed the lease agreement. Did all attorneys have office staff?

When we got there, I hesitated, and Paul took it from there. "Mom, I'll say good-bye. Have fun tonight. Pepper, can I walk you to your car?" Opal and I watched them walk away. Now, if she would please leave, I could sneak back to Waited4You. Paul and Pepper were walking too slowly for me to tell her the truth standing there.

I gasped when she turned the knob and the door opened. It wasn't locked, but being a business, I hadn't expected it to be. "Wait! I need to confess something. I wasn't going in."

"You weren't?"

"That was an excuse to make my getaway and give Paul a chance to ask Pepper out. So let's get out of here."

"But we're here now. Hello?" she asked the empty outer office. She went in and I followed, so I could close the door on the cold air.

There was an unoccupied receptionist's desk. The surface was completely clear. No family photos, coffee mugs, or note-pads. Not even a computer. I walked around and looked into the office behind it, Brennan's. The lightest possible touch of cigar smoke lingered, almost like someone in the room had thought about smoking one. A framed University of Virginia School of Law diploma hung on the wall behind the desk.

"Let's see how old he is," Opal whispered, as she walked by me and behind the desk for a closer look at the graduation year on the diploma.

"Opal, what if he comes back while we're in here?" I took the key out of my handbag and dropped it on the desk. If he caught us, we'd have cover. "What the hell?"

"Huh? I think he's about our age," she said, without looking back at me. "A little older. Not too much, though."

"Opal?" I inhaled her name, not able to say more. Hardly able to breathe.

Hearing the tone of my voice, she swung around. Other than pointing at the leather pouch and aged letter encased in a polyester sleeve sitting there on his desk, I couldn't move. The letter looked like it was written on rag paper and was maybe five inches wide and folded in half. I shut my eyes. Understanding crashed on me in waves. Each new realization hurt more than the one before it.

I didn't touch it, though I wanted to. One touch would contaminate evidence, but years of hundreds of touches made a document look old. Oil from human touch gave paper a certain scent. To me a perfume.

Opal, thankfully, had very few emergencies on the Potomac River, so I guessed it was her time in the Coast Guard that made her a genius in a crisis. I would have liked to study the spidery handwriting I saw, but she sprinted to my side and pulled my arm. "We're getting out of here. Now."

We ran to the door. "We should call 911," I said.

"We will once we're outside," she said. "Brennan Adler is Roberto's murderer."

Chapter Thirteen

"I need to speak with the detective working on the Roberto Fratelli murder," Opal said. "It's important." We waited outside in the cold for her to be connected. "Camille, can you remember his name?"

"Uh, Nick? That's all Janie said." He hadn't been with the chief on Saturday night, and he hadn't shown up at Roberto's condo when I left. Nor had he been the one to question Ella Coleman. Did he even exist?

"Yes, Detective? This is Opal—" She looked at me and rolled her eyes. "Chief Harrod? I was trying to reach a detective named Nick." He must have said that wasn't going to happen, because her next words were, "We just found the missing letter." He said something, and she looked at me. "Yes, the one that was stolen from the antique store when Roberto Fratelli was murdered." She told him she was with me and that we were standing in front of Waited4You.

I rubbed my temples, and after she hung up, she reached for my hand. "Camille, I'm so sorry. You must be disappointed."

"I can't believe it," I said.

"I wish there was some way this wasn't as bad as it seems, but for the life of me, I can't think of an innocent explanation for that letter being on Brennan Adler's desk. Can you?"

I shook my head. "It doesn't make sense. I can't believe he's a killer."

"I guess you could ask him tonight on your date?"

"Not funny."

"Too soon? Sorry, I just wanted to be sure you knew what a close call you had."

Chief Harrod's white car pulled up to the curb, lights on. He was followed by Janie in her BMW. Then two Marthasville police cars.

"Is the property owner in there?" Chief Harrod called to us. Without waiting for an answer, he cracked the door to Brennan's office building an inch but didn't enter. "Mr. Adler? Brennan? It's Ralph Harrod."

I shook my head. "No one's in there. The door wasn't locked, so we went in. I, uh, had something for him."

He stepped away from the door and turned on his heel to go speak to the officers. He looked up, then down King Street, pointing with two fingers the way flight attendants do. I automatically looked down at the sidewalk for lights to guide the way to the nearest exit.

Opal and I inched over to Janie. We wanted to confab without it looking like that's what we were doing.

"Why's he here? Where is the detective who is supposed to handle this case?" Opal asked, looking like an amateur ventriloquist.

Janie checked to be sure the chief wasn't in hearing range. "He wants to be reassigned and for some other detective to take this one." She tilted her head in Harrod's direction. "But he won't let him. Now tell me what you saw."

"It was the letter I found when we were inventorying Waited4You," Opal whispered. "Just sitting there. Pretty as you please on his desk. We went in to—"

"Don't tell me how you happened to be there," Janie said.

Opal pointed to me. "She needed to drop off—"

"I said don't—"

Opal took Janie's arm. "No, I have to tell you this. We just left the new key to Waited4You in there because he's the landlord. We need it back because he's a killer. Get it!"

Janie's eyes widened, and she nodded. "I understand now. I'll see what I can do," she whispered.

"I have no idea what you two are talking about . . ." I said. "Wait, now I get it." They thought I needed protection from Brennan. "And I don't agree with you."

"Did someone let you in?" Chief Harrod had left the cluster of uniformed officers and was within barking distance of us.

"No, like I said, the door was unlocked," I said.

He checked his watch. "This would be easier if he was in there."

"Let's wait for him. That's how this should be handled," Janie said.

Suddenly I saw Brennan Adler walk up King Street from the opposite direction. He was so handsome he seemed like a dream appearing in the twilight, holiday lights, and leftover snow.

"What in the hell is going on here!" he yelled when he saw the police presence in front of his office. Wait, dreams didn't talk like that, nor did they yell.

"Brennan, can we go inside?" Chief Harrod shook his hand and patted him on the back with his other hand.

"Of course, Ralph. Just a sec." He walked a couple of steps closer to me. "See you at seven." I didn't respond. I didn't know how I felt, and I had no idea what the look on my face revealed to him. My emotions bounced from disappointment to disbelief, which meant there was nothing to be disappointed about. Roberto was murdered and the letter was stolen. The letter was on the desk of the man I was supposed to have dinner with in less than two hours. In the beat we stood there, his expression changed. I saw confusion on his face and something else. What? Hurt?

Brennan, the chief, and two officers went inside. The other two uniformed officers remained standing sentry by the front door.

"You need to get to work," I reminded Opal.

"Yeah, I do. Are you going to be okay?"

I nodded. She said good-bye to Janie and walked downhill to where the *Admiral Joshua Barry* waited for her. If only I could get on a boat and sail the Potomac River to the Chesapeake Bay. "Janie, do you want to come in out of the cold?"

"I'd better stay out here. I don't want to be out of the loop."

I unlocked the door to Waited4You but stopped and looked back when I heard people coming out of Brennan's office.

"Ride in my car, Brennan."

He wasn't in handcuffs, but it looked like he was being taken in to be questioned. When he walked around to get in the car on the passenger side, he didn't look at me.

"I need to go inside Mr. Adler's office to be with them when they collect the evidence," Janie told me. "Every bit of this has to be handled by the book. Can you come by the office tomorrow?"

I told her I would, and we hugged good-bye. I had everything I wanted. The murder was solved. Then why did I feel like this?

Chapter Fourteen

The murder wasn't solved. Brennan had not been arrested or even held. Janie texted me that his statement explained how he'd ended up with the letter and that he had an alibi for Saturday night during the time frame when Roberto was killed.

"I don't see the suspect," Opal said in a stage whisper. She had finished work for the night and docked the *Admiral Joshua Barry* and was calling to tell me the coast was clear. Paul had sensed I wouldn't want to stay at home alone tonight and very sweetly asked if I wanted to take one of our nighttime walks along the water. I loved the idea, but I wanted to be sure Brennan wasn't sitting waiting for me at Vola's. Who was I kidding? I played back how Brennan had looked as he walked to Chief Harrod's car, how he hadn't looked at me. No way was he waiting to start our romantic evening.

Even after all that had happened since Saturday night, I didn't want to go back to my comfortable, predictable job. Especially not after talking to Denise and Deb this morning. Tonight, though, I was nostalgic for order. I didn't like having this many feelings. I didn't want Brennan Adler to be guilty, but I did want the murder solved. Now I was in this gray zone of not knowing if he was guilty or innocent. It was the worst of all possibilities.

The temperature hadn't dropped much more after the sun went down. It had been biting cold all day. I was bundled up, all the way down to hiking boots that would give me traction for the patches of ice. I put warm jackets on Stickley and Morris, leashed them, and headed out. Paul, the dogs, and I would meet Opal and David at the pier. Marthasville was such a dog-friendly city that we even had a public-access dog park near the city marina. I wanted to take my guys there for a bio-break before we met up with the others.

There were plenty of cars on the streets and the restaurants were filled with people, but unlike during the day or on warmer evenings, I saw few pedestrians. I was walking along the side of the Torpedo Factory Art Center toward the waterfront when a biker passed me and then stopped and dismounted. When he walked his bike back to me, I reached in my pocket for my cell phone.

"I saw the new key on the desk, so I guess I have you to thank for the police hauling me in for questioning this afternoon," Brennan said. His voice was low and hard.

I swallowed and walked a few more steps before I said anything. Then I stopped and unloaded. "You have the nerve to be mad at me?" The cadence I heard in my words sounded very Robert De Niro. "Hauled in? That's a bit dramatic, if you don't mind me saying so. It looked like you and Chief Harrod were tight. If you had an innocent explanation for having that letter, you should have told the police you had it all along! You knew they were looking for it, and you knew they were going under the assumption that whoever stole it murdered Roberto

Fratelli." I didn't like standing still, because I was getting cold. Nor did I like standing in the dark between the buildings, because I didn't know if I could trust him. The dogs and I started walking again.

"No, I didn't!"

"Which part?" I asked.

"I didn't know they were looking for the letter or that they knew it existed, certainly not that they thought it was missing! Or even that they thought the letter had anything at all to do with Roberto Fratelli's murder."

Was that possible? That he didn't know one of the theories the police were working on was that Roberto Fratelli had been killed by whoever stole the letter?

"You took it. Do you admit that much?"

"Yes, I took it. But then when I had it, I didn't know what to do with the stupid thing." He walked his bike up to me. His bike shoes clacked on the bricks. And his gears clicked.

"Why did you take it?" Wasn't it the property of Roberto or Waited4You?

"Because of you. I saw Opal find it under that chair. The whole setup was dodgy. The fact that it was hidden, everything. And since you couldn't trust anything Roberto Fratelli touched, I wanted to find out what it was. When I saw it was a letter supposedly to George Washington—"

"What! To whom?" The shock of the name stopped me again. The dogs pulled on their leashes and looked back at me in confusion. "Good lord, who was it from?"

"Supposedly—"

"Did it have a date on it? Opal said she saw one-seven-something."

"1758," he said.

"Holy sh . . . Wait, did you just say you took it because of me?"

"I didn't want you to try to sell it and get a bad name." We started walking again. Our steps matched perfectly, even though he was several inches taller than me. How could that be?

"Because I couldn't possibly tell the difference between an almost-three-hundred-year-old letter and a forgery? Don't worry about me."

"I didn't mean it like that."

"I only saw a little of the top of it, but you've seen the whole letter. How do you know it's a fake? I mean, there are tens of thousands of letters and other documents that belonged to George Washington."

"A couple of reasons. There's what I know about Roberto's ethics, but that's not the main reason I'm so sure it's a forgery. It was supposedly from Sally Fairfax, saying something completely different from how it's believed she answered him the first time he wrote to her after his engagement to Martha Custis. This letter is supposedly a response to his next letter to her. It might have been harder to see through if the forger tried to make it look like it was from Mary Philipse."

"No letters to Mary Philipse from George Washington, or from her to him, have ever been discovered. Are you saying a letter from her might have fooled you, or anyone else, because there would be no previous letter that it contradicted? There's not the context to place it in to analyze it?" I shivered in the cold and tightened my scarf closer around my neck. Brennan made a half step toward me, his arm outstretched, but stopped himself.

"Exactly. At least we agree on that," he said. "Besides, if there was intimate correspondence to or from a woman, it certainly would have been from Sally Fairfax. Everyone knows that." He sounded touchy, almost sensitive.

"What did the letter say?" I asked.

"It was hard to read that fancy handwriting and even harder to understand. The gist of it was that since he had said he chose her over Martha Custis, she would run away with him."

"It is fraudulent," I said, shocked. And, for some reason, I was now offended or hurt, or something. I didn't know which.

"Of course it is. George Washington never wrote that." He sounded as if the letter had bad-mouthed his mother.

"And Sally Fairfax didn't feel that way." I looked at my breath, white in the night air. "But I think you're a romantic, Mr. Adler." In the moonlight, I saw his scowl soften, and we walked on in the dark.

Now my mind considered the implications if people believed it was real. A letter like that could have changed our country's history. At the time, Washington had attained no more than the honorary rank of brigadier general. If he had run away with a married woman, it was doubtful he'd ever have gone any further. Certainly, he would not have been called on to lead the Continental Army. The letter was ridiculous.

"What was the paper like?" I asked. "Since it was out of the folio, you must have felt it."

"I do not appreciate you reporting me to the police!"

I had expected an answer to my question about the paper, and this turn surprised me. It brought me back to the present day with a thud. I didn't need to look over at him to know his frown was back. "I never said you couldn't be a romantic murderer." Take that.

"Look, I don't know anything about old paper. I'm just a country lawyer." *Sure.* "The other angle the police are working is that the thieves from a couple of months ago came back. Like they wanted to get whatever they could before he left," he said.

He and Chief Harrod must be friendly for that amount of oversharing. "Chief Harrod told you that?"

"Of course." Wow.

I shook my head at the way Janie Fairfax kept everything to herself and Chief Harrod was just the opposite. "Did Roberto say anything to you about that break-in when it happened?" I asked.

"No, but we didn't have that kind of tenant-landlord relationship. I went for months at a time without talking to him."

"Even though you were right next door, just separated by an alley?" I asked.

"Hey, it worked for me. Anyway, maybe the burglars thought security was lax in the transition."

"Was it ever anything but lax?" I asked.

"It seemed like he was taking extra precautions after Labor Day, and that was when the break-in occurred." Had Chief Harrod left anything out?

"What kind of additional precautions? He had an alarm system before the break-in. Obviously, since it went off. A person heard it from the sidewalk and phoned it in."

"Ah, that was typical Roberto." Brennan chuckled. "It made a lot of noise but wasn't connected to the police department or a security company." He couldn't have told me that before? "That's why I didn't rush to change the passcode for you when Opal asked me to. I was going to suggest you get a real system."

"I will. The police have been checking the alarm records. I'll tell Janie they can stop looking."

"Why tell her instead of the detective on the case?" he asked.

"I've yet to see him. I've only heard rumors that there is such a person." I didn't mention what Janie had said about him wanting off the case. I didn't owe Brennan anything. The chief could tell him over a beer. "He should be fired. I think he's lazy."

Brennan laughed at that, but I had no idea why he thought it was so funny.

"What extra precautions did he start taking after the break-in?" I asked.

"He was there more hours. I could hear him." We walked a little more, closer to the waterfront now. "You're a local and even a native. Is that why you're so plugged in?"

"I guess," I said, but I was thinking it was pretty rich that he thought I was "plugged in," since his BFF was the chief of police.

"We should work together."

I didn't answer, simply out of spite. I was fifty-five years old. Surely that made me immune to a school kid's heartache. I hated the way he had made me feel this afternoon.

"Whaddya say?" He took off his bike helmet and ran his hand over his head. "You know I didn't kill Roberto Fratelli." We stopped walking.

It hadn't been a question, but I answered him anyway. "I never thought you did." I didn't know how I knew, but I knew.

"I wish you had asked me about the letter first instead of calling the police."

"So we're back to that? Calling the police was the right thing to do." By that, I meant end of discussion. "It's in my interest for the police to find Roberto Fratelli's real killer. I don't want that hanging over my opening, the Common

Good events, or heaven forbid my son's swearing-in ceremony in January. I'm meeting with Janie tomorrow. Maybe she'll have news of progress the police have made."

"Good, and you'll tell me what she says?"

"Not so fast," I answered. "I want something in return. Do you know why Roberto never paid Ritchie for the tables he made?"

"Ritchie who? And what tables?"

We ambled on, him pushing his bike, and I explained about the faux Victorian tables. He seemed to know nothing about them. "All I can say is that I never once heard of him not paying vendors or dealers."

"Maybe Ritchie owed him money?" I suggested. "That would explain him giving Roberto the tables to sell and not receiving anything in return."

"It's more likely Roberto paid him under the table—and not a Victorian one, if you catch my meaning."

He was more relaxed now, and I felt I could go back to teasing him. So I did. "You seem to know a lot about him. None of it good. Are you sure you didn't kill him?"

He chuckled. "Go easy on me. I've had a bad day."

We were at the pier, near the Chart House restaurant, and Paul was walking our way. Lights shone all around, so we no longer depended on moonlight. Suddenly I was aware there were dozens of people around us. Watching the balloon man make animals. Listening to a guitar-playing street performer. Couples sitting on benches eating ridiculously expensive ice cream cones even though it was November, maybe to reward themselves after a long day of sightseeing and shopping. Sometimes they juggled their waffle cones so they could keep holding hands or snuggling together to stay warm.

Brennan put his hand on my arm to get me to look at him. "Here's something else I know about Roberto: his cancer was back, and he had only months to live. I hoped he could live out his last few months in peace, wherever he wanted. This is a hell of a thing to have happen. And I'm sorry his life ended the way it did."

Chapter Fifteen

Wednesday

"It looked bad for Mr. Adler in the beginning. Like we said, whoever stole the letter knew where it was hidden. But he told us he saw Opal when she found it under . . ."

I stopped listening to Janie. I hadn't seen Brennan in Waited4You on Saturday. Where had he been standing and how had he gotten in? Did he let himself in the back door regularly? Should I mention that to Janie? I would drive myself crazy if I kept thinking like this. I needed to know more before I incriminated the man any more than I already had.

"Can I see the letter?" I reached for my paper cup of hot tea.

"Why?"

"Just curiosity. I don't think it's real, but I would like to know more about it. Did you hear that it was supposedly written to George Washington from Sally Fairfax? If it's authentic, a lot of people are going to be upset."

"I did hear that, and who would be offended over something in a centuries-old letter?" she asked.

"It would change the way we think of George Washington."

"Why? You just said it was *to* him, so he didn't write it."

For some reason—maybe her innate restraint, maybe something else—she didn't want me to see it. Or at least she wasn't going to help me get a look at it. It was time for me to hold back too. Not as tit for tat but because until I knew the contents of the letter, it was dumb to make any more guesses that might come back to bite me later.

"The letter is on its way back from University of Virginia. It was taken there to be examined for authenticity. I was told they already performed a preliminary test on it this morning."

"I can tell you now that it's fake," I said.

"It's real." A young man, tall and broad shouldered, stuck his head in the door. He looked familiar.

"Camille Benson, this is Detective Harrod." Janie smiled at him. "Really? They said it's real?"

"Nice to meet you, Detective . . . did she say Detective Harrod?"

"Nice to meet you too. Call me Nick."

"As in Chief Harrod?"

"He's my father."

So this was Nick as in Nick, the detective assigned to Roberto's murder investigation. That explained Brennan laughing when I'd said I thought the detective on the case should be fired. It seemed like something Janie should have shared when we talked on Monday, or at any point since then, especially after all Opal and I had said about Chief Harrod slow-walking the investigation. Son of the police chief of Marthasville wasn't all this guy was.

He turned to Janie. "Took them only about half an hour. Those academic people were all over it."

"Is it back in the evidence room?" Janie asked, as excited as he was.

"I had to leave it with them in Charlottesville. They want to do more tests. They said it's one of the few surviving letters anyone has seen to George Washington from Sally somebody."

"Fairfax."

Janie Fairfax laughed, uncharacteristically. "No relation. At least none I know of."

I shook my head and buried my face in my hands.

"What's the matter?" she asked. For some reason, her voice quavered before she regained control. By the end of the question, it was toneless.

"I hope they don't make their initial assessment public." I raised my head and looked at her, then at Nick, who was still standing in the same spot. "You're the guy with the puppy."

He stared at me for a beat. Janie's jaw tensed. I didn't need to mention the unpleasantness with Roberto at the store on Saturday afternoon. You didn't have to be a body-language expert to figure out that Janie already knew. The incident hovered in the room with us like it was waiting for its own chair. Something tangible, and therefore dangerous, rather than a memory.

"Yeah." He hadn't moved from his post in the doorway. Almost as inscrutable as Janie.

I remembered Ella saying Chief Harrod should talk to his son. And Janie saying Nick wanted to be taken off the case. It was because he could be considered a suspect. A person of interest—wasn't that the TV term? But his father wouldn't hear of it. I stared at him without speaking, but I was obviously sizing him up. I didn't try to hide it. "I don't see you as a killer. I think you reacted the way a lot of people would if Roberto

123

went after their puppy." *A lot of people* would have gotten angry, but how many would get violent, needing to be restrained?

They both exhaled. Nick stepped into the room and sat in the chair next to mine. "I'm just a cop. Through and through and third generation. I should not have lost my temper the way I did. I'm sorry you and your friend had to see that."

I shrugged off his apology. "Did you wait to come to Roberto's home until I was gone because you knew I would recognize you as the guy who argued with him the day he was killed?"

He held up two stop-sign hands. "No, that's not what happened at all. I've been trying to get off this case for that very reason. I'm afraid any progress I make on the case will be looked at with suspicion. I was trying to talk someone into taking me off the investigation at the time. That's why I was late."

Time to change the subject. "I'm afraid the value of a letter like that—if it's real—makes Brennan Adler look even worse," I said. I wasn't ready to share any more of my thoughts on what the letter could be worth until I saw said letter. Maybe I would never give my opinion on its worth, since it was a fake. "Doesn't it?"

"He has an alibi. He told us he was riding his bike at the time, and we have him on a street camera on Eisenhower Avenue," Nick said. Like his father, he spoke slowly, with a hint of a southern accent and a distinctive rhythm to his speech.

I didn't see how the image could possibly be so clear that you could identify a man at night, in motion, especially someone wearing a bicycle helmet. But then, what did I know about the police department's technology?

"He lawyered up," Janie said. "I got a call from her this morning."

Nick did a double take. "He did what? Why would he do that?"

"He says he intends to take an extended cruise on his boat."

Nick leaned forward and put his elbows on his knees. "That doesn't sound good. Was it already planned? Like when the store had a new tenant, he would go?"

"No. All I know is he got mad about something and decided he wanted to take off," Janie said. "He plans on being gone six months. She's going to advise him to wait until after the case is solved."

"Do you think it was Dad that pissed him off?"

So Brennan was leaving Marthasville. The air in the room was very dry, and my eyes teared up. I hadn't noticed it before. I cleared my throat. "In the few minutes I saw him with Chief Harrod, it looked like he was being handled with kid gloves." I didn't mention Chief Harrod's oversharing with him on another avenue of investigation.

Janie nodded in agreement. "I know. That's how it seemed to me too."

I didn't want to hear any more. "Did you tell Nick about the break-in and the stolen books?"

"Yeah, she told Dad and me about it," said Nick. "It's interesting. Dad has known Helen and Noah Margalit for years. He's going to talk to them. That'll go over better. It's possible the thieves came back. I mean, why not? They got away with it the first time."

"Possible? We've eliminated everything else. I think that *is* exactly what happened!" Janie showed more emotion than she had all morning. Or maybe all year.

"I'm trying to learn more." Nick stood. "Gotta get back to work."

"I was hoping I could get a look at the letter." Another end run around her. Sorry. Not sorry.

"I have a copy I can email to you, if that would help. I'm curious to know why you think it's a fake."

"Yes, why do you care what it says since you think it's a fake?" Janie asked. She had noticed the trick.

"There might be a clue to the reason the forgery was created and who the forger was. I can go over the wording and check if it is consistent with the eighteenth century," I said. "I want to see if there is anything intentionally or overly salacious that might give away the forger's motive. There was a letter supposedly from George Washington to Martha Custis dated July 20, 1758, that was found to be a forgery by looking at the content and the wording."

That letter, supposedly written during the French and Indian War, when Washington had fought for the British for the last time in his life, started by saying they were on the march for the Ohio, meaning Fort Duquesne in the Ohio River Valley in what is now Pittsburg. In reality, the British army had still been making plans and Lt. Colonel George Washington didn't even know if his brigade would fight in the battle. Next, the tone did not fit a couple, in this case George and Martha, who had been together only three times. We don't know if they were engaged at the time, but he would not have written about love the way the writer did in this letter. There were also little, less obvious, clues. Like George Washington didn't use the word *courier*; he preferred *express*. Content could be a big factor in authenticating a document.

"Anytime George Washington's name is mentioned in correspondence, these theories pop up," I continued. "Like with Catharine Greene, General Nathanael Greene's wife. She liked to dance and her husband didn't, but he didn't mind if she danced with other men. She danced with George Washington. Years later, when more was written about her pretty amazing life, you can imagine what they said. But it was worse, since he was already married to Martha Washington. He met Sally Fairfax years before he was married, and I believe he had feelings for her. Then there's Mary Philipse, and no letters to or from her and George Washington have ever been found. I believe Martha Washington was the love of his life. They were together only three times in 1758, twice in March and once in June when he visited her in New Kent County, so it's unlikely they were head over heels in love before they married. Still, there's no evidence that Washington was ever unfaithful to his wife, or that it was anything but a happy marriage. Yet these stories keep popping up about his truuuuuue love."

"Like it wasn't Martha? That's what people like to imply?" Janie asked.

"Right."

"Are these forgeries always done for the money?" Nick asked.

"Usually that's behind them, but the fake letter from George to Martha before they married might have been created for a different reason. His two letters to Sally Fairfax were uncovered in 1877. This fake letter to Martha came up in 1886. Some scholars think a well-meaning person may have produced this over-the-top love letter to Martha to protect George Washington's reputation. After all, depending on how you interpret what he wrote, he could have looked like a real jerk writing to his friend's wife when he was engaged himself. Later, during their marriage, he did write very romantic letters to Martha, but the declarations in that particular letter didn't ring true." I paused. "Getting back to our letter, ordinarily, correspondence would be more valuable if it was signed by George Washington. In this case, it's worth more because it was written to him instead of from him. Did the forger, or the dealer, or Roberto, get lucky? Or did he know that much about Washington's life? I wanted to see if the forger made any historical mistakes, like the 1758 letter saying the British army was on the move when it wasn't.

"Then there's the fact that it was Roberto who had it. That's a big point against its authenticity. It's so unlikely."

"Are you saying Roberto's shady business practices reflect on the letter?" Nick asked.

"Yes, I am. The university is probably doing tests on the paper and ink. Hopefully, they'll have a historian look at the content and context. But the letter's history has to be taken into account too—and in this case, we know Roberto was selling fake Victorian furniture." I didn't mention that I might have more information on those stolen books later, because I didn't feel like I was standing on firm ground with that. I would wait until I was.

Nick took down my email address to forward a copy of the letter to me but didn't leave. I took the hint that I needed to go because they wanted to talk about police business. I stood and put on my warm coat and buttoned it up. "Nice to meet you, Nick. I'm sure you're both very busy." Since courthouse security forbade visitors from bringing in cell phones, I'd have to wait until later to see the correspondence I was sure was a fraud.

Deciphering the writing on that letter was going to be a hard slog. I deserved something for it. "Did you do background checks on Ella Coleman and Ritchie Potts?"

"That's confidential," Janie said. Everything was confidential with her, but I kept that sentiment to myself too.

Nick leaned on the back of the chair he'd been sitting on. "I think we can tell *her*, since it's a nonstory. She doesn't look like the type to go off and try to solve the murder herself." He laughed.

"True," I said. "All I want is to stay out of the way so you can find Roberto's killer as fast as you can. I don't know if anyone is going to want to shop at Waited4You until the town has closure."

Nick reached over and closed the office door. "Ritchie Potts is clean. All he has on his record is a car accident on Labor Day. He was at fault but no big deal. He had auto insurance and everybody ended up happy. Ella Coleman and some of her sorority sisters shoplifted cosmetics years ago when she was in college. Nothing to show either are murderers. Janie told me you were curious about him because of the fake tables, and we did take a closer look, but that's all we came up with. Then there is the former husband/current husband thing. He was at home all night, according to his phone's location tracking."

For that we needed privacy? When Nick opened Janie's office door for me, Chief Harrod stuck his head in. "Nick! A word." Father and son walked out and down the hall. I sat back down and looked at my young friend.

She looked pale and tired and even more closed off than usual. "Janie, if you ever need to talk about anything, I'm here. So is Opal."

She sprang up from her chair. "I'm good," she said, with fake cheer, as she looked out at the hallway in the direction the two men had gone. I had tried. That was all I could do.

Chapter Sixteen

"By God, you *will* tell me where you were on Saturday night!" Chief Harrod's gruff voice assaulted us as we walked to the elevator. I reflexively turned to the office door behind which the loud conversation was taking place. The nameplate said it was his son's office.

"The hell I will!" Nick yelled back, giving as good as he got.

"Camille, thank you for coming over," Janie said. Then she quickened our pace to the elevator. Having tried and failed to cover their angry voices with her own, her plan B was to get rid of me as fast as she could.

* * *

"Good thing I'm not the overly sensitive type," I said to Opal as I enjoyed a Greek salad for lunch at Mykonos Taverna. "She gave me the bum's rush."

My news about the guy with the puppy being the detective who had been ghosting us, not to mention Chief Harrod's son, had the same effect on Opal that it had had on me. Maybe not exactly the same. Opal's reaction was to fling her arms straight up in the air. Splat! A slab of chicken fell out of her *kotópoulo* sandwich and onto the table.

"Let me get this straight. Brennan Adler has an alibi. Ex-wife Ella has an alibi. Ritchie can't-remember-his-last-name wasn't anywhere in the area—"

"Potts, and it looks that way." I told her about the police checking his phone's location. "So they must have given some credence to your theory of a jealous husband knocking off his rival. You have to admit, that would be a crazy way for the unsexiest man on the planet to die."

"I'm sure stranger things have happened, but I don't know when." She picked up the piece of chicken off the tablecloth and popped it in her mouth. "That leaves us with one suspect without an alibi, Nick Harrod, the person no one wants to talk about."

"If everyone who had words with Roberto Fratelli becomes a suspect, the police will need to bring in extra help," I said.

"*Words?* Camille, it was more than that. If we hadn't been there, Detective Nick would have hit him."

I nodded because I had to agree. "He's a big guy. One blow could have killed Roberto."

"One blow did kill Roberto."

A waitress topped off our iced-tea glasses. "Are you talking about that poor man that owned Waited4You until somebody killed him?" I truly hoped that last sentence was all she had heard of our conversation. "I saw on the internet it looks like the police chief's son might have done it."

My mouth dropped open. "Where on the internet?"

"Maybe in the online edition of *Marthasville Daily News*? I can't remember. No, wait! That was where I read about the love letter somebody other than Martha wrote to George

Washington. I heard about the detective who's also the chief's son being a suspect from the Marthasville Facebook group. Or where *did* I hear about that?" She tapped her order pad on the side of her head.

A suspect? I desperately wanted to look at Opal so we could roll our eyes, but I also wanted the young woman to keep talking. She chewed on her pencil and looked around. "Maybe somebody here told me? Anyway, Mr. Fratelli was right here that very night. That *very* night." Got it. "With a woman!"

If she'd listened in on our conversation, maybe she'd done the same that night with Roberto and Ella. "Do you remember anything about that evening?"

"Do I ever. They weren't at my station. They were at the bar. Still, I heard more than Sheila! Obviously."

"Obviously?" Opal prodded her. I had a feeling she didn't need much encouraging, but it couldn't hurt.

"Sheila told the police they were fighting. But they weren't!" She walked away to take a diner's order two tables away.

I looked at the bar. It wasn't in a separate room. It was on the side wall of the dining room. A waitress could easily have overheard a conversation between two people sitting there. That I could imagine. What I couldn't picture was Roberto, the meanest man in Marthasville, sitting on a barstool, drink in hand, talking to a woman. Just being.

"They weren't fighting?" I asked between bites.

Opal and I looked at one another and shrugged.

The waitress was back. "He told her he was having some health problems. It sounded very, very serious. Baaad. Then she got all excited and jumped up and said she had to go."

"Then what?" Opal asked, wide-eyed.

"They left. That was all." The waitress pivoted and took off for another table.

I leaned in and whispered, "Opal, I have more to tell you, but later. Not in here." I looked to see where our waitress was. "Do you think what she just said means anything?"

Opal had started scrolling through something on her phone. "That two waitresses have two different accounts? Nothing useful."

*　*　*

We finished our lunches and headed back to Waited4You. The icy spots had melted, but it was cold, and we walked fast. My toes were grateful to be in my warm boots. As long as the streets were lined with gray slush and icicles melted and tumbled from awnings, my winter-white slacks and coat were off my wardrobe rotation. I was back to my typical black jeans and black cashmere sweater.

The night before I had told Opal, David, and Paul about running into Brennan on his bike and what he'd said about Roberto being ill. My unfortunate phrasing was that he didn't have long to live. None of us ever passed up the opportunity to make a sick joke, especially when given an opening like that. David had said the disease was "spot on."

"At least the waitress was right about what Roberto went there to tell Ella," I told Opal now.

"And she got up and stormed out? If anything, it reinforces my opinion of that woman. She is stone-cold," Opal said.

"Why do you think that? I mean, why *reinforces*? What did she do before to make you think she's stone-cold?"

"In the restaurant, I looked up who was posting that Detective Nick Harrod was a suspect, or that he should become one. It was none other than Ms. Ella Coleman. She has it on the Marthasville Facebook group, Instagram, and Twitter, and that's just what I could easily find. Who knows where else she put it? Besides, even if she and Roberto didn't fight in the restaurant, they did argue outside Waited4You." Opal pulled her jacket tighter against the wind. "Wait, how do we know that?"

"Janie told us," I reminded her.

Opal stopped and pointed a finger at me. "And she probably got it from Nick Harrod."

I cocked an eyebrow. "So you're saying there's a chance it's not true?" She shrugged, and we were walking again. "I don't know who to trust anymore," I admitted. "Other than you."

"Ditto. If you're thinking that maybe you can trust Brennan Adler, stop. The letter was on his desk. Just keep your doors locked, okay?"

"I will. The murderer is still out there. I have another suspect to tell you about. This is the theory Janie supports." I filled her in on the stolen books Helen Margalit had found in the alleyway.

"Camille, you should have led with that. The case might be solved!"

"I didn't want to say anything in front of that waitress. Anyway, finding someone who committed a robbery a few months ago? I don't know. How are the police going to do that?" We were almost back to Waited4You. "The thief *could* have dropped the books because he heard the alarm and thought the police were coming, but it seems, I don't know, not very likely."

"You mean, what kind of idiot thief tosses what was probably the most valuable thing he stole?" she suggested.

"Great minds, but what if the books weren't rare and valuable? Helen still had one of the books, and she gave it to me. It might not be old at all. The other night when I tried to tell, I came up dry. It was like nothing said it was a fake, nor did anything say it was legit. Before I spend money on having it appraised, I should have *some* opinion on it. The date on the copyright page gives the publication date as 1921, but . . . it was like I couldn't make a decision. I'm going to the Barrett branch of the library to see their rare books. Maybe I can relearn some of what my parents taught me about spotting a book not as old as a bookseller is pretending it is."

"First, you need to get your confidence back. Next, don't you have your own rare books to compare it to? Sorry. Rhetorical question. I just remembered who left those books there," she said.

Chapter Seventeen

"Janie, it looks like someone at the University of Virginia talked to reporters about the letter," I said when I called her after lunch. "I'm disappointed they would do that."

"How do you know they did?"

"A waitress at lunch saw the article. She said she read it in the online edition of the *Marthasville Daily News*." Was that what she meant by her question? "Wait, are you asking how I know it's in the paper, or why I think it was UVA that gave them the information?"

"Uh, I guess the first."

"I have it on my screen right now." Before I made the call, I'd pulled up the article in case the young woman had confused what she saw on Facebook with what was in the *Marthasville Daily News*. "It's definitely out there. There's an anonymous source but no direct quotes."

"I'm looking for it. Here it is." She read a word here and there as she scanned the article. "Now the second question. Why do you think someone from UVA leaked the story?"

"Well, not many people knew about the letter before this article. And because it doesn't say where the letter was found.

It doesn't even mention that it went missing from Saturday night until Tuesday. I figure it was someone with half of the story." Was it just yesterday that we'd found it? Could I be sure it wasn't a month or a lifetime ago?

Janie gave a little laugh. "You're right. Hmm. Maybe this will be good for tourism for the city, Camille. Look at it like that. You know, every cloud." In the last five or six years, Marthasville had become a *destination*. Dollars spent by tourists increased every year. That was partly because of our proximity to Washington, DC, but also because of our waterfront and our history.

"The same waitress told us about some talk online about what happened between Detective Harrod and Roberto Fratelli the day of the murder. I hope that gets cleared up soon."

She thanked me for the call and hung up without commenting on the detective.

My next call was to my son.

"Mom, I can't talk. Can I call you back later?"

"Sure, Paul, but hon, don't make a public statement about the letter. Not until we talk. Okay? Bye." Last night when I'd told him what Brennan had said about the letter being written from Sally Fairfax to George Washington, it was minds blown all around.

"Wait, Mom. My phone is blowing up over it. This is about *your* letter?" I wouldn't exactly call it *my* letter. "Dr. Branch wants it to be featured in Common Good for the Commonwealth." Dr. Charles Branch was Paul's predecessor as mayor. He had not run for reelection, so the transition was expected to be smooth—no hurt feelings and no blame games. When he'd decided to retire from practicing medicine, Dr. Branch had known he couldn't travel with his wife, as he'd promised her for decades they would do, unless he gave up politics. "The theme is *There's Always More to Learn*, and it's about lifelong education. A historic letter written nearby and found here is a great way to illustrate that, right?"

"Not if it's a fraud, and that's what I think the letter is." I put him on speaker so I could see the time on my phone. I needed to leave soon for my meeting.

"But *you* only saw the top part of it, right?"

"Right, but—"

"If a university, not just any university but one of the top schools in the country, says it's real, it might be. Dr. Branch thinks this could put Marthasville on par with some of the Massachusetts cities that are known for their history and get plenty of tourism dollars because of it. Like Concord and Lexington. And he's been great to me."

"What about the circumstances around how it was found? That's not exactly a fairy-tale story," I reminded him.

"You're right. They'll have to decide how to message that. Maybe that's what Doc wants to talk to me about tonight."

Roberto Fratelli's murder had already begun fading into the background. The tragedy was something to be messaged. Would anyone in town even remember what he looked like after this year's Common Good events? Next there would be Marthasville's holiday traditions, like the waterskiing Santa and Carols of Christmas, ending with Olde Year's Day at the Torpedo Factory Art Center on New Year's Eve Day. The First Night celebrations included the countdown street party in the city hall courtyard, Battle of the Buskers, where street performers competed, and fireworks on the Potomac River at midnight. We would all move on.

"Can you just hold off until UVA has time for a more comprehensive analysis?" I asked.

"I'm having coffee with him tonight. I'll see what I can do. Do you think they'll be able to say for sure maybe tomorrow?" he pleaded. He was in a tough spot, and he wanted good old Mom to fix this.

"That's not how this works. I doubt they will give their final opinion tomorrow, but when they do, other experts will research and debate the letter."

We agreed we would talk later. He had a meeting to get to. So did I.

Chapter Eighteen

Our city's library had been started in the 1790s as the Marthasville Library Company. Back then it was a subscription library, meaning patrons had to pay to use it—unlike today, thankfully. The Local History/Special Collections, or LH/SC, Branch Library was located inside the Barrett Branch on Queen Street. According to the website, its mission was to "acquire and make available to the public materials relating to the history and genealogy of Marthasville, and the Commonwealth of Virginia." The collection included books, maps, pictures, ephemera, photographs, microformat publications, manuscripts, oral history, periodicals, newspapers, and multimedia and electronic media materials. The core of the rare-books collection was from the original collection of the subscription library.

Caroline Pak, the local history librarian, led me through the lobby to a door in a glass wall that separated the researchers' room from the rest of the floor. "Our collection represents the types of books held by a library from that time period." I could almost see my reflection in the serious young woman's glossy black hair. Her oversized red eyeglasses slipped a little, and when she pushed them up, I saw a tiny tattoo of a book on her arm, just below the back of her hand and delicate wrist.

She unlocked the door, and we went into the large, serene room with two of its walls lined with bookcases. The books were behind glass, as Caroline and I were. The need for redundancy spoke to their value, but it looked like the books were napping. Since Barrett is a public library, appointments were not required. A reference interview, however, was. For that, we sat at one of the several rugged wooden tables. She folded her hands and smiled. "What are you researching, Ms. Benson?"

How could I answer that? Should I say I wanted to remember everything my parents had taught me so I could get my confidence level up enough to function like the midfifties person I was? I told her that I was the new owner of Waited4You. "Actually, I'm trying to recalibrate my senses to keep from buying forgeries of rare books."

"Recalibrate?" she asked.

I told her that my parents had been the store's founders, two owners ago—or if you counted me, three owners back.

She looked over her glasses at me, like I was one very interesting specimen. "You know there's technology for that now?" Had I imagined her glancing at my white hair? No, unfortunately, I hadn't.

"I want to be able to make a decent initial assessment." I looked at the glass cases. "Could I just look at a couple of the books in there? Maybe you could tell me which section has the oldest books in it."

She stood. "Go ahead. Take out any of those you want to see."

"Really?" The interview was over? I'd passed? Wow.

"Would you like to take a few books home with you?" Finally, I caught on that she was teasing me, and laughed at myself for falling for it.

"Yes, I'm joking, and no, you can't take any rare books home with you. Those aren't even rare books on the shelves in this room, and researchers don't get to just pick up any book they see." She was funny. Even though the joke was on me, I laughed again. "Our rare books are kept in, believe it or not, the rare-book room."

"Quite a coincidence," I said, teasing back. She got the joke and laughed.

"That's a separate room. I'm afraid researchers are not allowed in there." She walked to the door. "I have a couple of books in mind that you might like. I'll be right back." When she got to the door, she said, "Don't touch anything." Haha.

Soon she was back with a tray holding two books. She sat it on the table in front of me.

"Should I wear gloves?"

"We don't require them for paper books." She looked at what I wore. Some called my black slacks and black turtleneck sweater my uniform, but I preferred the term *wardrobe*. "You should be okay, since you're not wearing light colors. You don't even want to know how many white blouses I've ruined."

"With what?"

"Red rot." Caroline paused to be sure I understood the scope of the peril I faced. "It's from leather that's deteriorating. If it gets on your clothes, it's all over. There's no getting it out."

"Thanks for telling me." In the past few days I had been around murder, theft, forgery, and a business that might go under before it even opened its doors, yet surprisingly, this red rot menace still scared me. I took it seriously. She gave me some preliminary instructions. I had to cradle the book's spine and cover the way you held a baby. Also, when I turned the books' pages, I needed to lift them gently and not flip them. Got it.

I opened the first book, *The Romance of Historic Marthasville*, which had been written in 1923. I held it up and smelled it. "Mmm."

"I do that too."

I jumped in my seat; I hadn't known she was *right* behind me. Over my shoulder. "You almost gave me a heart attack. For a second, I thought you were red rot."

"Sorry. I've been told I hover. In an audit we discovered a theft, so now we observe people the entire time they're with a rare book. I didn't mean to be intrusive."

"You had a theft too? That's terrible. I learned someone stole some books from the store a few months ago . . ." I let my words drift off. Waited4You had nothing like the book I held in my hands. "I'm suspicious of the one book that was recovered." I looked down at the book I'd opened. It had lived. It had been properly cared for, but it also had been opened, read, closed, loaned, and borrowed. When I thought about *Boys & Girls & Families*, I didn't feel any of that. The pages of a children's book should be roughed up, at least a little. Such books should be chewed on, slobbered on, slept with, and loved. *Boys & Girls & Families* had wear consistent with a book left in the rain that had not had the benefit of a professional book restorer, but it hadn't lived. The book had been written in 1921, but I didn't believe my copy was anywhere near that old. It wasn't a first edition. "The other stolen books were returned to the former owner, but I don't know what happened to them. I haven't found them."

"That's the man that was murdered?"

"Yes, Roberto Fratelli. Is there a reason people steal books, other than because they're portable?"

"Collectors will pay astronomical sums for the exact book they want. In 2020, a collector, Stephan Loewentheil, paid almost ten million for a first printing of Shakespeare's First Folio. The most ever paid for a book was when David Rubenstein spent fourteen-point-two million for *The Bay Psalm Book*, one of the few copies out there of our country's first book. It was printed eighteen years after settlers landed at Plymouth Rock."

That gave me something to consider. Had the thief been looking for one particular book? Too bad I didn't have the others.

Caroline looked around the room before going on. "Old books connect our past to our present."

"I think someone who steals a book is stealing from the future. In a way, I hope the stolen books *were* forgeries, since they were left out in the rain," I said.

"Oh, yes!" she said. She sat back down and leaned forward, eager to talk. "A recent study found that moisture is a greater danger than increased temperature." She saw I was interested and went on. "Moisture affects the tensile properties *and* the pH value of paper! Deterioration of paper can be delayed hundreds of years by proper storage." And I thought I geeked out on topics like this. I couldn't hold a candle to her. She took a breath and went on. "Pages were stolen from ours, not the entire book." She spoke solemnly, like we shared a tragedy.

That was so far from the truth that I looked down in discomfort. The theft of Roberto's fakes didn't deserve Caroline's sympathy. All week, or at least after I'd seen the copper stickers, I'd held on to this fantasy that I would find some redeeming quality in the man. Not that it affected my strong belief that his murder deserved a thorough police investigation, but it would have been nice.

Caroline sat quietly as I looked at the *The Romance of Historic Marthasville*. I tried to remember the instructions for the safe handling of the volume. This book spoke to me of time and lives and continuity and beauty and every good thing that could be counted on.

She waited for me to tenderly close the book before speaking again. "Uh, may I ask you something?"

"Sure." I couldn't help but be disappointed. I had been enjoying myself so much chatting with her and being around the beautiful old books. *Please don't ask any questions about the murder, or the letter.*

"People usually come here to research genealogy, historiography, or some aspect of Marthasville or Virginia history. You said you didn't care which rare books you saw. What are you looking for? Are you really trying to hone a skill?"

Thank you. Thank you. A topic other than what I expected and dreaded.

"I'm looking for a feeling. My parents helped me develop the ability to spot evidence of a forgery, or at least when something about a book has been changed. Maybe the paper isn't right, or maybe the binding. Now I'm trying to remember what they taught me. They were both so good, especially my dad. Not that he would appraise a book, but when one was offered by a dealer, he was able to decide if they should walk away or have an analysis done on it."

She nodded. "You want to see if you have the knack?"

"I guess you could say that." I pulled the second book closer. The title was *Constitution and By-laws of Potomac Lodge No. 8, Independent Order and Odd Fellows*, from 1843.

"I think this is particularly interesting. See what good condition the paper is in?"

145

I gently touched a page and nodded. "It looks strong."

"An older book is sometimes in better condition than one published in the 1940s. During World War II, changes were made to the papermaking process and the ingredients used in it. More sawdust was used for pulp and more chlorine was added, making newer paper more brittle than older paper." She smiled and then went on. "That book does have some boxing. Do you see it? It looks like blotches or freckles, and it's usually around the edge of the page instead of in the middle. We don't know what causes it. That and spine and hinge damage are our biggest problems." She hesitated, then said, "We were . . ." She stopped again. "Sorry, I'm interrupting you."

"Please, go ahead."

"I should let you look at . . ." She pointed at *Constitution and By-laws of Potomac Lodge No. 8*. It seemed she had something on her mind that she wanted to tell me, so I closed the book. She and these two books had helped me more than she would ever know, since now I felt confident saying my found book was a fraud. I was happy to hear whatever she needed to say. "We were certainly surprised when the audit uncovered the missing pages."

"Do you know when the theft was? Like how long the pages had been missing? Was this a regularly scheduled audit?"

"We weren't due for another audit for several months, but we received an anonymous tip to check the books in the Local History Library."

I jerked up straighter. "Wow. This is getting curiouser and curiouser. Could the tip have been from the person who stole the pages, and felt guilty later? I mean, he would be the only one that would know the pages were missing, right? Or maybe someone who saw the person do it."

"She. The tip was from a woman."

"So you audited your collection page by page?"

"Oh yes."

"You're certainly knowledgeable about books. How long have you worked here?" I asked, carefully putting *Constitution and By-laws of Potomac Lodge No. 8* back on the tray.

"Since college. I have a master's in library science, specializing in archives management, and another in museum education."

"Impressive." I hesitated. "Do you think it's possible for a university or a lab to determine if a manuscript, say, a personal letter, is not a forgery in less than an hour?"

"To say it's *not* a forgery? I doubt it. Sometimes they can say something *is* a fake, certainly when there's something glaringly wrong, rather quickly. They could date the paper and the ink, but I doubt any trustworthy academic would stake their reputation on a finding that a work was authentic in that short period of time." Of course, she was right. I knew that. After all, I had a PhD in art history. Why hadn't I trusted my own judgment, education, and life experience?

I stood, and she came over to get the books and the tray, which she slid toward her on the table until it was in front of her. She opened one book and then the other and inspected each.

"Do you know which pages were stolen?"

"The free endpaper."

I stared. "I expected you to say a map or a hand-colored lithograph." Even the lowly *Boys & Girls & Families* had amazing illustrations.

She shook her head.

"A blank page?"

"Just a blank page."

Chapter Nineteen

I turned from Queen Street to North Columbus to get back to King Street. In the short drive back to Waited4You, I thought about how I'd learned more about myself than about rare books in my time with Caroline Pak. The pristine condition of *Boys & Girls & Families* screamed that something was wrong. Why hadn't I been able to say that definitively two days ago? I hadn't learned more since then. Maybe all the stolen books were misrepresented, just like the one given to me by Helen Margalit.

A fake is an existing work altered with the intention of deceiving, a forgery is a fraudulent imitation, and a facsimile is any reproduction. And it was the inscription, added by someone, that made the book a fake. It wasn't a century-old book. Even if it had been legitimately bought off of Amazon, with royalties going to the author's estate, it hadn't lived the life Roberto had told us it had. The children's book was a fake because of the notation by *Aunt Minnie*. The crime wasn't that the book's original publication year was 1921; we bought classic books all the time. It was the addition of something designed to deceive that made the book a lie. Similarly, the reproduction Victorian table Ritchie Potts made had been fine until the descriptive card lied about its true age.

There was also the copyright page information indicating *Boys & Girls & Families* was a first-edition book. Aunt Minnie's inscription meant it could not be claimed that its pristine condition was because it had never been in circulation. Supposedly, it had been gifted to some child. You couldn't have it both ways. I knew the dust jacket was new, and now I knew the book wasn't old and rare.

The reason for the deceit was, apparently, money. Roberto could charge more for the book. That left me with two more questions. Who were the thieves, and who had created the books? Was either their production or their theft related to his murder? Roberto could have written in the Aunt Minnie note, but could he have forged the copyright page? That was doubtful. As for the other part, I didn't believe the returning-burglar theory. It was too convenient. But if that was what happened, I hoped the police proved it soon.

Occasionally even the best dealers could be fooled and put a replica, like the table, on the market. That was what Roberto had wanted us to think happened when he used the *Casablanca* defense. I hadn't believed him, and the sales records showing he'd sold several identical tables were proof.

Maybe Roberto had been fooled by Aunt Minnie?

The reality was that the antiques business was largely unregulated. I, however, shared the values of my parents before me, who had chosen to keep their self-esteem, be able to sleep at night, and have repeat customers, who also happened to be their neighbors. In my case, I could add *and not be killed*. Cheating the wrong person might be what had gotten Roberto murdered. Not that there was a right person to defraud.

As I neared King Street, I decided to go home and take the dogs out. Maybe I'd bring them back with me to—

What the . . . ?

The city hall courtyard was crowded with people, maybe fifty or so, many of them with cameras and microphones. More lined the sidewalk in front of the courthouse building across the street. Rather than turning onto King Street, I went across the intersection and took that route home. The reporters could be here for a lot of reasons. I looked down the block, and oh yes, about ten people were milling in front of Waited4You. This was about either Roberto's murder or the letter. But today was Wednesday. Roberto had been killed on Saturday. Why had the reporters shown up now? I told my car to call that fount of wisdom: Opal.

"Have you seen the news people around city hall?"

"Nah, I've been on the boat since lunch, but I heard about them."

"What's going on? Did Roberto become more popular now that he's dead? Or have they made an arrest? Please tell me that's it. That would be great."

"I wish. Most of them are here because of the letter. Maybe some of them because of the cover-up."

"There's a cover-up?" That was news to me. Marthasville didn't do cover-ups—though it had more to do with our not having anything to cover up than our high moral standards.

"In Ella's online posts, that's what she calls it. She still wants this detective, Chief Harrod's son, investigated. Like the waitress said. And, ya know, she has a point. If the guy has an alibi, let him say what it is. You, or I, or Brennan Adler, would be hauled in if we refused to answer that."

I rubbed my forehead. "What about the letter?"

"Some of those people are there in case the letter is returned from Charlottesville today. They want to see it. Or at least take photos of the armored truck or whatever."

"Whoa, they're bringing it back here in a what?"

"If someone has found the missing letter from Sally Fairfax to George Washington here in Marthasville, it will be a big deal," she said.

"Or a very big embarrassment for the city."

"You know you're my oldest and dearest friend, right?" she said.

"Buuuut," I prompted.

"The University of Virginia is, well, the University of Virginia. If they say it's authentic . . ." She sounded apologetic. And now she sounded like Paul.

"It was found in a store owned by someone we know bought and sold other forgeries," I countered. Maybe that was circumstantial evidence. Roberto *could* have had a document of historical importance.

Nah. Why was I doubting myself again? "Let's change the subject. Did you see the article in the *Marthasville Daily News* this morning?"

"No time. What'd it say? Wait, is this the one about the letter?"

"No, this one is about the murder investigation. I want to hear your take on it. Chief Harrod put out a statement saying they were considering reopening the inquiry into an old robbery of the antique store. He said something about determining if there was a connection between that crime and Roberto's murder."

Opal laughed. "You mean he made the connection! He knew what he was doing."

"That's what I thought too. I think he wants everyone to think the police are making progress solving the murder."

"But it's not progress if they're not really related, right? Maybe to take the spotlight off his son?" she suggested.

"You don't really suspect *him*, do you? Remember, he's also the guy with the puppy." I heard water sloshing in the background. "Are you swabbing the deck?"

"Yup. And since you told me he won't give an alibi, I do suspect him! I've decided I will until he gives one. Who knows, maybe he doesn't have one. Investigating the old robbery and the speculation about the letter distract attention from the chief's son."

"I wonder if Chief Harrod leaked the information to the *Daily News* about what UVA said about the letter. I'm home now. I'll call you back." I pulled into a parking spot for car charging and hooked up. Rather than going straight inside, I leaned against the side of the car to think.

I'd meant what I'd said earlier about Chief Harrod handling Brennan Adler with kid gloves. It seemed premature for the police chief to give the media the story about the robbery, but he had. Could he also have leaked the story about UVA's analysis of the letter? If he had, at least he hadn't said it was found in a certain local attorney's office. Why had he stopped before going that far? Which would have been unconscionable, but it would have helped his son. Was he doing Brennan a favor, or Nick?

Chapter Twenty

The dogs couldn't believe their luck in getting a midday car ride. I parked in my assigned space in the parking lot behind Waited4You and checked the online edition of the *Marthasville Daily News*. There it was. A second article about the letter had been added. The headline was *Team Martha or Team Sally? Time to Choose Sides*. I felt ill.

Young George Washington's letters to Sally Fairfax, wife of George William Fairfax, certainly indicated a flirtation at the least, maybe even a hopeless love on his part. Her husband's sister was married to Lawrence Washington, George Washington's half brother. Lawrence had brought his brother to the Fairfax home when George was sixteen and Sally was eighteen. Over the next few years, his letters to her grew warmer, and at some point she asked him to send them to her through a friend.

On January 6, 1759, when he was twenty-six, he married Martha Custis, but the previous September, while he was engaged, he'd written the famous letter to Sally that academic types have argued over for more than a century. In 1877 the *New York Herald* published it. The next day it sold for thirteen dollars, along with another letter from him for a whopping $11.50. Tongues wagged and doubts lingered. The letter wasn't seen by the public for years, but when it was rediscovered in 1958 in Harvard's Houghton Library, the excitement and speculation began again. The letter was authentic, the real deal.

From his camp at Fort Cumberland, George Washington wrote:

> *You have drawn me my dear Madam, or rather have I drawn myself, into an honest confession of a Simple Fact—misconstrue not my meaning—'tis obvious—doubt it not, nor expose it,—the World has no business to know the object of my Love, declard in this manner to—you when I want to conceal it—One thing, above all things in this World I wish to know, and only one person of your Acquaintance can solve me that, or guess my meaning.*

No modern-day cryptographer could have been as opaque. In Sally's next letter she seemed not to have understood his profession of love, or she pretended she hadn't—if a declaration of his love was in fact what it was. He wrote back:

> *Do we still misunderstand the true meaning of each others letters? I think it must appear so, tho I would feign hope the contrary, as I cannot speak plainer without—but I'll say no more and leave you to guess the rest.*

According to the article, the letter hidden under the chair at Waited4You was purportedly her answer to the second letter. I was still waiting for Nick's email with his copy of the fraud that was being perpetrated on my town. Roberto *could* have been the forger, but that didn't fit. I had seen his hurried scratches on invoices and other records, but no examples of calligraphy or imitation older English writing.

We came in through the back, and now the two dogs ran, yapping like crazy, to the front door. The cluster of people I'd seen earlier was gone, but someone was there. Bark about an exciting day.

A young man pressed his forehead to the glass and looked in. He scanned the room from one side to the other. He was startled to see me standing there, and when he recovered from the shock, he pointed to the *Help Wanted* sign. Maybe he was about to leave me a note applying for a job.

He wore a sweater vest and puffer jacket, and he held a pen in his hand, which he used to motion to the sign once again. "Can I come in?" I could hear him just fine, but he acted out turning the doorknob and pulling the door open to enter the store.

Brennan was walking past and saw the pantomime. He slowed, and from the way his head was cocked to the side, he was obviously listening in and enjoying the show.

Since I didn't know how many hours a week Pepper was available to work, I wanted to have a few more résumés ready to review. If I was going to have a staff trained by the day after Thanksgiving, I did need to get busy interviewing and hiring. I unlocked the door. The young man looked to be in his late twenties and had dirty-blond hair and a see-through moustache he should have given up on long ago. Wasn't going to happen for him. Suddenly he pushed his way in. Too eager. He was in my face. A warning sound went off in my head. Why did he look familiar to me? When he reached inside his jacket, my first thought was how thin he was beneath the bulk

155

of the jacket. The sweater vest was roomy on his slight chest. He reached into a pocket and pulled out a phone, holding it up to me. He was the jerk who'd photographed me Saturday night for the *Daily News*! I cringed again thinking of that very unflattering photo.

"Do you think Roberto Fratelli walked in on the rare-book burglars?" he shouted. As he held the phone up to my face, he grinned in a self-satisfied way at his turn of phrase. *Rare-book burglars* had a nice ring to it, I guess.

I backed up and looked at the dogs. They had never been called on to protect me, so I had no idea who would end up protecting whom. Then a low growl came from Stickley. His efforts weren't needed, because in a couple of quick steps Brennan loomed over the man and hooked his arms behind him. He turned the guy to the door, his feet dangling inches off the floor. I remembered how Brennan had looked that first day when he stood behind me at the window. I had thought then that he looked like he could be dangerous.

The younger man arched his back and looked at me. "Well, do you?" he shouted, still holding on to his phone. With Brennan's grip on his jacket, the guy's sleeves rode up over his bony wrists. I hated how much force Brennan was using on the smaller man.

"No! Why would anyone come back to steal more counterfeits?" I yelled after him. I wanted it to stop.

"Go to city hall where the other reporters are!" Brennan swung him around and pushed him outside. When he let go of him, the kid's legs buckled, and he sank down to the sidewalk.

"Nah, they're arguing about two chicks, Martha and Sally." Then he jumped up from his knees and scurried away.

Brennan closed the door but held on to the knob, not turning around.

"Thank you?" I offered, in case that was what he was waiting for. I was trembling so hard I felt weak. All I wanted was for him to leave.

"No, thank youuuuu." His voice dripped with sarcasm. I was so not in the mood for whatever was behind that. "He'll publish that or put it online, and the police will suspect me again. Now I'll never get out of this place." This place? I thought he liked Marthasville.

I inhaled and tried to steady my voice. "What does the burglary have to do with you?"

"Nothing, except it meant there was a suspect that wasn't me. And you just undermined that theory."

"Why does everyone want to blame the person who can't be found? Doesn't that sound a little too convenient?" *Just leave.*

He huffed and yanked the door open. If he slammed it, I would never speak to him again, which made me as immature as him. Besides, he was still my landlord, so I had to speak to him. He stopped the door before it hit the frame, then walked away.

Chapter
Twenty-One

I sat at the old metal desk in the stock room and brought up music on my computer tablet. I was in the mood for "White Room" by Cream, mostly for the perfection of the guitar playing. The right song could make you feel alone, if that's what you were looking for. That scene between Brennan and the reporter had terrified me, and until I could find some calm, a musical cocoon was all I wanted.

At first, Roberto's unique filing system had seemed impractical. He had a folder for each month; records weren't filed by subject. An invoice was followed by a sales tax filing, which was followed by a letter from a dealer, or that month's electric bill. I was used to it now, and liked it.

I was looking for an insurance claim filed in late September or maybe in October. True, he had the stolen books back, but thanks to the rain, they weren't in salable condition. I checked those folders and came up empty. Then, because why not, I went through November. There were no claim forms, letters, or printed emails from an insurance company, not even a note about the books. That might mean the books were worth so little that it hadn't been worth his time. Or that he didn't want to call attention to the theft. I was happy he hadn't filed a claim, since it saved me the trouble of returning any check that might show up from the company.

My phone rang, and I turned the music down.

"Is this Ms. Benson?"

I told the caller it was, and he introduced himself as Ambrose "call me Amby" Jones, editor of the *Marthasville Daily News*.

I was about to hang up on him, but Camille Benson, owner of Waited4You, stayed my hand. "If this is about the death of the previous owner, I don't have any information to give you. You'll need to speak with the police." *Like I'm betting you've been doing all along.*

"My call is about something completely different, I assure you." He chuckled. "Would you be interested in writing a regular column for the newspaper on antiquing? Tips and tidbits. I'm sure you know what I'm talking about."

Maybe the influence of the music wore off, or maybe the source was something else entirely, but suddenly the other Camille found the strength to leap up and overpower Camille the business owner. "Would you be interested in calling off your intrusive, sneaky photographer?"

"What? What in the world do you mean?"

I would give him about two seconds to convince me he wasn't pretending he didn't know what I was talking about, and then I was going to hang up. After all, the photograph had been in his newspaper, even prominently positioned. "He was here the night of the murder and again today."

"Are you talking about a small guy trying to grow a moustache?"

"That's him."

"He doesn't work for me. He's a freelancer. On behalf of the newspaper, I sincerely apologize. How about if I promise to be very careful about what I buy from him in the future? Wait, I can go even further. I won't buy *any* photos from him again. He's green, and he thinks he can do anything he wants to get a photograph or a story."

I sighed. "Can I think about it? The Sunday morning photo really stung." I was mollified by his apology. As I spoke, I Googled Amby. His headshot showed a middle-aged man, more scalp than hair, and a good-natured grin. He had one of those faces that reminded everyone of someone.

"Ah, Ms. Benson, your beauty is so well known, one photo couldn't possibly change anybody's thinking on that."

I laughed out loud.

"Too much?" he asked, cajoling.

"A little." I was still laughing.

"How about it? Will you write a column? Say, monthly?"

Camille the business owner was back in the game. "I'd love to." We hung up, and I was happy the two Camilles were once again united.

I went back to looking at Roberto's records. There was a paid invoice for a reorder of the embossed *W4Y* stickers. The copper-colored disks were simple, functional, and tasteful. They were the Martha Stewart, not the Marie Kondo, of office supplies by conveying the beautiful essence of an antique store. Less isn't always more, they reminded us. In the notes section, the vendor had written in, *Original artwork supplied by customer.*

A sheet of white paper was stapled to the invoice. On it was a sketch of the little logo. It was an oval with a horizontal orientation, about the width of a quarter. Under the drawing, Roberto had written, *Copyright Roberto Fratelli.*

I felt like I'd had a glimpse at a different person, not "the meanest man in Marthasville." When I'd first heard he was keeping the whimsical name my parents had given the store, I'd wondered if he had a softer side. Then the stories of his tirades and harsh responses to visitors had gone around town, so I'd assumed he'd kept the name out of laziness or a desire to take advantage of the reputation my parents and the intervening owner had built.

How had he created something this sublime? I didn't know how, but he had. I leaned back in the old desk chair, then rocked forward. Hearing the squeaking, Stickley and Morris ran back to me from their perch on the rugs. I needed a different spot for those, because I couldn't chance UV rays dulling the vibrant colors, but people had already gotten used to seeing my boys sitting there. I noticed a few people stopping to wave at them. The dogs would stand and wag their nubs. With each of these encounters, Waited4You was closer to opening and further from being "that place where that man was murdered." Maybe I would put a sheet over the top rug.

I straightened the papers from the September folder and replaced them. As I closed the folder, I noticed a pencil drawing on the inside cover. It looked a little like a desk with a chair behind it. I rocked back and forth, listening to the chair creak and thinking more about the stolen books. Roberto hadn't filed an insurance claim. Was it because the books had been misrepresented? I had seen only one book, the children's book. That was a fake, so there was no reason to think the others were authentic. Cheating customers was one thing; insurance fraud might have been going too far, even for him. Anyway, his loss wasn't nearly what it would have been if the books had been true rare books or had some attribute that would make them valuable to a collector.

He had the books back, but where were they? When we'd inventoried the stock room, I hadn't seen any books that fit Helen's description. Nor had any of the boxes of merchandise smelled moldy, like they held something wet. Roberto hadn't wanted them back when Helen first tried to give them to him, but then he'd changed his mind. Did that mean they were evidence of something? That could certainly explain his behavior. Or maybe he didn't want anyone else to have them. That would be consistent.

I sat up straight. Some forgeries were not reported because the gallery owners did not want their professional reputations tarnished. Had Roberto been duped? That didn't feel right. It would mean he'd thought the books were authentic before they were stolen, and just the opposite after. "He didn't want the thieves caught and he didn't want a court trial!" I said to . . . Morris. "Hey, where's Stickley? And stop trying to look so innocent." I felt something against my foot under the desk. "Stickley! What are you doing?" His hip and nub of a tail were up in the air, and he sniffed and scratched at the baseboard. "That does it." Pulling him out wasn't easy, as motivated as he was, but I was able to since I was the leader of the pack. I shooed both dogs back to the showroom and reached for my cell phone.

I Googled the pest service I used at home and dialed their number. "I think I have a mouse," I told the person who answered. She put me on hold to check the calendar, and I took that time to replace the papers for the October file. I was about to put them back in what looked like the September folder when I caught myself. No, that *was* the October file.

But there it was again. The drawing. This time the perspective of the desk was from the side. You could clearly see the chair. It was a one-piece unit. Roberto had sketched the computer desk Ritchie Potts had designed. The one that reminded me of Elsa Peretti's work. I picked up the November file next. There was another drawing on the inside of that folder. Same desk. This time a view from the back was depicted. There were details on all three versions I hadn't seen on the photograph of the piece when it won the award. How had Roberto known so much about Ritchie's design? My guess was that those sketches meant he'd found the pioneering design extraordinary, an industry changer, like I did. Had he seen the real thing at Ritchie and Ella's house? I would love to see it myself.

I shook my head and went back to thinking about the theft. I imagined that night. A thief or thieves running away down the alley, in the rain. How could they tell anything about the quality of the books they'd stolen? It would be tempting to imagine a Thomas Crown–type cat burglar, but if you were expert enough to figure out a book was a fake in the rain at nighttime, you were good enough to catch that before you left the store.

The police chief, commonwealth's attorney Janie, and my landlord were all ready to connect Roberto's murder to the theft. I was the only holdout. Maybe the theft had been a link in the chain of events that led to the murder, but there was much more to the crime than a mysterious bad guy who hadn't been found, and would never be found, returning and killing him. Roberto Fratelli had been frail and thin and could have been shoved aside easily. Killing was overkill.

The Police sang their 1979 song "I'm Sending Out an S.O.S.," which meant I had a phone call coming in from Opal.

"I'm off tonight. I have an idea. And this one is pretty good," she said.

"Before you say any more, I'm exhausted."

Of course she said more. "I keep thinking about the waitress saying that Ella and Roberto weren't arguing at the restaurant but Detective Harrod saying they were. I'd like to know for sure what happened when they got to Watied4You instead of taking anybody's word for it."

"Meaning you don't want to take the detective's word."

"Exactly. Let's ask Janie if we can see the video footage of the two of them walking to Waited4You. What do you say?"

"I like it. I'll call her now."

"I already did. We're going to her condo tonight." I put the three folders in my satchel as she gave me the details. "She lives in West End at Watergate at Landmark. I'll pick you up at seven thirty, okay?"

"Only if it's in The Car," I said.

Chapter
Twenty-Two

I wrote one last article for the premier issue of my newsletter, which still didn't have a name. The topic was "undecorating." Transforming a time-stamped room was often as simple as taking away accessories. Many of my friends were amazed by how fresh a living room or bedroom looked and felt after their dust catchers were donated to a good cause or packed away.

The next hour was spent setting up displays. I thought back to how my parents had sold pieces they didn't particularly care for. My mother loathed hobnail milk glass in anything other than serving pieces. I agreed. I couldn't imagine holding a hobnail glass tumbler. The feel would distract from the taste of the beverage. She said if it was a matter of quality, give your opinion; if it was just differing tastes, let the customer buy all he wanted. I would use that rule in deciding what to do with some of the less beautiful merch Roberto had left me.

My holiday theme was "Christmas lite," but I would probably end up calling it something else. While I worked, I auditioned seasonal and nonholiday music selections and put on "Off the Cuff" by Ragan Whiteside. It was perfect, and I made a note to find out if the flutist had holiday music out.

I moved a wooden dining room table front and center. Roberto had covered it with a mishmash of 1950s kitchen tools. There were small items like vintage aluminum measuring spoons, a wooden rolling pin, and two red-handled spatulas strewn around the table and sitting in an incomplete set of jadeite mixing bowls. I took all of that to the back and brought out pressed-glass stemware and cut-glass serving dishes and two coordinating tartan plaid tablecloths. I set the table for a dinner party. Each place setting was different, but I thought they looked cohesive enough to tell a story. One of the glasses for each diner held a Christmas ornament, to which I attached a sticker noting how many of each piece I had in the storeroom. I arranged Depression glass stemware on one side of the table and carnival glass on the other.

I set the more expensive cut-glass serving pieces in the center of the table on cloth I'd folded to use as a runner. I added a two-handled loving cup in cranberry-to-clear, a graceful green-to-clear six-inch champagne cooler, and a clear jelly compote. All were from the American Brilliant Period, 1876 until 1914. They were super heavy because of their high lead oxide content.

Stickley and Morris barked. Then I heard a knock and turned to see Pepper at the door. She wore a black skirt, which ended halfway between her knees and ankles, and a black blouse under a kelly-green wool winter coat. "I hope you haven't been standing there too long. Do I have the music too loud?" I asked when I unlocked the door and let her in.

"Just walked up. I brought my résumé," she said, holding the paper out to me.

"Thank you." I gave it a quick read. She could have emailed it, but she'd made the effort to come by. So far, so good. "The job is part-time, but I'll need someone after the holidays too. Is that okay?"

"Sure! Wait, you're a Ragan Whiteside fan?" She came up on her toes in excitement. The gesture was completely at odds with her somber clothes.

"I am," I said.

"Isn't she amazing?"

"I love her music. Do you think it'll work playing in the background here in the store?"

She looked around. "If this was the old kind of antique store, no. But with the vibe you're creating, definitely!"

I finally did something right! Whew. "I was thinking Mindi Abair music would work too."

"Vocal or just sax?" she asked.

"Just sax. I want it to be almost subliminal."

"Agree!" she said. "You know she has a Christmas album. Perfect, right? And Kayla Waters! She's local." She turned in a circle looking at the changes I'd made. "An ongoing part-time job would be even better. I love music, but the money isn't great." Pepper would be a perfect part-timer to have on board.

"Weekends are busy days for the stores in Old Town. Unfortunately, that's also when most estate sales are held. Opal's been great, but I can't keep calling on her. She has her own business to run," I explained. "I know of one estate sale coming up the first weekend in December with a pair of William Haines side chairs that I would love to get for the store."

"I don't know who or what that is. Sorry."

"Haines was a successful actor in the 1920s and '30s. He refused to deny that he was gay, so the big studios dropped him. He quit acting in 1935 and started an interior design business. The chairs are beautiful."

"Ms. Benson—"

"Please, call me Camille."

She smiled, and I hoped I wouldn't accidently call her Brenda Starr. "Camille, I don't know much about antiques, but I think I'm good with people. Oh, and by the way, I know I look like I'm going to a funeral, but we're performing tonight. I have a solo." With each sentence, her speech accelerated. I hoped she wasn't nervous.

"That's exciting. What are you playing?"

"'The Swan' from *The Carnival of the Animals*."

"That's one of my favorites! I doubt if Paul has ever heard of it, but it's romantic and lush and—"

"Uh, I have an extra ticket."

"That's so nice of you, but I have plans." I was disappointed, but Opal and Janie were counting on me. Was the prospect of inviting me what had caused the nerves?

She looked down at the floor. "Actually, I wanted to ask Paul if he wanted to come and hear me."

Ah. "That's a great idea. Want his number?"

"Sure." I was already writing it down for her. "I'll look at this"—I pointed to her résumé, which I'd placed on an oak parlor table, circa 1910—"and call you tomorrow." Sure, I could have interviewed her then and there, but I wanted her to make that call to my son. The cello was such a passionate instrument. Those two were as good as in love.

Chapter
Twenty-Three

West End was one of Marthasville's fastest-growing neighborhoods. In Marthasville that term— *neighborhood*—didn't refer to a subdivision with a cul-de-sac. Rather, it was an area of town with a couple hundred to a few thousand people.

Each neighborhood had historic attractions. For instance, before Prohibition, the Old Town neighborhood had boasted over fifty bars and "comparatively loose morals." Today it was down to thirty-five bars.

A West End landmark, Fort Ward, was the best preserved of the extensive network of Union forts and batteries built to protect the capital during the Civil War. Today, besides the museum, tours, and other events, the forty-five-acre park was a first-rate place to jog. One of Paul's favorites. This neighborhood's other draw was that it was the hub of Marthasville's craft beer scene. Port City Brewing Company's name was a nod to colonial Marthasville's importance as a seaport. A century later the city was home to the largest brewery in the southern United States, which ended up being another casualty of Prohibition.

Janie lived in the part of West End we called condo canyon, and Watergate at Landmark was one of the largest complexes. She had left Opal's name with the gate, and we were given a pass to put on the windshield of The Car. The security guard whistled in admiration at the 1990 Corvette ZR1, which had its top down. The exterior paint color was competition yellow, and the upholstery, which wasn't original, was black. It had a six-speed manual transmission, which made me feel like this was a real car and Opal was really driving.

"C4s were the best, weren't they?" the guard said.

"Sure are for my money," Opal answered as she let out the clutch.

*   *   *

"We're early, but I'm sure it won't matter," Opal said as we took the mirror-walled elevator from the lobby to the seventh floor. The Car was so fast it wasn't unusual for us to arrive before we were expected.

"I hope not. Janie is such a private person, you never know when you're crossing boundaries." I pulled off my white wool ribbed beanie and smoothed my hair back into its ponytail. The matching gloves I'd already stuffed into my pockets. If you're going to be a passenger in The Car in November, you had better dress for it. Especially at the speeds Opal drove.

As I was about to ring the doorbell, we heard high-pitched barking from inside. I pulled my hand back. "She has a dog? When did she get it?"

"Like you said, she's a very private person."

I looked at the number again. "We're at the right apartment. Seven twenty-five. What if she has company? She is expecting us, right?"

"Yes!" Opal shook her finger at the door. "She said for us to come here and she would show us the video clip on her computer. Wait, I think I hear someone."

Before Opal could press the doorbell, the door opened. Janie gasped when she saw us. Nick Harrod stood behind her, one arm in his wool coat and one in midair. She had an embarrassed expression on her face, and the look on Nick's was sheepish. I didn't see the look on the collie puppy's face, because he ran by us and out into the hallway fast as lightning.

"This is your puppy?" I asked her.

"Un-huh. Well, *ours*," she said. "Oh no!"

The dog sprinted down the carpeted hallway as fast as his scrawny puppy legs could go. The four of us ran after him, and Nick reached him first. He scooped him up in his arms, and we walked back to Janie's apartment door.

"What's his name? Her name?" Opal cooed, offering her palm to be sniffed.

"She, and it's Rizzoli," Janie answered.

"For Jane Rizzoli, like in *Rizzoli & Isles*?" Opal asked.

"Yeah, she was a police detective too." Janie smiled at Nick.

"Has she grown since Saturday?" I asked, scratching the top of her head just behind an ear on my way to the sofa.

"Daily. Seriously, I think she grows every day. Would you like anything to drink?"

"Maybe some answers," I said. "Nick, you were *here* Saturday night, and that's why you don't want to give your father your alibi?" I remembered Chief Harrod keeping an eye on the door to Waited4You and his annoyance. Nick was who he'd been waiting for. And Nick had been otherwise occupied.

"Yeah." He put the collie puppy on the carpet and dropped into a white leather chair, which matched the sofa.

Rizzoli ran up to Opal, and she picked the dog up and held her in her lap. "Chief Harrod doesn't know you're dating?"

"Nope." He looked over at Janie, who was sitting in a wing chair upholstered with distressed plaid in the shade of white known as oatmeal. Even her decorating choices were unrevealing. Very private. Safety first. "I would shout it from out there." He pointed to the balcony, then reached for her hand. "But *someone* wants to keep the fact that we're dating in the vault."

"I just don't like for everyone to know my business," Janie said, looking down at the beige carpet.

Opal leaned forward, over Rizzoli's head. "Sweetie, you've seen Ella Coleman's posts about what happened between Roberto and Nick the day of the murder."

I had a brief moment of insight into and agreement with Janie's guardedness when I thought about the waitress blithely passing along the notion that "it looks like the son might have done it" and referring to Nick as "a suspect" when her source was nothing more than a troll on the internet. Janie still needed to fight back. I nodded. "Giving Nick an alibi would shut her up."

"But would it? Wouldn't she just say I was protecting him?" Janie teared up and bit her lower lip.

"What if she does? The truth needs to come out," I said. "Can I have a cup of tea? I'll help." Before she could turn down my offer to turn a knob on the stove to boil water, I was up and halfway to the kitchen.

"Uh, uh—" I'd left her no choice, and she stood and followed me.

I checked the kettle for water before turning to her. Turning a dial was literally all that was involved. "You haven't told him about the stalker you had in law school, have you?"

She shook her head and looked in the direction of the living room. "I . . . I can't talk about it."

"He loves you."

"I know," she said, bobbing her head and smiling in spite of herself.

"Opal and I made a promise to Fran to watch over you forever. I can't give you advice that would be bad for your mental health, but neither can I let someone be accused of a murder he didn't commit. Surely you can see that having these rumors out there could hurt Nick's career." He seemed like the kind of person everything came easily to, but in a town the size of Marthasville, insinuations, like diamonds, were forever.

Her shoulders slumped, and she covered her face with her hands. "No, no."

I cupped her face in my palms. "Have you considered seeing someone? Get help for the trauma that's obviously still in there?"

She shook her head. "I'll try. I need time." She shook her head to push the ugly memories to a dark corner. "For now, let's look at the video footage."

I reached over and turned the burner off.

"Don't you want a cup of tea?"

"Nah, too late for caffeine." I went back to the living room. The surprise at seeing Nick there had subsided, and I could ask him a few questions about the case. "Nick, something's been bothering me, and I hope you can help." The puppy was where I had been sitting, so I squeezed in at the end of the sofa. Janie started to shoo him off. "He's fine. How did Ella know about what happened at Waited4You? Weren't we four the only people in the store at the time? It was just Roberto, Opal, you, and I."

"We were. You're right. That's a very interesting question," he said. "I remember the door was propped open when I came in. Maybe she was walking by?"

"I blocked the door until you had the puppy," I said. "No one walked by. Wait, I take that back. I did see someone, but it wasn't Ella. It was a waitress from Mykonos Taverna. I don't know which one, but her coat was open and I saw her apron."

"All I know is she calls for my head on a platter every single day on either the Nextdoor website or the I Love Marthasville Facebook group."

"Truth!" Opal said. "What did you do to make her so mad?"

"I never met the woman in my life. I have no idea."

"No telling," I said, shaking my head. "On a slightly different topic, have you found out what the murder weapon was?"

"It was flat and left a trace of mineral oil when it hit Fratelli. The killer must have taken it with him, because luminol didn't show blood on any of the items in Waited4You. Can you think of anything in the store he might have used?"

"Why are you assuming it's a man?" Opal asked, swinging her arms and waking up Rizzoli, who was dozing.

"He was hit with something heavy, so we're leaning in that direction, but we're not committed to it," Nick said. "Could've been a strong woman, I guess."

"If it had mineral oil on it, it was probably made of wood," I said. "Do you know anything about the shape?"

"Flat, or at least the part that made contact was."

"Wooden with a level surface? Could he have been hit with a tabletop?" Opal suggested. "Like a small table." She pointed to Janie's contemporary end table by the sofa.

"We considered it, but we don't think so. Would've been hard to get that much force with a table. Besides, there wasn't any blood on the tables in your place. Nothing lit up with luminol."

"Sorry, I can't think of anything like that." I shook my head. "I can't even think of anything not made of wood. Roberto didn't leave any cookware, or I would suggest a frying pan. If luminol didn't show blood on anything, does that mean the killer brought the murder weapon in with him and took it when he left?"

"That's a possibility," Nick said. "He didn't have to bring it in. Could've just taken it when he left."

"Nothing was missing except the letter. I wish I could be more help."

"I know. Oh well, we'll figure it out."

I liked his confidence.

"Have you located the brother Ella Coleman told you about?" I asked.

"She couldn't remember his name and couldn't find the phone number. Our investigator has a lead on a sister's child in New Jersey. She's following up on that."

Had I imagined it, or had Opal just signaled to Janie with one squinted eye while Nick was talking? He might have caught it too, because he looked over at Janie, then hoisted himself up from the chair. "Gotta get back to work." She went over to him, and they stood close. He wrapped his arm around her small waist and kissed her cheek.

"You look tired," I said. I didn't envy the position he was in. Why wouldn't his father reassign the case to someone else? Anyone he arrested would say he was trying to save himself. Hell, that's what I would say.

"He's very tired." Janie walked him to the door, and Opal and I talked about how much we loved the upholstery on her dining room chairs.

As they were kissing, both their cell phones rang. They checked the screens, and he waved that he was going to the hallway to answer.

Janie read hers and then relayed what had happened. "A photographer from the *Daily News* was found dead," she said. "Just outside the newspaper's offices on Seminary Road."

Chapter
Twenty-Four

"Janie, are you sure you don't need to go to the crime scene? We understand if you do." I remembered how Chief Harrod chided her on Sunday for not coming to Waited4You the night of the murder.

"This is important, and it won't take long. I'll wait a half hour or so to give them time to secure the area." She sat between Opal and me on the sofa.

While she logged on to her computer, I told them about my telephone call this afternoon with Amby Jones, the *Daily News* editor in chief, and him asking me to write a column on antiquing.

"Free advertisement is what that is!" Opal reached her arm over Janie's back so we could high-five.

"I hope he doesn't hire the crazy freelancer to fill this position," I said. "You don't think he will, do you?"

"What crazy freelancer? Like paparazzi?" Janie asked.

"Nah, aren't those photographers? This guy takes photos and asks questions. He took that glamour shot of me getting in the police car on Saturday night, and he came back to Waited4You asking questions about the case."

"That's all the town needs now is an overly zealous reporter. Did you see the press gaggle we have here for the letter?" Janie asked as she typed.

"I've had ads in the newspaper for years," said Opal. "Wonder if the deceased person is anyone I know. You said he was a photographer?"

"Yeah," Janie answered, but she'd waited a beat.

"Then he's probably not anyone I know, even though they send photographers for events like the canine cruise, and sometimes to get photos of monuments during fireworks shows. I'll send Mr. Jones an email later with my condolences," Opal said.

"He was murdered?" I asked.

Both women stared at me. Then Opal looked at Janie. "She's right, isn't she?"

"How did you get that from what I said?" Janie moaned.

A police detective and the commonwealth's attorney would not be called in if we were talking about a ninety-six-year-old dying of a heart attack in his sleep. "Skill," I answered, since that was kinder than *common sense*. "And you didn't correct me when I said 'crime scene.'"

Opal giggled, and Janie blew out an exasperated sigh. "Ready to watch the footage from Saturday night?" The laptop was open on the ottoman, and she clicked on the attachment with the video. "Here we see Roberto walking east on King Street. Ella's following close behind him. He looks like he's trying to ignore her, but as you can see, she's still talking. We haven't found anyone that heard what she was saying."

I put on my glasses and leaned forward. "It looks like she's asking him to 'wait' and 'slow down.'"

"But why is he taking off like that?" Opal stroked the now wide awake Rizzoli's coat as she spoke. "Didn't he ask her to come to Mykonos Taverna to talk to him?"

"I think he had to hurry to get back to Waited4You to meet someone," Janie said.

"You do? You no longer think the book thieves came back and he surprised them?" I asked.

"Both could be true." She was leaving out so much more than she said.

I wanted to ask her how you could surprise someone you had arranged to meet, but I didn't. Instead, I tried to imagine that particular string of events. Roberto had had an appointment to meet with someone—though setting up his tête-à-tête with Ella just beforehand and taking a chance on being late didn't make sense—but instead the robbers from before were there.

Nah.

"If he went there to meet someone, why didn't he turn the lights on?" I asked. "The lights were off when Opal and I went in. Isn't that what you would do? I don't think he planned to meet anyone in the store. He may have known his killer and let him or her in, but I don't think it was planned."

"If he turned the light on, people from the outside could have seen him in there," Opal interjected. "You and I might have seen the place lit up, since we were having dinner across the street. And remember, he had no business being in there after the papers were signed. He lied about giving you all the keys. A whole restaurant full of people could have seen him."

"He could have at least turned on a light in the stock room. I think he went back to get the letter."

"I'll need to leave soon, so let's get back to the videos," Janie said. "Now we need to change to a different camera." She brought the laptop onto her lap. She closed the video on the screen and opened another. "Ella and Roberto are in front of Waited4You. The camera was behind their backs, but you'll see that he pulls a key out of his jacket pocket and opens the door."

"The little sneak," Opal said. "Too bad we don't have a better angle. The case would be solved if we could see in there. See how she pulls his arm? What do you think that means?"

"That she's guilty," I said.

Again, Opal and Janie exchanged a look. This time I was sure I hadn't imagined it.

"Camille, she didn't go into Waited4You, and everything points to Brennan Adler," Janie said.

"Wait, you two talked about this already, didn't you? Is that the real reason we're here? To talk about Brennan?" Of course it was. Janie could have told us what was on the tape over the phone. But then we wouldn't have uncovered her and Nick's secret relationship.

"Weeeell," Opal said.

I turned to Janie. "What about Brennan's alibi? Just this morning Nick said there was a photo of him riding his bike."

"He got that bit of information from his father. I don't work for the police chief." She sounded defiant, even angry. "No, I don't work for the police, and they don't work for me. I'm an elected official, and unlike the chief, I don't even work for the city manager. Technically, neither do my employees, since they work for an elected official."

"Soooo, you can bring a case without the police?" Opal asked. Her eyebrows were way up on her forehead.

Janie shrugged, and I couldn't tell if that was a yes or a no. I turned to Opal. "I think she's trying to tell us that if she wants Brennan Adler arrested and charged, he will be."

Janie held up one finger. "Things won't go that far. First, Mr. Adler had the letter—"

I cut her off. "If he already had the letter, where's his motive? It certainly wasn't to threaten or torture or pressure or whatever Roberto Fratelli into giving it to him. Remember how the stock room looked? Someone had gone through every box."

"We only have his word for when he took it," Janie said.

"But we know when he saw where it was hidden," I reminded them.

"Roberto could have moved it later, and that was why Brennan had to search the stock room." Janie was determined to find a way for Brennan to be guilty, no matter how convoluted the path. I pinched the bridge of my nose.

"Plus, if Roberto knew Brennan took it, he might have wanted to silence him," Opal said.

"Whose side are you on?" I pleaded.

"Yours! I don't think you're seeing this clearly. You don't want him to be guilty."

"Second, he's in a hurry to leave town," Janie said. I had no answer to that. "Next, was he at Waited4You at all on Saturday?"

"If he saw Opal pick up that chair, he had to have been."

"Did you see him?"

I felt like I was on the witness stand and I'd promised to tell the truth, the whole truth, and nothing but the truth. I shook my head. I was not going down for perjury. No, sirree.

"How about you, Opal? Did you see him?"

"Nope, and he's a guy a woman would notice, if you know what I mean."

Janie wasn't through making her case. "For argument's sake, let's say he was there and saw you find the letter under that chair but neither of you knew he was there, when would he have come back to get it?"

"After we left," I answered. "And using his key, if that was going to be your next question."

"And he came in through the back," Janie said.

"How do you know?" Opal asked.

Janie rolled her eyes. "Nick is working really hard on this. He's spent a lot of time looking at any video he could from every camera in the area, and Mr. Adler didn't come in through the front door. Still, the most damning evidence against Brennan Adler is the value of that letter."

"The letter is fake!" I said.

"You know that from seeing it for a few seconds? And just the top part of it too." Opal was not letting me off easy.

"I know enough history to say it's not authentic. Martha Washington burned a lot, maybe most, of her husband's letters after he died."

"Oh, were you there?" Opal laughed.

"Some days it feels like it." I laughed too. Janie's mood lightened, but she was still serious.

"She could only burn the letters she knew about," Opal said, as she reached behind Janie and patted my back.

"So George Washington hid this letter from his wife? That sounds like something a forger would say to explain why it's just now shown up," I said. "What about the letters scholars know about? The Papers of George Washington project at the

University of Virginia has over 135,000 of George Washington's public and private papers. Do you think Roberto Fratelli would have this one, but they wouldn't?" It felt like I finally had a point on the board.

Janie shook her head. "You don't think you're maybe being a teensy bit naïve? I mean, so much leads to Brennan Adler. By the way, I had your new key taken in as evidence, so he doesn't have it."

"Thank you," Opal said. "But evidence? It didn't exist when Roberto was murdered. Good girl. I'm impressed."

I just shook my head. "You saw the video. Ella is obviously trying to keep him from going inside Waited4You. Aren't you curious to know why? Does Ritchie Potts have an alibi?"

"Ella alibied him. She said he was home all evening," Janie answered.

"That ali don't by, does it?" I asked. "No. How would she know where he was if she was in Old Town at a restaurant with Roberto?"

Janie stretched her arms overhead. "His phone says he was. Remember, Nick said it didn't move."

"Camille, sweetie, let's talk about your safety," said Opal. "Remember when I asked Brennan Adler to help you change the code on your alarm? Did he?"

"No, I did it myself." That much was true.

"That's good," Opal said. "That means he can't disarm it."

"But from what you told me, that security system is pretty much useless," Janie said.

"What?" Opal jumped up.

"Yeah, it's not connected to an alarm center. It just makes a lot of noise," I said.

Opal scrubbed her forehead. "And Mr. Brennan Adler didn't mention that to you? Even after a murder and a break-in? I rest my case."

"A new system is being installed next week." I sounded sheepish, or evasive, or maybe even both. Time to change the subject. "Janie, is UVA still saying the letter is authentic?"

"They've clammed up."

Wonder why? I harrumphed.

"They're getting conflicting opinions."

Her phone pinged. "Here's a photo of the man that was—and yes, Camille, you were right—murdered tonight." She held her phone out for us to see. "This says his name is Gil Harris."

The headshot showed a man I had recently met. "He's not employed by *Marthasville Daily News*. He's the freelancer."

"Was," they said together, correcting me.

Now he would never have that moustache.

Chapter
Twenty-Five

The night was clear. About a thousand stars shone over us. We could appreciate the beauty because we were bundled up in the right clothes. Hats, gloves, and scarves.

"Opal, don't we need to be in the right lane?" We were in the middle lane of South Walker Street, at the intersection with Duke Street, waiting for the light to change. The Car was in the wrong lane to head east.

"We're getting on I-395."

"We're not taking Duke Street to my place?"

"I thought we'd take a different route."

I knew that tone. "Where are we going?"

"Seminary Road." She went for a nonchalant manner, but I had known her way too long to fall for that.

"Not to the crime scene. Please tell me we're not going there."

She reached over and turned on the audio system. "How's this?"

"We Built this City," sung by Starship, filled the car. She cranked up the volume and yelled to be heard. "You can't be mad when you're listening to this. Admit it."

The song was from the album *Knee Deep in the Hoopla*. I started laughing, because that's what *this* city was in because of the letter. I looked at the car lights ahead of us on the high-way and the tall buildings filled with people living their lives as we zoomed past. "I love West End," I called out.

"Oh, okay, sure," Opal yelled back as she reached for her phone.

Starship was replaced by Pet Shop Boys singing "West End Girls." Whatever.

We took the Seminary Road East exit off I-395, and she turned the music off. I was still thinking about hoopla over the letter, supposedly written by Sally Fairfax to George Washing-ton. All afternoon the online edition of the *Marthasville Daily News* had fed the speculation with their hourly updates.

* * *

The *Marthasville Daily News* building sat well back from the road in what once had been a stately old home. Three or four hills, which were either natural or had been landscaped in, made it look like the lawn was unfurling to the street. The driveway went on forever and was wide enough for two cars to sit side by side, or for one to make a U-turn if circumstances called for a quick getaway. Opal parked at its entrance, on the left side.

"Do you think we'll be in their way?" she asked.

"Surely everyone who's coming is already here." Every kind of official vehicle I could think of was there, including two gray Ford Interceptors. Unmarked, but they might as well have been marked.

Nick did a double take when he saw us. Opal had described Brennan as a man you noticed, and the same could be said about The Car. Nick reached us almost before we shut its cute doors.

"What're you doing here?"

"Good question. That's what I want to know too." Janie's BMW was parked behind The Car, and she stomped up, arms swinging. I managed not to laugh at her earnestness.

"Did you follow, I mean, tail us?" Opal asked.

"It wasn't exactly hard."

"Camille knows the deceased," Opal announced importantly, like that explained anything at all.

"Know him? I wouldn't go that far." I shoved my hands into my pockets because I was cold and, unlike Opal, I was able to speak without waving them around. "He came to Waited4You. Twice. Saturday night and today," I explained to Nick.

He looked at me, and as he followed the one-two-three of what that might mean, he squeezed his eyes shut. Janie stood next to him, and her face showed the struggle she was having to keep from reaching out to take his arm. "If this is related to the Fratelli murder, it's another case I have no business investigating."

My thoughts on this man's murder ran in a different direction. Brennan had manhandled the guy and thrown him out of Waited4You just this afternoon. I'd told Janie and Opal about the dead man's two visits to the store, but I hadn't gone into detail about this afternoon's scuffle. I'd conveniently left out any mention of Brennan or his temper. I squeezed my hands in my pocket into balls. My fingernails dug into my palms through the gloves.

"Camille, what are you thinking?" Nick asked.

Brennan had accused me of implicating him in Roberto's murder, not once but twice. Here I was, about to do it again. "No . . . I mean, nothing." Cooperating with the police, the good guys, was one thing; being a tattletale was something else.

Chapter Twenty-Six

Janie told Nick more of the details—based on what she knew—of the two times I'd seen the dead man. He took out a notebook. "When was he at your place today?"

I thought back over my very full day and tried to answer. "I'm not sure."

"It would help me trace his movements if you could just narrow it down."

"I'd say between two and three o'clock." I held up my arm. "I don't wear a watch, so I honestly don't know." It was only a matter of time before footage from the traffic camera showed the police what had happened between him and Brennan; then Janie and Opal would swear I was protecting him.

A white sheet lay on the ground at what looked like the mathematical middle of the expanse of grass and flower gardens. A crime scene truck idled in the driveway. Several people, all wearing coveralls, masks, and booties, worked around the sheet. Two rows of tiny flags stuck out of the ground, making a path to the sheet. When the techs walked to or from the body, they stayed to that corridor.

"Do you want to see the body?" Nick asked.

"Yes!" Opal answered.

"No!" I said.

"He was asking me, not you two," Janie said, settling the matter. "I'll wait on the driveway for now."

"Opal, should we go? It's been a long day."

"Now, are you sure you don't want to stay and see the body? Oh, come on," Nick teased.

"Quite sure." I turned to go to The Car but came back. "You heard about the ceiling tile that was moved in my stock room?"

"Yeah, it was in the report."

"This guy is very thin, like emaciated."

"I noticed," Nick said. "I think I can take it from here."

I had done my civic duty and was happy to leave when I heard Amby Jones's unmistakable voice in the near distance. In the photo on the newspaper web page, his hair and clothes had appeared tidier, his health better. It was dark out, but that was definitely the man I had talked to on the phone and Googled. He was part of a small gathering of people farther along the driveway, closer to the *Daily News* building.

I took Opal's arm and whispered, "You know who that is?"

"Yes, I do. This would be the perfect time to express our condolences, don't you think?" She nodded at me, twice. "I'm right behind you."

* * *

"Mr. Jones? I'm Camille Benson." The woman and man with Amby drifted away. The look they shared told me they were happy for the chance to escape.

He spread his arms wide. Wait, he wasn't really coming in for a hug, was he? Yes, he was. I pulled back, but I was a little too late. My arms were pinned to my sides, which made it hard for me to signal the hug was over by patting his back two times.

"I'm Opal Wells." She thrust her hand up to his face between us, and he let go of me.

"Of course I know you, Ms. Wells. A longtime advertiser with us." He pounced at her for a hug, but Opal ninja'd out of his reach. She pivoted so that she was perpendicular to him and pointed to the lawn. "Isn't this tragic?"

His lunge, the too-muchness of it, and her move reminded me of something. I took in Amby Jones's big head and short body. He was the man I'd seen crossing King Street on Sunday morning with Ella Coleman. I was as sure of that as I was that the bobblehead-collecting craze was over.

He wagged his big head. "So sad. So sad."

"Mr. Jones?" Nick walked up. "Quick word, please."

"Of course, of course." This was a man who specialized in repeating himself.

As Nick walked away with Amby, he looked at Opal and me over his shoulder with suspicion. We shrugged innocently.

I sniffed the air. "I smell oranges. Do you?"

"Yeah, all of a sudden."

We could hear Nick talking to Amby up ahead. "This is good. We can stop here," Nick said, causing Amby to freeze midstep. "We're asking everyone to stay off the grass. We're still hoping for shoe prints." The newspaperman exhaled and righted himself.

"Amby Jones knows Ella," I told Opal. The men were about five feet away from us, so I had to whisper. "I saw them together on Sunday." She looked straight at me, but her gaze was distant, unfocused. "Did you hear me?"

"I'm eavesdropping," she whispered. "The guy's cell phone is missing, but his wallet was still in his pocket. Had a few hundred dollars in it. Nick wants to know if Amby had recently paid him. Amby says he had and hasn't seen him since. Okay, they're done."

"That's odd."

"Just one of my many talents," she said. "I don't think it's so odd. Anyway, it came in handy, didn't it?"

"I meant, it's strange that his cell phone would be stolen but not his wallet, with that much cash in it." I knew he had a cell phone—first, because who didn't? and second, because my privacy had been trespassed by it.

"Maybe this wasn't a mugging?" she asked.

"He had a smartphone, but it wasn't a superexpensive model." I looked back at the big lit-up building. "I wonder what was on it."

"Maybe he raked the wrong person's muck."

"We need to make nice with Handsy Jones," I said.

She wrinkled her nose. "Fine, but you first," she said. "Here he comes."

"This would be easier if I trusted him. If he knows Ella, I don't," I whispered. "Mr. Jones—"

"Please call me Amby." His eyes followed Nick as the detective walked to the figure under the sheet on the lawn, keeping between the flags. "So sad, so sad," he repeated, looking down. I so wanted to beg him to stop doing that. I would pay him.

"Amby, it looks like Gil Harris was leaving the *Daily News* building when he was attacked," I fished.

He gazed at his own building, then his eyes ran down the driveway to Seminary Road. "Do you think so?"

"We have to assume that, Amby," Opal added. "So sad, so sad." The mockery was lost on him.

"But I mean, it looks like he's facing the building." For some reason, Amby was becoming uncomfortable.

"What was he working on for you?" I asked, ignoring what he'd said. Of course, he was right; the dead man was facing that way. If anything, I would guess he'd been headed *to* the building. Something told me I would get more information from Amby if I used anything other than the direct approach, so I'd said just the opposite of what was right in front of our eyes.

"Now, now, I told you I wouldn't use Gil Harris again, and I haven't."

"What stories or photos had he already turned in?" I pressed. Whatever was on his phone was probably lost, but not what had already been transmitted to the newspaper.

He hesitated. "I don't know if I should . . ."

"Amby, I think I saw you on Sunday, late morning. Weren't you going to brunch at Vicissitudes?" He stared at me with his jaw hanging open. What was that about? "You were with Ella Coleman." He pulled a handkerchief from his pocket and wiped his brow. Oh. The picture came into focus.

"Brrr." Opal shivered. By anyone else, it would have been overacting, but this was Opal being herself. Or was it? "Could we go inside and get warm before we get back in that convertible?"

"Of course," Amby said. "Right this way."

Right this way. Now he had me doing it. At least I was only repeating for emphasis in my head.

"Nick," Opal called out. "Can you have someone watch The Car?"

"Anything else?" he yelled back.

Amby Jones led us up the hill and into the brick building, which was smaller than I'd thought it was. I realized I'd never been inside before, though I had seen it all my life. The landscaping, or maybe the bright lights, made it look imposing. Or maybe I still saw it the way it had looked to me when I was a kid. Just a child's memory.

"I feel warmer already," Opal cooed. She needn't have gone to the trouble. Amby Jones was so out of love with both of us.

"I see everyone is still here," he said. "Such dedication from young journalists today."

We stepped into an open area. There was a receptionist desk, but beyond that were only cubicles in two rows, four deep. Half of the eight were occupied, and pairs of eyes looked over their blue fabric half walls at us. The body of a murdered man had been found on the property of the local newspaper. Any journalist worth her salt would want to be part of writing that story, but did he really expect us to believe that's why they were here this late? Oh, Amby. Because of their proximity to where the photographer's body had been found, they would all be questioned. Statements would be taken. The more sensitive among them would think about the time she'd been putting her groceries in the car and found a can of something in the corner that she hadn't been charged for. None would completely shake the notion that the police could read minds.

They were quiet. Maybe the police had told them not to talk to one another about what they'd seen or hadn't seen. Maybe they had done as instructed, or maybe they had been blabbing since the body was discovered,

193

"My office is over here," Amby said, leading us to the right, keeping to the front wall of windows and avoiding the maze of workstations and eyeballs.

"Do you want to check your emails to see if he sent you anything this afternoon?" I asked.

"I doubt there would be more. I just paid him," he said, admitting the dead man had been there recently.

"In cash?" I asked.

"No, no." So Harris had cashed the check at a local bank? Not if Amby meant "just paid him" literally.

The front wall of Amby's office was glass. The two sides were lined with bookcases filled with trophies and framed certificates. A massive oak desk was the room's centerpiece. He dropped into his chair, and it groaned. After turning on a desk lamp and then his computer, he said, "All I have from him is a photo of the front of the store taken today. And an email with the audio clip."

I walked behind his desk and leaned over. "Can I see the photo? Wait, what's that on your screen?"

"That? It's tomorrow's print edition front page."

I glanced at Opal and read it aloud. "*Marthasville Police Chief Reopens Months-Old Antique Store Break-In.*" I scanned the paragraphs. Chief Harrod was quoted twice: once to say there was a chance the burglary was related to the murder of Roberto Fratelli, later to brag about his consistent practice of leaving no stone unturned. That last line would come in handy when the returning-burglars scenario was disproven. It had the added advantage of defending his slow pace in finding Roberto's killer and solving what until tonight had been the only murder in Marthasville all year.

"Isn't that what was in the paper today?" Opal asked.

Amby cleared his throat. "It's an update on what happened." He sounded uncomfortable with his own answer, as he should have been.

I gave him the side-eye. "This morning's paper said he was considering reopening the case. This says he has. That's not exactly a light-year ahead."

"This is Marthasville," he said, palms up. "We don't usually have a lot of news around here, in case you haven't noticed."

"Until now," Opal reminded him.

"I might run another piece on the letter," he grumbled.

"Amby, how are you getting your information on the letter?" I asked.

"Our sources are confidential."

"So it's Chief Harrod?" I asked.

"I didn't say that! I *didn't* say that!" He sounded indignant, but also like what I'd said was a little bit true. If he started repeating himself again, Marthasville would have a third murder for the year.

"I'm still going to tell him you said exactly that." I would never do that.

"Some jerk at University of Virginia has me on speed dial."

I looked over at Opal to see if she was taking all this in and did a double take when I saw what she was doing. She stood in the corner of the room. She was looking out the window, then out the office door, then repeating the sequence.

"Does this jerk have a name?" I asked.

He shrugged his shoulders. "I never thought I would say this, but we may have too much news. Let me see, where is his email?" the newspaperman said.

I walked around to Opal. *What are you doing?* I mouthed.

"On lookout," she whispered.

"On the lookout for what?" Handsy, I mean, Amby, yelled across the room.

"With all these windows, someone had to have seen something that will help the police," she said. "*They* could come back to get the informants. You know, stitches for snitches."

His eyes widened and his feet shuffled under his desk. His vinyl chair mat kept him from getting up.

"Mr. Jones? Amby? Are you all right?" I held out my hand to let him know everything was okay. And except for the murder about a hundred yards from his door, all was well. No one was coming for anyone.

He swiveled his chair and exhaled. Suddenly, moving faster than we'd yet seen him manage, he pressed down on its arms and leveraged himself up. In two steps for me and three for Opal, we were in front of him, our hands on his shoulders, pushing him back to a seated position.

"I want to see the photograph," I said.

"Okaaay," he said. I didn't trust this new calm act. What was he planning? "I'm opening the attachment now, as we speak."

I couldn't help but smile when I saw Stickley and Morris looking through the Waited4You window. "When was this taken?"

Amby put on a pair of reading glasses. "Says this afternoon at two thirty-five."

I reached over and clicked the other attachment to the email.

"That's the audio file," he said.

There was blank air, then I heard myself say, "No! Why would anyone come back to steal more counterfeits?" Did my voice really sound like that? Ugh.

After that, Brennan said, "Go to city hall where the other reporters are!" We heard scuffing and a yowl from Gil Harris.

Opal huffed and put her hand on her hip, eyebrows raised. Later I would explain why I hadn't told her what Brennan had done to the photographer this afternoon.

"Nah, they're arguing about two chicks, Martha and Sally." The clip ended.

"That's all I have."

"Why did he record the audio instead of videoing that?" Opal asked.

Amby shrugged again.

"What about the photo he took on Saturday night?" I asked.

"What about it?" He shook his head. A splotch of red traveled from his neck to the jaw. Poor baby.

"Would you please forward that to me?"

"Uh, don't know if I can do that." Holding out on me was his big plan?

"Why not?" Opal asked. "Amby, tell us the truth. Just like the name of the restaurant." She tilted her head and smiled in a knowing way.

He looked to the side at me, like he didn't dare take his eyes off Opal but desperately needing me to translate.

For a few seconds, I was as lost as he was. "I have no idea what she means." Aha. "She's confusing *vicissitudes* with *verisimilitude*."

He gave his head a quick shake. "I gave the rights to it back to him."

"How does that work?" Opal asked, her vocabulary problem in the distant past.

"He gave me the check back, and we voided it, along with the agreement."

"Does that mean the money they found in his wallet was his payment for the photo he took *today*?" I asked.

"Maybe a little of it. We don't pay freelancers that much, but he wanted what was coming to him. He came here wanting to be paid right after he took it." According to Opal's eavesdropping, Amby had led Nick to believe the money in the dead man's wallet was what he'd paid the kid.

He opened his top desk drawer and pulled out a check. He, or someone, had written *VOID* across it in black ink. "You see." I did. I saw the date was Sunday, not today.

"Would you forward the audio file and both photos to me?" I asked. "Mr. Harris isn't going to complain."

"I can send the photo from today. And the audio file. Doing it now."

"Thanks. I can always use another photo of my dogs. Go ahead and send it to me, but I also need the photo taken Saturday night." Technically it had been taken on Sunday, since it was after midnight, but I didn't want to get literal with Amby. No need for that. Other than the way I was threatening and coercing him, we were keeping the transaction friendly. Still, I wouldn't want Camille the business owner to see what I was doing. I recited the Waited4You email address to him in a low voice.

"*That* photo doesn't belong to me any longer. It hasn't since a couple of hours ago," he said as he typed.

"So Gil Harris was here twice?" I asked.

"Yeah. Two times too many." He relaxed in his chair, looking like he had won.

I wanted Saturday's photo more than I wanted to ask why he'd told Nick he hadn't seen Gil since he paid him. Time to get to work. I made a point of looking at the wedding ring digging into his fleshy finger. My gaze lingered just long enough for him to register what was happening. He sat up straight.

The energy in the press room changed, and it wasn't just the cold air blowing in through the open double doors. Nick was there and ready to interview one and all.

Unfortunately, he looked to the side and saw us in Amby's office. Opal waved and called out, "Over here, Nick," like he wasn't already walking toward us with a big scowl on his face. She was great at making the best of a bad situation.

I gave Amby a no-nonsense look, the kind I'd occasionally given Paul when he was a kid. "Hurry up and send it to me." I smiled and hoped he wouldn't realize that if he stalled until Nick got there, he wouldn't have to give me anything.

"But I don't have the rights to the first photo," he pleaded.

"You have the original email he sent to you with it attached." Didn't the guy know emails are forever?

His hands shook as they hovered over the keyboard. I raised an eyebrow. He composed a second email to me and added the attachment. "Uh . . . uh . . ." He hadn't hit send and Nick was getting closer.

"I want that email," I said.

"You and everybody else," he hissed, stalling for time.

"Ella is lovely, isn't she?"

"Uhhh," he whined.

"Ooone," I said. Nick was almost at the office door. "Does your wife still volunteer at the Little Theater of Marthasville?"

Amby hit send.

"Camille? Opal? What are you doing here?" Nick didn't sound angry or annoyed, but his tone was a little patronizing.

Opal was in my line of vision, and she and Amby had begun a nonverbal conversation. She tried to reassure him about something. Oh, yes, who didn't need to know about his brunch date and who would never hear it from our lips. The person with the matching wedding ring, that's who. Married to Handsy Amby, the woman had enough problems. I wouldn't add to them. Just as long as that second email landed in my in-box in a reasonable amount of time.

My work here was done. I nodded to Nick on my way out. "We were expressing our sympathy to Mr. Jones. This must be very upsetting for him and the newspaper staff."

"We're here for you, Amby," Opal added, and fluttered her fingers to wave good-bye and good riddance.

"Oh, yes," he huffed. "Oh, yes."

"Not so fast. Camille, a word."

I leaned over Amby and hugged him. "Who else wants that photo?"

"Camille?" Nick yelled from the outer office.

I let Amby off the hook and walked out of the office.

"Huh?"

I made the mistake of looking back at him when he made that sound. He had a stupid-happy look on his face, then it morphed to confusion, then to something silly. This was directed at Opal. She touched her lips with two fingers, then pointed at Amby with them. The expression in her eyes, though, was straight out of *Godfather Part II*.

"Your eyes," I whispered. "Point to your eyes, not your lips."

I caught up with Nick outside, now the really cold outside. That was fine with me, since I wanted to be anywhere but in Amby's office waiting for him to unmix Opal's messages.

"Do you think this might be related to Roberto Fratelli's murder?" he asked.

Opal came out behind me and heard the question. "Gosh, Nick, why don't you go ask the police?" She bounced on her toes and swung her arms. He pulled back, stunned at her animated self. "Detective, one minute you're all *What are you two doing here?* And the next you want us to help with the case!"

"I never said I wanted your help on the case. Just your take on it." He lowered his voice. "Janie says you're good at that kind of thing, Camille."

"She is." Janie walked around us and inside, followed by two uniformed officers, a young man and a young woman. "We'll start getting statements."

"Nick, what are the chances they're not related?" I asked.

He exhaled. "Yeah, I know." It was a hard truth.

"If the two murders are connected, your father and Brennan's pet theory of the burglars returning goes down the drain," I said. "It's unlikely this kid has anything to do with a rare-books theft from months ago. The truth isn't always what you want it to be." I told him about the article scheduled for tomorrow's *Marthasville Daily News*. As if he needed more bad news.

"That's gonna make the force look bad," he said.

"Can you ask him not to run it?" Opal asked.

"I hate to do that, since we haven't connected the Fratelli murder to this one. There might be no connection at all."

Opal sniffed. "Nick?"

"Yeah?"

I thought she was going to ask why he was kidding himself. Of course this murder was connected to Roberto's. Instead, she said, "Why do you smell like oranges?"

Chapter
Twenty-Seven

I had the emails from Amby Jones, so Opal and I walked back down the driveway to where The Car waited for us.

"What skills do you have other than eavesdropping that I don't know about?" I asked. "That was impressive hearing."

"That may be all. Speaking of skills, what about you putting the screws on Amby, I mean, Handsy Jones?"

"I know, right? I was in the middle of the blackmail before I knew I was doing it. If he hadn't reacted the way he did, I would have assumed he and Ella were meeting his wife for brunch or some other perfectly innocent explanation. What do you think she sees in him?"

"She was married to Roberto! How high can her standards be?"

I heard a voice behind me. "Well, if it's not Camille Benson sitting in a yellow Corvette." The man followed his teasing comment up with a loud, long whistle.

I looked around to see Frenchie, the crime scene tech from Saturday night. "This car gets whistled at more than I ever did," I said.

"What are you two doing at another murder scene?" he asked.

"We didn't find the body this time. We were at Janie's place, and she got the call," Opal explained, leaving out the details that needed to be left out. For instance, that Nick had been there and gotten the call too. Or that when the calls had come in, they were making out by the door.

"Just a sec." He gave instructions to a team of men hauling some serious lighting equipment and generators.

"What's all that for?" Opal asked.

"Gotta light up the night." Frenchie leaned his hands on the car door. Some car owners might not appreciate the fingerprints, but Opal wasn't like that. "We're looking for tracks in the grass. He was strangled, so there was someone else on the lawn." At first that sounded like overexplaining, but then I realized if he had been shot, the killer might not have been standing on the grass. Ditto if he was poisoned. Nick hadn't shared that.

I wouldn't mind if Frenchie stuck around. He shared information and he was cool. I scanned the lawn, not looking at anything in particular. I wanted Opal to see enough of the side of my face for us to communicate a *yaaas*!

"They think he was attacked someplace other than where he landed."

"Wasn't he strangled?" she asked. "Are you saying he was strangled a little bit someplace else, then finished off on the hill?"

Frenchie laughed. "Nah, there are some minor injuries, but the strangulation happened right there where he ended up. The killer had to walk up to him and walk away from him." He stood up straight and pointed to the body. "His knees were bruised recently, but not as part of this. You gotta wonder why he was on his knees."

I caught my breath as I replayed the scene with Brennan and the kid this afternoon at Waited4You. Brennan had wheeled him around and the guy's knees had buckled. He'd sunk down to the sidewalk. More people came to work the crime scene, and the movement pulled me out of my private nightmare.

"What? You two just showed up here to help out?" Frenchie teased.

Opal laughed. "The Marthasville police might have needed us. They still might. You never know."

I looked at her. "Actually, we do know. They'll never need us. Ever."

We all laughed as she started the engine.

"Wait, what is that? A real key?" he asked.

"Sure is!" she said.

"Drive safe in this thing, Opal. And Camille, we didn't know how you wanted us to leave those boxes Saturday night, so we did the best we could."

"Huh?" It was hard to hear over the noise of the car, so Opal killed the engine.

"Remember when we walked in, the boxes were all turned to forty-five degrees and touching?"

I nodded.

A portable light stand with four heavy-duty lamps came on. I shielded my eyes with a hand over my brows. "That's what fifteen hundred watts looks like." Frenchie laughed, but he was looking down, letting his eyes adjust too. "Anyway, when we went back to process the room, we saw you and the chief had separated them. I guess you were going through the contents. We left them like that. Sorry if it looked messy."

I hadn't moved them. And I doubted the chief had put that much effort into it. He was too busy looking for his son, and generally police chief–ing around. There were a lot of people working at Waited4You that horrible night. Any of them could have rearranged the boxes.

"Did you find anything in the attic?" I asked.

"Nah. No one had been up there in a year at least. We wondered if he moved the tile just to throw us off."

"There were no fingerprints or anything you could use at either door?" Opal asked.

"Nothing," he said, shaking his head, still disappointed.

"I watch a lot of TV, and quite frankly, Frenchie, I don't see how that's possible," Opal kidded him. "Should Camille and I have a look?"

He chuckled. "For a hot minute we thought we had something. It looked like a pick had been used on the back door. After we did some more checking, we found a small amount of rust. Those scrapes weren't made Saturday night."

"Like a lockpick?" Opal asked.

"No, more like something a craftsperson would use. And we don't know for sure it was a pick. Could've been a bit for a drill."

"Is that what's fueling Chief Harrod's campaign to pin this on a burglar from a few months ago?" I asked. Frenchie shrugged and looked around at the progress the techs were making.

I couldn't help but think if the lock had been jimmied, that would have helped clear Brennan, since he had a key to use. "His killer didn't necessarily need to break in. Roberto was supposed to give me all the keys, but he kept one. That's what he used to let himself in. Maybe there were no fingerprints on the knob because Roberto let whoever it was in."

"I think you should join the force, Camille." Frenchie was teasing, but hearing myself now, I hardly recognized my own voice. I was more confident than I had been when I'd first thought about buying Waited4You a week ago.

"Do you think the scrape on the lock could have happened during the break-in when the books were stolen?" I asked.

"All I know about that break-in is what I've read in the *Daily News*. But like I said, there was some rust in there. When was that?"

"Labor Day," I said.

"Then it could've happened then. Over my pay grade, I'm afraid. I bet Nick would love to talk about it, though."

"The locks have been recored, but I saved the old cores. Want them?" I asked.

"Why don't you hang on to them for now. I'll tell Nick you have them, and he can let you know if he ends up needing them."

"Sure."

"Good seeing you. Have a nice evening, ladies." If he thought I had led his team on a wild-goose chase by pointing out the missing ceiling tile, he was kind enough not to mention it.

"Detective! Over here," someone yelled out.

Frenchie looked over at the guy calling out to Nick. "Looks like they found something. Better get to work."

Opal put The Car in reverse and backed onto Seminary Road.

Chapter
Twenty-Eight

Opal drove us back to Old Town through fun, crazy, hilly back streets. When she braked at a stop sign, she asked, "Should we have waited to see what Frenchie found? Ten or twenty years ago, we would have stayed all night, but I'm really beat."

"So am I. Besides, I need to get home to the dogs. And I want to look at the photos Amby emailed me. I'm curious about why Gil Harris wanted the rights back to his photo. The paper had already used it once. Actually twice, if you count the online edition, where Paul saw it, and then print. I doubt they would run it again. Did he think he could make more money off of it selling it again?"

She checked the rearview mirror to be sure there were no cars behind us. "Maybe he was going to blackmail you?"

"Very funny." I looked up at the stars and tried to roll the kinks out of my shoulders.

Opal drove through the intersection. "What were you and Frenchie saying about the boxes in the stock room?"

"On Saturday you were outside when they called me in to look at the room. Remember we lined the boxes up against the walls? The murderer arranged them in kind of a crazy way. Touching each other and turned diagonally. When Frenchie's team went back to process the stock room, the boxes were separated. He thought Chief Harrod or I moved them. I didn't. I came outside. Maybe the chief did, but I doubt it. So who did?"

"Why don't you think the chief went through them?"

"Because he asked us to."

"But that was the next day when he said that," she said over the engine noise.

"He mentioned it to me on Saturday night." *Maybe tomorrow you can let me know what all is missing* had been his words.

"Camille, you said the killer put the boxes in that pattern. Maybe it was Roberto. Would he have had time?"

"Well, he was killed not long before we found him. According to the video, he went in at nine forty-five. If his killer was waiting for him, then obviously, no, he wouldn't have had time to move the boxes. If not, then yeah."

When we climbed the steep streets of the trendy Del Ray neighborhood of Marthasville, Opal changed gears and gave The Car more gas, and we flew. We could outrun anything. Or so we thought.

Chapter
Twenty-Nine

Stickley and Morris were on top of the duvet, making me their willing prisoner. My laptop was perched on my bent knees. I had spent the last half hour studying the photo taken today that had come to me courtesy of the email from Amby Jones. I started with that one, since, after all, Gil Harris had been killed soon after it was taken. The time had come to admit there wasn't anything on it but the two dogs looking out the window. I yawned again and opened the attachment for Saturday night's photograph. My expectations were low for finding a clue in the photo from four days ago, but I would give it a quick look, then get a good night's sleep.

I rolled Stickley's ears in my fingers. Why couldn't the *Daily News* have used the full photo? In Sunday's paper the scene was pared down, cropped on the side and over my head to my startled face and half-mast eyes. In the original photo the sales floor of Waited4You was lit up behind me. I tried to find Frenchie among the people working in the store and couldn't. The back of the room was dark. I remembered how surprised I'd been when Chief Harrod turned off the light in the stock room.

I admired the large oak mirror on the back wall, from France, as I had all week. At over four feet tall, it would be perfect over a mantel. With the frame's finely detailed floral carvings and the mirror's original beveled glass, it was a find. It was—really—from the nineteenth century and in good condition, with only light distressing from age and use. It had leaned against the wall when Roberto owned Waited4You, and it was still there because I hadn't found the spot to show it off at its best. Positioned there, it reflected the street. That didn't help a potential buyer *see* it in her home, the way she could if it was across from other furniture. I needed a spot for it, and then I had to hire someone to hang it.

On my screen I could see the storefront window display reflected in the mirror. Or rather, Roberto's halfhearted attempt at it. No spotlights, no interest. His preference had been to keep the front window unobstructed so passersby could see the merchandise inside on the sales floor. I, on the other hand, believed this prime real estate should have an attractive display to draw customers in. It should tell Waited4You's story. I reached for the notepad by my bed. *Mom and Dad photo in window?* With each minute, more of the adrenaline from Opal's driving of The Car was wearing off. I was getting sleepy, and I didn't trust myself to remember that idea in the morning.

I studied the photo from corner to corner. "Nothing to see here, folks," I said to the dogs. "This was a waste of time."

I did need to find a spot for the beautiful mirror. I selected it in the photograph and enlarged it. Maybe the floral motif on the frame or the wood color would get some ideas flowing. Below the carving on the top of the frame, I saw a police car. Maybe the one Mark Zhou had brought me home in?

I saw a light shape in the mirror and leaned in for a better view. My tired brain wasn't staying on track. What was that? Gil Harris's photo of the room included the mirror. The mirror reflected the storefront window, both what was visible through the window, like the police car, and what was reflected back by the glass. But what was that there in the dark? The section of the photograph wouldn't enlarge any more without becoming completely unreadable. I felt my head fall forward, and then I jerked awake.

* * *

My stomach felt funny. My phone rang, and I opened my eyes enough to know the computer was still open and sitting on my midsection. My bedside lamp was on, and it was dark outside.

"Hello."

"Camille, wake up. It's Janie. I need to tell you something." Had I not been half asleep, what she said would have struck fear in me.

"Is it morning?" I asked, trying to sit up. The movement woke the dogs up, and they gave me *WTH, Mom?* looks. My computer woke up too.

"Almost. Not quite," she said.

"What time is it?"

"Around midnight."

I laughed. "I've only been asleep for about an hour?"

"I wanted you to hear this from me. Chief Harrod is about to have Brennan Adler arrested for the murders of Roberto Fratelli and Gil Harris."

"What? Why?" Now I was wide awake.

"They will contact his attorney, and he'll be given the opportunity to come in on his own." She slowed down, either to breathe or to decide how much more to tell me. I didn't know how much more I could bear to hear. "The police have someone watching his boat."

"What happened after Opal and I left? Because something sure did."

"There were bike tracks on the grass in front of the *Marthasville Daily News* building."

"Bike tracks? That's all you have? Half the people in Marthasville ride a bike." I moved my computer so I could get up. My thumb must have pressed the brightness tab on the monitor, because all of a sudden the screen glowed. It was on maximum brightness and hurt my eyes, but when I looked again, I saw something new. An image I hadn't been able to see before.

"Janie, I think I have a photograph of the murderer."

Chapter Thirty

Thursday

I slept until Opal's call woke me up at eight o'clock. "What time are you going to Waited4You?" She was wound up, even by Opal standards.

"Around ten, I guess. I have an exterminator coming at eleven thirty." For some reason, that made her laugh.

"I'll see you around, let me see, tenish."

"What's going on?"

She had already hung up. I checked my texts, and one had come in during the night. It was from Pepper.

Unfortunately, it didn't work out last night for Paul to come to the concert. I wanted to say I really need a part-time job and I hope you will still consider me for a position at your lovely antique store.

What had he done now?

I tossed the phone into the folds of the plum duvet and stared at the white ceiling. I hoped I could remember the very vivid dream I'd had. In it I'd walked around Waited4You, touching all the books. When I turned my head and looked at my coral bedroom walls, I remembered more. There had been hundreds of them at least. Dozens were arranged on my new Christmas display table, which lengthened the more I walked. It grew and grew, but somehow the table stayed inside the gallery. In the dream I watched my hand as I reached out and touched each one. There were holiday books, gothic mysteries, biographies, books on architecture and gardening. Even in the dream, I knew I hadn't included books in my display yesterday. Only glassware and serving dishes, along with ball ornaments.

I looked back at the books I'd touched, but they were gone, and the table was covered in leaves. We were inside, but a breeze lifted and gently blew them around. Then I realized for the first time that I had a long line of customers. They were walking out the door with handfuls of leaves they hadn't paid for. It seemed I sold those, because I started yelling at the customers, "They're not free!"

I threw off the flannel sheet and duvet and jumped out of bed.

"My phone!" I slapped the covers until I felt something hard. The dogs stared at me from the foot of the bed. "You could have helped me find it, you know. You are *dogs*."

Janie answered on the second ring. "Good morn—"

"Have you found someone to enhance that photo I sent you?"

"It's just now eight o'clock, so no. I looked at it, and honestly, it looks like the reflection of a reflection of a flash."

"Janie, I think the killer was still inside Waited4You. Remember, Roberto had just been killed."

"Are you doing this to help Brennan Adler?" she asked.

"I wasn't able to tell who that was in the photograph either. It might even be him. So no. Did they arrest him?"

"Nick persuaded his father to hold off. He agreed to hold off for twenty-four hours. That should give them enough time to see what they can get from the photograph."

"I wanted to talk to you about the letter too. I know someone who can prove the letter isn't authentic. When will it be returned from Charlottesville?"

She stammered. "Don't know . . ." Maybe I'd caught this guarded person off guard.

"Or can you set up a virtual meeting with whoever has the letter at University of Virginia?" I asked. Maybe I sounded like I'd try to get her to believe in Brennan's innocence any way I could. I didn't care.

"Uh, sure." I heard her office door close. "I think the letter will be returned here later this week. Do you know a local expert? Paul and Dr. Branch are in the loop. We were going to contact the Smithsonian or the National Gallery. I still think the letter is real. If it is, we'll need expert guidance. We need somebody to tell us how to store it until the trial, if there is one."

"She's very local. Her name is Caroline Pak. Let me know what time I can bring her to your office." *Tell you how to preserve a fraud? Oh, Janie, that's so not what you need her to do.*

I looked at Stickley. "I know what you're thinking. That I should have asked Caroline first. You see, I'm not sure how I would ask her. Should I say, 'I need you to save Marthasville from becoming the laughingstock of the state'?" Next, I looked at Morris. "Because that's exactly what I need her to do!"

Chapter
Thirty-One

"Remember when Janie asked if you saw Brennan Adler here on Saturday, when he said he saw me pick up that chair? But neither of us saw him." Opal walked—very slowly, except for the quick turn at each wall—across the room. Side to side.

"I admit I didn't see him here at all on Saturday."

"Aha! Exhibit one." She whirled 180 degrees and swanned to the other wall.

"For what?"

"Exhibit two. Remember when you asked Detective Nick Harrod how Ella Coleman knew about his altercation with the victim, Roberto Fratelli?"

"Yeah, but—"

"And he said that was a very interesting question?"

"But—"

"Two individuals knew about something that happened in this very antique store without being in here. Coincidence?"

"Uh, I don't really—"

"No! Of course not. There's only one explanation." Dramatic pause. "The store is bugged."

"What? As far as Ella knowing about Nick and Roberto, I was thinking the waitress from Mykonos Taverna told her."

"Possibly." Not a bit deflated. "Wouldn't you like to knooooow for sure?"

"Yes, I would. Of course." When Opal was this committed, all you could do was let her go.

With a flourish, she pulled a black box out of her jeans jacket pocket.

"What's that?"

"This, my friend, is what is known in the business as a bug detector."

"Which business would that be? The tour boat business?"

Her dimples were on full display when she grinned ear to ear, the way she was smiling now. "The solving-of-murders business."

I was walking over to get a closer look but froze when I heard the last bit. "Isn't that the line of work the police are in?"

"This has become so complicated. Exhibit one—"

"Oh, please, no more exhibits. Just tell me."

"We have a detective that doesn't want to work on the case, and his father who wants him to stay on it. Said detective would be a suspect if he was anyone else."

"He has an alibi," I reminded her.

"But he won't tell anyone where he was, so it's not going to help him. Next, we have a suspect who is buddy-buddy with the police chief. Though who knows after last night's murder. So, you see, we have to handle this ourselves."

I shook my head. "So how does this thing work?"

"I'm not sure. I had to buy the floor model, and the guy who sold it to me lost the instruction manual. He said we would be able to find wireless signals, like microphones and hidden cameras. We look through this thingy." She pointed to a small lens near the top. "Then you press this button on the side. Allow me to demonstrate." She held it up to her eye and faced the left wall.

"What's supposed to happen?"

"When it detects a bug, which is a covert something, a red light will reflect from it." She methodically scanned that wall—step together, press the button on the side of the detector, step together, press the side button again. It looked like a virtual reality minuet.

"Opal, nothing is lighting up." The dance continued.

"Yet." The front door opened, and I thought how nice it would be to have a bell on it. "And now you sound as negative as Paul," she said.

"I'm not negative!"

"Oh, hi, Paul." Opal waved between steps.

"What did you do to Pepper?" I demanded, my hands on my hips.

"Huh?" He looked confused, but he had to know what I was talking about.

"I have a hit!" Opal yelled.

"Mom, what is she doing?"

"We believe we have a situation," Opal answered.

"We don't have a situation," I said to Opal. To Paul, I said, "I really like Pepper, and I'm going to hire her whether you like it or not."

"Uh, okay. And I like her too."

"Can we get back to business, please? There's something here!"

"She's crazy," Paul said. "Why did you ask about Pepper?"

"Opal's not crazy."

"Oh, no." He motioned with his head to where Opal stood. She inspected the wall, stepped closer, then inspected it again. "Did Pepper say she didn't want to go out with me? She did, didn't she?"

"No . . . well, she said something about it not working out. I can't remember her exact words. Opal, I don't think that's a bug."

"It's lit up like a Christmas tree! Of course it's a hidden microphone or camera. Ew, or maybe both. Paul, you go over and check it out."

"I'm too upset. Mooooom, I really like her."

Opal pointed to the counter on the back wall. "Paul, go! I'm not touching it. Find out what that is."

Incoming mayor or not, he went to the back wall.

"Opal, it's not a bug," I said. "That's my computer tablet."

"Oh," she said. Paul rolled his eyes and slumped back to me. "Then I'll move on to that wall." Nothing got her down. Not a thing.

"Opal, can you check the stock room next?"

"You two want to talk in private, don't you? All you had to do was say so."

"Yes!" Paul said.

"No, I want you to check out the ceiling. One of the tiles was moved when the murderer ransacked it going through all the boxes. Frenchie's people didn't find anything, but I doubt they have equipment as advanced as yours."

"I'm on it!" She saluted, turned sharply, and went to the back.

Paul slapped his forehead. "You're as crazy as she is."

"Sweetie, you need to be a little crazy!"

Opal was back soon. "No bugs in the back room!"

"Oh, so you don't need me?" An older man, with more than a passing resemblance to Santa Claus, stood inside the front door. The effect was muted by his khaki uniform and canister of bug spray.

"Earl?" Paul, Opal, and I said at the same time.

"Is that you?" I asked as I took his hand. I had known the owner of No Rest for Pests for years. "I hardly recognized you!"

He rubbed his white beard. "It's me, all right. Work's slow during the holidays, so I started looking for something to do nights and weekends. You know, maybe get a little something special for Mrs. Claus. I have five Santa gigs lined up so far."

"I have an idea. Earl, can I call on you to make deliveries?" I asked. "And would you wear your Santa costume?" With his size, he was a proper, traditional Saint Nick. He was tall, maybe six three or four, and big. Perfect.

"Sure thing! Now, do you have bugs or not?"

I walked with him to the stock room. "I may have mice."

"But she said—"

"Don't mind her," I said as I passed Opal. "There's a spot under the desk the dogs won't leave alone."

"Gotta scoot anyway," Opal said. "Today is a big paper-work day for me. I'll call you later, Camille."

I hugged her before I took Earl to the area where I suspected mice. Then I went back to the front to leave him alone to work—and to have words with my son. If he and Pepper had weathered the *How could Mozart and Bach be geniuses?* bump in the road, they should be dating by now. What had he done this time?

"Mom, you gotta admit Opal's over-the-top."

"There's a Marilyn Monroe quotation I like: *Imperfection is beauty, madness is genius and it's better to be absolutely ridiculous than absolutely boring.* I'm lucky to have someone that brilliant as a friend. Tell me what happened between you and Pepper."

"Yesterday afternoon she texted me while I was running. I read some of it at a red light, but then I dictated my answer to her. I heard back from her, but by then she didn't need to talk. She really doesn't want to go out with me? That's what she said? Are you sure?"

"It sounded like she thought you didn't want to date her. Let me see your phone."

He keyed in his password and handed it to me. "Oh, Paul! You really wrote this? Why, if you like her?"

I handed him back his phone. He read how the phone had interpreted what he'd said. **You're playing a solo? I'm running away.**

"So that's why she answered *never mind.*"

"Go to the concert tonight. You'll have to buy your own ticket. Serves you right. Take a nice bouquet of flowers. Use the same florist you used for the roses you gave me last Wednesday. Take them to the stage at the end. Got it?"

"Got it."

"And ask her to accompany you to some of the Common Good for the Commonwealth parties. I think she would like that."

"Good idea. I will."

"Camille, can you come in here?" Earl stood in the stock room doorway, flashlight in hand. "No sign of mice, and they do let you know when they take up residence, so you're good on that front." We went to the desk, and he shined the beam of light on the floorboard. "See that?" A tiny white triangle peeked from behind the baseboard. "I don't think I can get under there."

"No problem. I'll get tweezers and get that out. What do I owe you?"

"Nothing." He picked up his canister and holstered his flashlight. "Glad you don't have mice. Should I put Waited4You on the same schedule as your residence?"

"Yes, but not on the same day. I'll leave the dogs at home when you spray here and bring them here when you spray the townhouse."

"Sounds like a plan. Did you know someone from the police department is taking photos out back?" Earl asked as he wiped his hands with a handkerchief.

"Why?" Paul asked.

"I think it has something to do with the article on the front page of today's paper. Someone broke in here and stole some extremely valuable rare books and then dropped them when the police started chasing them." As he spoke, he squared his shoulders and looked around, like the culprits might still be lurking. Obviously, and unfortunately, Nick hadn't been able to kill the story.

"The article said that?" The few paragraphs I'd read on Amby Jones's monitor hadn't included anything like that. Granted, what I did read was suspect, but it wasn't as illogical as what Earl was saying.

"Not the article. That was in the comment section."

"You can't believe anything in a comment," Paul said.

"Earl, none of that is true. The books weren't valuable, and the police weren't chasing the thieves."

"Hmm, you don't say." He scratched his chin. "How about the comment in one of the articles about the love letter to George Washington? It said he could've dropped it out of his pocket when he was leaving the George Washington Masonic Temple."

"Again, not true," I said, rubbing my forehead.

"How do you know it's not?"

Paul patted the older man's shoulder. "The George Washington Masonic Temple wasn't built until early last century. The inside wasn't finished until 1973."

"You don't say."

* * *

I said good-bye to both men and went back to the stock room and looked under the desk again. Could I get that slip of paper out with my fingernails? There was only one way to find out. I kicked off my snakeskin—actually leather—slides and got on my hands and knees under the desk. The paper was thicker than regular computer printer paper and determined to stay put. "You think you're stubborn. Well, I am too."

"I believe that," a man's voice said. It was Brennan Adler. He was standing behind me, and my backside was up in the air.

Just then I felt the paper release from its hiding place. I pulled it out. A photo. There was nothing to do but back out from under the desk. He held out a hand, which I took, as I slid my feet into my shoes.

"The dogs found this behind the baseboard. It's a photograph. I hope it's of my parents. Maybe it was left from their time here." Thinking of the possibility made me smile. I turned on the desk lamp and held the photo under the light. "Looks like a Polaroid. I used to love those sixty-second cameras," I said.

"That would be nice, but it might not be old at all. Other companies make instant cameras still."

"This isn't from before . . . it's Roberto," I said. He stood next to a large piece of furniture, his hand resting on it. He beamed with pride. "He was young, and he doesn't look mad at the world."

"No, he doesn't. He hardly looks like himself." Brennan chuckled. I blinked, then looked down and tried to cover my surprise. Brennan was relaxed and in a good mood too. Did that mean he didn't know about Gil Harris's murder? Or that Chief Harrod planned to have him arrested? "What is that thing? A combination chair and desk?"

"Yeah." It was the computer desk Ritchie Potts had won an award for ten years ago. I pointed at the brochure, maybe a flyer or newsletter, he held in his other hand. "I wonder what this says. I can't read it. Let me get something to enlarge it."

"Hey? Are you okay?"

No, I wasn't. The decision to keep what I knew about the computer desk to myself had been easily made. I couldn't trust Brennan. That was either because of the reasons Opal and Janie had listed last night or arose from something in my DNA. I no longer knew.

"I'm fine. My loupe and magnifying glass are out here." I walked by him and tried to smile.

"I'm sorry the photo wasn't of your parents," he said, lightly touching my arm.

If only Opal and Janie could see me now. It would have been nice to believe in Brennan enough to tell him what I knew about the computer desk, but the words *old fool* played over and over in my head. I wasn't blindly trusting him. I was doing just the opposite. I was as suspicious as he'd accused me of being. His fingers had hardly brushed my sweater, but I still felt the touch.

I rummaged through a basket of tools under the refectory table that was now my desk. At least until I sold it.

He rapped his knuckles on it. "This is nice. Oak?"

"Yes, it's for sale. Sorry, I forgot you're leaving town."

"Yup. I enjoy time alone on my boat."

I found a magnifying glass. The loupe, in my handbag, had higher magnification, but with this, we could both read what Roberto was holding in his hand.

Why was Roberto standing next to a piece of furniture designed by Ritchie Potts? Maybe it wasn't the same, just similar? I read the headline out loud. "It says it's *New Workplace Furniture for a New Millennium*. This was designed in 2000?"

"Designed then? I guess so. Why does it matter?"

I looked at Roberto's joyous face, then turned away. How could Ritchie have won an award, especially one for an *emerging* designer, ten years after the design? Had Ritchie stolen Roberto's design?

Brennan hadn't seen photos showing the lowered well for the keyboard from the announcement of Ritchie Potts's German Emerging Furniture Designer of the Year Award. Nor had he seen the ergonomic footrests. Wait, neither had I. I had seen that section in the design drawings on Roberto's folders. I looked back at the old Polaroid black-and-white photo. The footrest was there. I saw it now that I knew what I was looking for.

Just how close were the two designs? The answer rested on the footrest. I needed to see one of Ritchie's desks.

Chapter
Thirty-Two

The intent way I studied the photo, or maybe the closed expression on my face, told Brennan there was more to it than I was letting on. "Looks like you know more about this than you care to share." Brennan shrugged. "I'm sorry you can't trust me. If you had gotten to know me, you would never think I was a killer."

"Where were you when you saw Opal find the letter on Saturday? We never saw you. How did you get in?"

He pointed to the door to the stock room. "I stood right there. I used my key to come in the back door. You may not have seen me, but I saw you. You were wearing slightly tight black jeans and a sweater I would have loved to touch. Oh yeah, you also had a cute scarf around your neck."

"You don't call Hermès cute. That's a sacrilege."

"Well, the shoes were cute. Can I say that? And you had your hair in a ponytail." He turned to go. "I guess no one saw me because Opal was engrossed with the chair, and you were busy, too. But trust me, I saw you."

After he left, I sat down and closed my eyes. After a couple of deep breaths, I had convinced myself again that less was better when it came to discussing the case with Brennan. What was I supposed to say? *Did you know the police have your boat under surveillance?* Or, *Hey, aren't you glad you weren't arrested in the wee hours of the morning?*

I was just grateful he hadn't come in half an hour earlier. He might have seen Opal checking the store for a hidden camera, thinking that's how he'd known about the letter hidden under the chair. Or heard me asking her to check the ceiling for a bug. A waitress had told Ella what happened between Nick and Roberto. Brennan Adler had walked in the back door, which he had the right to do.

I called Opal to let her know we no longer had a *situation*.

"This is even worse than I thought."

"How?" I asked.

"The murderer came back and removed the bug."

Right. Sixty-something-year-old Brennan Adler had vaulted down from overhead, then back up again like a stunt man in *Mission Impossible*. "I may have found something in the photograph Gil Harris took on Saturday night. Uh, it might be the killer."

"Camille! You couldn't have led with that?"

"I really wanted to tell you this morning, but I didn't want Paul to hear it. In case I'm wrong and it was nothing. Then when Earl came in, I knew it would have to wait." I told her about the reflection of a reflection of a shadow.

She hesitated. "Yeah, I can see why you might not want to put that out there. It sounds straight off of *True Detective*."

"Are you making a joke because that would mean he was still there when we found Roberto's body? Who would try to take both of us on?" I laughed at the very thought of it.

227

"Only a fool." Opal snorted. "But how could anyone stay hidden with all the cops there?"

"The only rooms with a light on were the sales floor and the stock room. Maybe the kitchen? I can't remember."

"Hmm, Frenchie did say he hadn't been dead long. Gosh, we're lucky Chief Harrod didn't try to pin this on us."

"He might have if he knew his son would be suspected."

Chapter
Thirty-Three

It was time to meet Caroline Pak at the Marthasville court-house in Janie's office. I put on my coat and gloves and set the security alarm. On the sidewalk, I blinked at the light bouncing off every surface and put on my sunglasses. The brightness of the day had no respect at all for the feelings that weighed me down.

We met at the bottom of the brick steps outside. "You brought the books with the missing pages and you didn't bring your cell phone, right?"

"Right."

* * *

Janie led us to a conference room, and we talked on the way. "I haven't gotten the email from Nick with the copy of the let-ter," I told her.

"Oh, that," she said. "You may have noticed we have a leak. Someone's been telling the *Marthasville Daily News* all about the letter. Chief Harrod shut down most outside com-munication on the case."

"I just assumed the chief was the *Daily News* source," I said.

"He probably was," Janie whispered. "For now, we're not telling anyone the contents of the letter."

"If he's mad about the accusations against Nick, they were on Facebook and came from one person, Ella Coleman." What wasn't she telling me? "You're thinking that only Brennan and the forger, of course, will know what it says? You hope someone will show their hand by quoting it?"

"Something like that," was her cryptic response. "If it *is* a forgery." Did that mean she still suspected Brennan? And that she had more faith in the letter than she should?

I was curious to read what the letter said, but I didn't *need* to see it. I already knew it was fake. The language of the time was damn hard to decipher, even when the writer wasn't trying to hide what was really being said, and I couldn't imagine trying to compose a letter using it. Still, it would have been interesting to Google a few lines to see if they were copied from something the forger had found on the internet.

"How's the investigation of last night's murder going?" I asked.

"He was strangled with somebody's bare hands. His cell phone was stolen, but the police don't need the actual phone to get his call history. That's what they're doing now." My mind flashed back to Nick's confrontation with Roberto on Saturday. He'd held Rizzoli with one hand and reached for Roberto's throat with the other. I couldn't unsee it, even though I knew he had been at Janie's condo at the time of the murder.

Nick was in the conference room reserved for us, waiting patiently. Janie sat down next to him. I took the chair on the end and Caroline sat on my left. There was a lowered screen in the front of the room. A recorder sat on the glossy mahogany table. I tried to read Caroline's body language for doubt or stress, and she seemed at ease. She wore a brown sweater dress and knee-high boots.

"Ready to go?" Nick asked, over his shoulder, as he got up and closed the door. When he was back in his chair, he initiated an online meeting with someone at the University of Virginia via a laptop on the table. After a greeting, he told us the meeting was being recorded. He gave a bright smile and began. "Of course, we've met before, but for the tape, I'm Detective Nick Harrod and we're at the Marthasville court-house building. I'll let these fine people I'm here with intro-duce themselves." He motioned for us to go around the room and give our names.

"I'm Janie Fairfax, commonwealth's attorney for the City of Marthasville."

"I'm Caroline Pak, the local history librarian at the Local History and Special Collections Branch Library here in Marthasville."

Next it was my turn. "I'm Camille Benson, owner of Wait-ed4You Antiques, where the letter was initially found."

Someone in the Charlottesville group harrumphed.

Nick invited them to introduce themselves. There was one woman and a man. It looked like they were in her office, since she sat behind a desk cluttered with paper, and he'd brought a chair to sit at her side. The camera on her computer moni-tor was turned so we could see both of them. The projection screen in the front of our room was split. We saw them on the right side and ourselves on the left.

Could one of them be the person who had Amby on speed dial, as he'd put it?

Nick's good looks were not wasted on Dr. Delinda Bis-hara. She cooed that she was professor and chair of the PhD program at the Corcoran Department of History. When she said she specialized in eighteenth-century American history, I could have sworn she was trying to say something else completely. She wore a turtleneck sweater with pearls, and she never let go of them.

Nick was patting his pockets and didn't notice her attention. "Damn, left my phone someplace," he said under his breath to Janie. She pressed her lips together to keep from grinning. He'd had it when he left her condo to go to the scene of Gil Harris's murder, so he must have gone back to her place from there.

Dr. Farhad Harold told us in a solemn tone that he was a curator at the Albert and Shirley Small Special Collections Library. "We understand the letter was found in, let's say, a rather interesting circumstance," he said.

"Yes, sir," Nick said. "It was first discovered at what would, several hours later, become the scene of a murder. It was taken from there and found again."

"Where?" Dr. Harold asked.

Nick hesitated. *Tell him it's none of his business.* My mouth was ready to jump in if he mentioned Brennan's name. "I'm not at liberty to say. Nor do I think it's pertinent." I exhaled. "We tested the glue from the duct tape used where it had been hidden against the residue on the folio I brought the letter to you in. It was a match. It's the same letter."

Dr. Harold straightened his glasses and looked at the camera. "Mrs. Benson, I understand you question the letter's authenticity. Can you tell us why?"

"Objects, like letters to George Washington, don't just show up the way this one did. That was my original red flag." There was a stack of notepads in front of me on the table, and I pulled one onto my lap.

How did he know that??? I wrote, and passed the pad under the table to Janie's lap.

"I'm sorry, what are your credentials?" Dr. Harold asked.

"I have a PhD in art history," I said.

Dr. Bishara leaned forward, her elbows on the desk. "I tend to agree with Dr. Benson. As a subject matter expert, I can't imagine Fairfax writing a second letter of a personal nature to George Washington after she already rebuffed him the first time. By then he would have been married."

Dr. Harold waved a hand in the air. "We had a paper forensics expert age-date the paper. That was done the morning Detective Harrod brought the letter to us. We were happy to give him that initial assessment in hopes Marthasville would remember us kindly if the city choses to donate it to a museum." He cleared his throat. "The time frame, while it's just a range, is appropriate for a letter from Sally Cary Fairfax to George Washington. That's an early opinion, and we have other strategies we can use to authenticate historical documents."

The notepad tapped my thigh, and keeping my eyes on the screen, I reached for it. You never knew when a skill acquired in junior high would come in handy.

The nerve! Assuming we'll give the letter to them! Janie had written. Under that she'd added the answer to my question. *Nick told him. Dr. Harold is convinced it's real.*

"We can account for that," Caroline said. "You see—"

Dr. Bishara interrupted. "You can't properly evaluate a manuscript without taking into account the historical, political, and personal context of the writer and his or her times." It was hard to tell in a virtual meeting, but I could have sworn she looked at Nick as she spoke. She paused and gave her colleague a sideways glance, showing her disdain for either him, his credentials, or his field. "And *that* takes an extensive knowledge of history. The idea that Sally Fairfax would write back to her old boyfriend to say she'd changed her mind and would await his instructions, and go anywhere to be with him, is ludicrous." That was what the letter said? *Hot stuff.* "She was looking forward to becoming Lady Fairfax. For that to happen, she had to be a loyalist! And remain married to George William Fairfax, which she did."

Caroline spoke louder this time. "I can explain—"

Both Dr. Bishara and Dr. Harold tried to cut in, but Nick was having none of it. "Ms. Pak, go ahead, please."

"I can explain why the paper's age-dating showed what it did," she said. "Dr. Bishara, would you please hold the letter near the camera on your computer?"

The professor pulled on a pair of white gloves and gently unfolded the letter. If the paper had a straight edge, I would look like an idiot. I'd made a calculated guess and was about to find out if I was right. I looked at the screen on the front wall. The left edge of the letter had two slight moon-shaped indentations. One hollow was near the top and the other was about three-quarters down. Caroline opened her bag.

"Keep holding it up, please." A huff of irritation from Dr. Harold. "I have with me two books from our collection," she said. "In an audit, we discovered both books were missing the flyleaf. They had been stolen."

"Just a second. What are the titles?" he asked.

"I'll get to that later," she said. Good for her, not letting him sidetrack her. "Two of our books from the mid to late eighteenth century had the free end plate stolen out of them. The plates in both were plain paper." She opened the first book, then closed it again. Why had she done that? I couldn't move. I was an idiot to believe this stupid-ass dream. Being in the chair at the end of the table put me in the direct firing line of Drs. Bishara and Harold. They could surely see the tight look on my face. The dread. I wished I were sitting anywhere else. Caroline opened the other book and smiled before she held it up to the camera on the laptop. I let myself breathe again. All thanks to my brilliant dream.

Nick said, "Would you tell us what we're seeing for the benefit of the recording?"

"In this book, all that is left of the endpaper, specifically the free endpaper, sometimes called the flyleaf or the first free page, are the two slices that are the opposite of what you have on the letter in question." It had all been there—the flying leaves, the free leaves.

Since she was holding the book open in front of the laptop's camera, I was looking at its cover. I looked at the projected image on that big, beautiful screen. The two half ovals, one near the top of the page, the other closer to the bottom, were obviously what was left when someone had ripped off the flyleaf.

Caroline was speaking again, but this time she wasn't interrupted. The Charlottesville experts were pictures of despair. "I'm sure you both know why thieves sometimes target the blank page of an antique book."

Dr. Harold nodded and lowered his head. "Sometimes they're used to forge a painting. This time . . ."

"What is the date of that book, Caroline?" Janie asked.

"This is a first-print run of *Cecelia*, by Frances Burney, in 1782."

"What should we do with *this*?" barked Dr. Harold, flinging his hand, now filled with disdain for our once coveted and beloved letter. "I guess we could use it for teaching or calibrating testing equipment."

"It's from this book, and it should be returned to Marthasville for it. I mean, when it's no longer needed for the investigation," Caroline said, in a *Not so fast, buster* tone. "Not all of our books still have the endpapers. Once the cover detaches, with time, the end leaf comes off too. So a lot of books don't have them. We'll want that one, which was intentionally removed, back."

I kept my eyes on the screen while I wrote a few words on the notepad. *Are you going to sic red rot on them?* I passed it to her.

"I'll drive down for it as soon as we finish here," Nick said. So much for the armored car ride planned for the letter. "Fake or real, it's still evidence in the murder."

There were hurried footsteps in the hallway. I doubt I would have paid any attention to it if Janie hadn't simultaneously slid her arm to the laptop and ended the session. Since she did it so quickly, Charlottesville never knew what happened to their connection. The door flew open and Chief Harrod stormed in and stole our oxygen.

"A meeting on the letter? Nick, my admin just told me. I would have been happy to join you. A word?" Those Harrod men did like their *words*. He nodded at Caroline and me. "Ladies." He walked out, expecting Nick to follow him. Which he did.

"I told you to spend your time on the Fratelli murder investigation. I know you think you should be taken off the case, but I told you I do not agree . . . Look, we just caught a break on last night's murder. That newspaper publisher's memory miraculously cleared a little more."

Janie's eyes were squeezed shut. Being there when some-one else's family had an argument was just as painful as I remembered. In the last few minutes, I had seen two public disagreements—one virtual and one with the Harrod men—and that was two too many. I couldn't wait to get out of there. Caroline and Janie scrambled to their feet, which told me the feeling was mutual. It was bad enough for Nick to be dressed down by his father in front of Janie, but for it to be within earshot of two more people—ouch.

Thinking of family, I needed to call Paul. Hopefully, I wasn't too late to stop him from making his first mistake as Marthasville's mayor, even before his tenure started.

"Caroline, thank you so much. You were great." I shook her hand, and we walked to the elevator.

"Camille, I have that recipe you wanted," Janie said. I hadn't thought of that code in forever. Fran, Opal, and I had used it for years. Too bad it no longer fooled anyone. But then, it *had* just worked on Caroline. She shook my hand and told me good-bye. She got on the elevator, and I followed Janie back to her office.

"What you heard back there wasn't as bad as it sounded." It sounded pretty bad. "The chief is determined not to show Nick any favoritism. I wanted to be sure you knew that."

I gave my head a quick shake, like I'd already forgot-ten about it. The hell I had. He was showing him nothing but favoritism. "Who was Gil Harris? Have you located his family?"

"That's what you asked after Roberto Fratelli's murder. You think of the family first, don't you?"

Maybe she was trying to pry into my family history. Maybe not. Sharper people than she had tried and failed. Besides, I would not be pulled off the subject that easily. "Where's he from?"

"Suffolk, Virginia. His parents should be here later this morning. The Suffolk police chief told them a few hours ago. That's not a visit any cop wants to pay. He knows the family, so it was even harder." She took a deep breath and turned her head to the side.

"You look so much like your mother when you do that," I said.

"So I've been told. His parents think he was a bigger deal in journalism than he was."

"Oh, no."

"Gets worse. They think he was killed because he was about to break a big story. Like a DC story—like, big as Watergate." She blew out all the air she held. "Camille, please help me. I don't want to hurt their feelings."

"Sweetie, we'll think of something." I would. The rare moment of vulnerability showed her trust in me. Now to come up with a plan. "Hmm, what can we tell them?"

"Hmm," Janie repeated. "Something—"

"I've got it. Amby Jones is a B-plus student in lying. Not great, but okay. Good enough. Opal and I saw through him. Nick didn't. We can ask him to embellish their son's relation-ship with the newspaper?"

"Amby's had a lot of practice embellishing the truth lately. He corrected the, as he called it, mistaken impression he may have left Nick with," she said, with a little laugh. "Nick figures Amby wanted to seem like a big spender, and that's why he said the money in the victim's wallet was what he had paid him." She looked at the closed office door. Her phone beeped, and she picked it up. "The latest clarification is the fact that Gil came to the newspaper twice yesterday."

"Interesting," I said. "He knew he had to clear that up before the employees were interviewed, since they would have seen Gil come back. Did he tell Nick about Gil wanting his rights to the photo returned?"

Janie nodded. "That's why we're taking seriously your idea that there's some clue hidden in it. It might be—just maybe—the outline of a man in the dark. Are you going to be okay if that man is Brennan Adler?"

"Isn't Brennan in the clear now that the question of the authenticity of the letter has been resolved?"

She seemed to consider the question, but wasn't the answer obvious? "If the letter and murder are related, then Brennan Adler is back to being a suspect."

I jumped out of my chair. "What are you saying? The theory was that if the letter was authentic, its incredible value would be his motive. Are you saying proving it's a fraud also implicates him?" I was furious at the unfairness of what was happening. That could not possibly be good for my blood pressure. "It's one thing for me, a private citizen who has nothing at all to do with the investigation, to think about what fits or doesn't fit." She rolled her eyes when I said I was uninvolved, but I went on. "I can truffle-hunt all I want, but *you* can't."

"The letter was missing. It was in his office all along. Those are the facts," she said. "I'm sorry."

"There could be a connection between the forgery of the letter and the Waited4You book theft," I said.

"Then please sit back down," she said with a smile, intending to calm me.

"The thieves stole a few books that were labeled as rare books and threw them away almost immediately. You know that part. Maybe they realized they weren't as old as Roberto had labeled them, so they were no good to them to use for what we just saw. You've heard of something not being worth the paper it was printed on? Well, the paper in this case of Caroline's books is worth a lot." I stopped to take a breath. "The theory has a couple of holes, though."

"Like what?" She put her fist under her chin and waited.

"First, the book Helen Margalit gave me was pretty certainly printed well after 1921, but Roberto didn't leave the others—"

"Maybe he destroyed them?" she asked.

"Or he could have sold them to an unsuspecting buyer, maybe at an antique fair or some kind of market. Anyway, we have no way of knowing for sure if they were also fakes, but I think it's a good guess they were. Next, it was dark and raining when his alarm went off. How could they tell anything about the books once they got outside? Obviously, if they saw they were fakes when they were still inside the store, they would have left them."

"You're saying since those books didn't suit the thief's purpose, he stole the flyleaf from books in the library's collection, since he could be sure they were from the time period he needed?" She leaned back in her chair and looked at the ceiling, thinking hard. "The chief's plan of reopening the robbery investigation is looking really smart now."

"I laughed when I read Chief Harrod's statements in the *Daily News* – yesterday and today. There's no investigation to *reopen* because Roberto wanted to drop it. And we both know the chief fed that to Amby to make himself look good."

Janie raised an eyebrow.

"What does that look mean?" She didn't answer me, so I threw out a guess. "Or family reasons? He doesn't want his son's name brought into this. Go ahead and accuse me of defending Brennan if you want, but I will do anything I can to keep him from being railroaded."

"Then let's get to work." She pulled a memo pad into position. "Your theory about what was behind the theft of the books connects two of our mysteries, but not to the murder," she said. "Nor does it tell us the thief's identity. I need more. I'll admit Brennan Adler doesn't fit in that role. Why would he go there at night in the rain? He had a key, so he could go in anytime."

"So you were seriously thinking he might be the forger? Since only the forger would need the paper. He agrees with me that the letter is a fake. If it was his, wouldn't he say just the opposite? I don't know him well, hardly at all, but *that* really doesn't fit," I said.

"What would fit? What's your read on him?"

"He saw Roberto for what he was. If he was a master forger and needed paper from the 1700s, Waited4You would be the last place he would look. I think he's a decent man, and I think he truly wanted Roberto to live out what time he had left wherever he wanted to . . ."

"Camille?"

"I think I just figured out where Roberto planned to go after he sold the business."

"Where?"

"Nowhere. I mean, here. Marthasville." I told her about the hoarding or overstocking or whatever it was of the processed foods.

"That's the saddest thing I ever heard," she said.

"The police have got to find out who killed him." I still believed that.

She nodded, "And I'll talk to Nick about Brennan. He's never suspected him. It was mostly me. Sorry."

I had no answer for that. Opal and I had promised to look after her, but I didn't have to like everything she did. "I was hoping that the face in the photograph, in the window in the mirror, would tell you. Now that I've said it out loud and had some sleep, I agree it's a long shot." I laughed at myself. "I remembered something else. Chief Harrod reassigned the officer standing by that door before that photo was taken. He told him to help with traffic control. If this was someone leaving— someone who wasn't supposed to be there—"

"Like the killer?" Janie asked.

"No one would have been at that door to see them," I finished.

"Or stop them. Now I have another mystery to add to the list. That's all we need." She rat-tat-tapped the tip of her pen on the notepad.

"Want another?"

"Not really, but you're going to tell me anyway, aren't you?"

I nodded. "As you saw, two library books were missing the flyleaf. What I don't get is why someone would kill Roberto to get the letter back. Why not just create another?"

Was there another letter to George Washington waiting to be discovered?

Chapter
Thirty-Four

In the late afternoon, I worked on a display of quilts. Quilting was the stitching that sewed together the quilt's three layers—the quilt top, the middle layer, which was the batting, and the backing. I wasn't a snob about hand quilting versus machine quilting, but I wanted anything I sold correctly labeled. Each type of quilting had its advantages. Hand-stitched quilts got higher bragging rights for the craftsperson. Machine-quilting stitches were more tightly sewn, and the finished product looked crisp. For quilts that would be washed frequently, like in a nursery or on a child's bed, a machine-quilted choice was much better. Most of my stock looked pedestrian to my eyes. The designs on each of the seven quilts were vintage. I'd seen them all before. Who hadn't? None looked like a collage or told a new story, which I favored. I remembered my mother's words and smiled, thinking how little my preference mattered. Each of the quilts would be perfect for someone's home. My job was done when they were labeled as what they were.

My phone rang, and when I answered it, I heard someone crying and trying to speak. "Janie, is that you?"

"Oh, Camille! Nick is missing. He was on his way back from Charlottesville, and he should have been here an hour ago. He's not answering his phone."

"Janie, remember, he didn't have it with him this morning. Are you sure he's not just tied up in traffic?"

"There was a threat. It was phoned in last night to 911. We didn't know what it meant at the time." She sobbed again. "Do you know what kidnappers do to people in law enforcement?"

An icy serpent slithered through my core. I wanted to tell her not to get ahead of herself, or as Opal would say, *Don't borrow trouble*. The truth was, I was terrified. "What is his father doing to find him?"

"Everything."

"Miss Fairfax, a word!" The chief had come in, and I found the aggressiveness in his voice, if not comforting, then confidence inspiring. Like an anchor. For once I welcomed it.

"Janie, should I come to your office? Janie?" She didn't answer me, nor had she ended the call.

"We found his phone," Chief Harrod barked. "It's at Watergate at Landmark. Isn't that where you live?"

"Yes, it is. I need to tell you something." When she told him about their relationship, she would also be giving him Nick's alibi for Saturday night. Not much of a silver lining, but it was something.

"Later. The state police found his car someplace on I-64, but he's not in it. And the car wasn't involved in an accident, but it has two blown tires."

"He had a flat? That's all?" The relief in Janie's voice almost broke my heart. If what he said had been good news, he, as a police chief and Nick's father, would have been celebrating. It was just news, that was all. I wanted to scream, *Janie, think. Two flat tires.*

She hung up, no doubt to explain why Nick's phone was where it was, sitting accumulating frantic messages. I sat there holding my phone in both hands. Chief Harrod had just foreclosed so many benign scenarios.

Chapter
Thirty-Five

I called Opal, and she agreed to meet me at the courthouse, almost before I finished asking her. Janie had left word at the front desk, and we were escorted up to her office by a young, uniformed officer. He and the entire building were in mourning. The intensity, the pressure, the quiet were all prayers for Nick's safe return, and also a solemn promise for what was in store for whoever was behind this.

Janie was in the meeting room we'd used earlier rather than her office, and she called out to us when we went by the door.

Chief Harrod sat at the end of the table, chair pushed back, thinking, coiled tight. If it was possible, he had aged since this morning. A female officer stood at attention nearby. Mark Zhou, wearing headphones, sat at the conference room table with a landline phone, two cell phones, a compact printer, and a recorder. With the chief present, the command center was wherever he was.

"Thank you both for coming. Still no sign of him." Janie was keeping a tight rein on her emotions. The questions raised by finding Nick's disabled police SUV but not him had finally caught up with her. "We just hung up with Dr. Bishara and Dr. Harold and the head of security at UVA. Gosh, Dr. Bishara looked like she was as upset as I am. They're checking all the security cameras on campus to see if anyone followed him out of the parking lot."

"All the fella cared about was that damn letter," the chief said, staring at a spot on the table.

"The letter might be missing too," Janie said to us. "It wasn't in the car."

Opal sat down in the chair next to Janie and put her arm around her shoulders. "What did the caller say? What did he threaten?"

"She," Chief Harrod corrected. "She said it would be better for everyone involved if the letter, quote, 'stayed disappeared.'"

"If the call was made last night, how do you know she was talking about Nick being kidnapped, or taken hostage, or whatever this is?" I asked. "And the letter wasn't missing last night. It was at UVA. We saw it on-screen this morning,"

"She said she was afraid someone was going to get hurt if the letter came back to Marthasville," Chief Harrod said. "That 'stayed disappeared' part tells me the caller knows something. Maybe it's not related to this . . ." His voice trailed off.

"She knew last night that the letter would be taken and that it's a forgery," I said.

"Camille, we're telling you all this in case you know something that can help." Janie looked at me like I was a horse she had led to water and was now begging to drink. Like I would know what she meant. When I did grasp what she was saying, my head jerked on its own.

"Are you asking about Brennan Adler?" I hadn't been out with the guy, even once, and now we were the Bonnie and

Clyde of Marthasville? Hadn't she said just a few hours ago that she didn't believe he'd killed Roberto? That it didn't fit? Then she'd come pretty darn close to accusing him of forging a letter to George Washington. And now this?

The bottoms of the chief's balled-up fists hit the table. Every other person in the room jumped. "Dammit, when were you going to tell us about him roughing up Gil Harris for you yesterday afternoon?"

I felt like my whole life was in a vise. Brennan felt I was trying to get him convicted, and Janie, Chief Harrod, and Opal thought I was protecting him. It took all I had to keep my eyes on Harrod's red-hot glare instead of turning away,

Chief Harrod looked over at Mark. "Keep his boat under surveillance. Is he on it now?"

"I'll check," the younger man said, already typing.

Janie stretched her arms out to me. "Camille, please. Nick is in more danger with every minute we lose."

If I overthought that, I would be mad as hell. Not to mention disappointed in Janie. "Did you trace the call?" I asked.

"We can't get into that," she said.

"Yes, we can," Chief Harrod said. "This is my son's life we're talking about. It was made near the river, in Founders Park. The south end of the park." That was near Chart House restaurant and also where Opal docked the *Admiral Joshua Barry*. "The phone belongs to a student at Marthasville High. A woman came up to him and his girlfriend with a sob story about losing her phone and asked to borrow his. The school resource officer talked to both of them. They said the woman was bundled up and they didn't know what she looked like. They thought she was old, but when the officer pressed them, he learned this could be anywhere from thirty years old to a hundred."

"So the warning call was made from Marthasville, but his car was found on I-64, somewhere around Charlottesville? What does that say?" I asked.

"Maybe someone followed him," Chief Harrod said, rubbing the top of his head with his knuckles.

Mark pulled his earphones from his face and said, "Chief, Mr. Adler is still at his residence."

I looked at Chief Harrod and then at Janie. "I expected better from both of you."

He threw up his hands. Did he know he was grasping at straws?

"Do you think they're going to demand a ransom for Nick, and for the letter?" Opal asked, before they felt they needed to respond to what I'd said.

"I wish they would hurry up and do it," Janie said.

"Maybe Nick, but not the letter," I said. "It sounds like the caller knows the letter is a fake."

"I agree," Chief Harrod said.

"But does she know that we know it is?" I asked. He raised an eyebrow. "I haven't seen anything in the online *Marthasville Daily News* about the meeting this morning. Have you made it public?"

"No, I was putting that off."

"Then don't. Can you ask Dr. Bishara and Dr. Harold to keep the letter's status to themselves for now?"

He turned to Mark. "On it," the young officer said, somehow dialing and typing at the same time. The printer whirred to warm up.

Janie looked confused.

Opal touched her arm. "This way whoever is behind this will think he's in a very strong negotiating position. Do anything to get the talking started." She looked at the rest of us. "Looks like whoever is behind this is local. Where on I-64 was his car found?"

Before anyone could answer, Mark said, "Chief, 'scuse me, but I have UVA campus security wanting to connect. And this photo just came in." He handed Chief Harrod a piece of paper from the printer.

"It's his car. And a close up of the tires. Two were punctured." The intensity of his look should have burned through the paper and the table it rested on—that's how much power it took him not to break down.

"Punctured? Not slashed?" I stood, my hands on the back of a chair, not able to sit down.

"Yeah, that's what I said." His eyes were still on the same spot.

I leaned over for a closer look. Each photo took up half the page. The top was taken from the front of the SUV, showing the passenger side tires. Maybe the way the car tilted had been the gut punch for Chief Harrod. It was for me. A million years ago Opal and I had laughed about where the old Crown Victorias were today. No one was kidding now.

The lower photo showed the tread of one of the tires and the hole. Then I picked up my handbag from the chair by the wall where I'd left it and found a loupe. "May I?" I asked as I reached for the paper.

"Be my guest." The chief pushed it closer to me. I sat and examined the close-up of the tires on Nick's Ford Interceptor.

"This might be a long shot, but I'd like to get Frenchie on the phone and ask him to look at this," I said.

"On it," Mark said, without waiting for the chief to give him the order. Today, in this room, everything was on the table. He motioned to the screen. "Okay to connect UVA security by video?"

"Go ahead," the chief grumbled.

"The state police are already on," the campus security chief said when he saw us. "Chief Harrod, sorry not to be more help. I had a student that thought he had seen something, but it went nowhere. He thought he saw your son changing his tires in the parking lot." Someone behind him said something, and he turned around. "I've been corrected. He thought he *heard* him changing a tire. Whatever that means."

"It could mean he was using a cordless impact driver to loosen the lug nuts," Opal said. All eyes shifted to her, those in the room and in Charlottesville. "But I don't think so. Few people have two spare tires. That's what you call a pessimist. Camille, you have a different idea, don't you?"

"If someone drilled small holes in the tires, would they look like that?" I pointed to the photo I had returned to the table. "And would the drill make a similar sound?"

"Yeah," several people said at the same time. "I think so."

"On Saturday night, when the investigators were looking at the back door to Waited4You, they saw where someone had tried to get in. I want Frenchie to let us know if the tool that made that mark could have made holes in those tires."

"Tried to get in that night?" Janie asked.

"No, the marks were older. Like maybe a couple of months." I knew this was a stretch.

"You're implying they may have been made by the person or persons who broke in to steal those books?" Chief Harrod was so intensely focused that his eyebrows threatened to impede his vision.

"They don't know whether or not those marks were made on the evening of Labor Day, but it's possible."

"Frenchie is waiting to be added to the call," Mark Zhou said.

"So add him," said the chief. I wasn't going to attribute his rudeness to worry, since it was his default mode. "Frenchie," the chief said, in place of a greeting.

On the screen, we watched as the off-duty crime scene investigator walked through a lobby someplace. When I saw the gigantic bust of George Washington, I knew where he was.

"You're at Mount Vernon?" I asked.

"Yeah, here for the Madeira wine tasting. Mark sent me the photo of Nick's tires, and I just sent a photo of the marks made on the doorknob at the antique store, by the pick, if it was in fact that, to the state police. Mark, do you have it also? If you do, can you put both on the screen?" Was there anything this guy couldn't do?

After a few clicks by Mark, we were looking at two photos on the screen in front of the room. The old lock on my back door was on the left side, and one of Nick's flat tires was enlarged on the right side.

"Frenchie, could those have been made by a drill bit?" I asked. "Like used *with* the drill on his tires, and *without* on the doorknob?"

He whistled through his teeth. "Definitely could have been. I'm not ready to swear the same tool was used on the tire and the door lock, but let's say I'm eighty-five percent sure it's a match."

The officer from the state police was, if anything, a little less ambivalent. "Looks like it could be. I'd be willing to say yes." Then he shrugged and changed the subject. "Chief, you were informed there was no sign of a struggle, right?"

"Yeah."

"We've gone over the car more thoroughly, and still nothing." Another officer came in, and he stood up and went out of camera range. He was back in a few seconds.

Chief Harrod looked at Mark. "This thing secure? Ya know, private?"

"Yes, sir."

"We know from what the car tells us that he got out on his own steam. We saw him. And there was nothing on the perimeter alert. No motion. No motion trail. If he got out of his disabled vehicle to talk to someone, they were parked in front of him."

"Or he could have gotten out to walk?" the campus security chief suggested.

"We think if he was going to do that, he would radio in. He didn't have his cell phone with him." He cleared his throat.

"According to the dogs, he didn't walk far," the state police officer said. "I just got a report from a second team of dogs. He didn't go far from the vehicle——"

As the man spoke, Chief Harrod looked at Janie, then Opal and me, then he interrupted him. "Janie, if you'd rather be at home, I understand. Maybe get some rest?"

"Someone has him." She had seen through his attempt to shield her. "I'm staying here."

Both Mark and Frenchie reassured the chief that officers from various jurisdictions were all looking for his son. "We're going to find him. Between officers and dogs on the ground and helicopters in the air, I know we will."

Before they ended the call, Frenchie asked for the cell phone number of the state police officer.

I thanked him for logging on. "I hope I didn't waste your time. We don't even know when the marks were made on the Waited4You door."

"Ah, it felt good to be doing something, anything. Only wish I could do more. Chief? Janie? Want me to come in?"

"Not yet," Chief Harrod said.

Frenchie spoke to someone we couldn't see. "I gotta go to work."

"I said you didn't have to come to the station. We don't need you yet."

"Chief, I'm not coming to the office. I'm going to see Nick's car." He hung up.

Chapter
Thirty-Six

"Camille, I'm sorry," Janie said, "but exactly what does the damage to your door have to do with finding Nick?"

I'd thought she had followed all that. Her mental strain was taking a toll.

Chief Harrod leaned closer and answered her. "If we've identified a link between what all's happened in Marthasville this week and Nick's disappearance, we've saved ourselves a lot of time. Now we won't be chasing our tails looking at old cases—who's out on bail, family members with grudges, people like that." I thought Janie had sounded annoyed or even petulant, but Chief Harrod's response was gentle, kind, and understanding.

"There's a chance the person or persons who stole the books have Nick?" she asked.

Chief Harrod looked at a new message on his phone and stood. "If we didn't have anything saying Fratelli was murdered by them, we do now." Proof of a connection between all the crimes, the murders, the forged letter, and the book theft gave solace to this father's mind.

Mark began unplugging and packing up his equipment, and the uniformed officer followed Chief Harrod out. "They have a real command center set up for us," Mark said. He looked at the door. "Ms. Benson, your son called the chief. It was very nice of him. You wouldn't know it by, well, you know, but it meant a lot to him."

"Thanks for telling me that," I said. I wondered if he would cancel going to Pepper's concert.

Opal was trying to get my attention. She looked at Janie, then back at me. "We shouldn't leave her alone," she whispered.

"I'll be okay," she said. "I'll go with them."

I placed my hand on her shoulder. "Do you want me to go to your place and take Rizzoli out?"

She looked at me like I hadn't spoken English. Finally, she answered, "That'd be nice."

"I need your house keys," I said.

She pulled them out of her handbag and slid them across the table. Then she, like the chief, zombie-walked out of the room, leaving Opal and me there alone. Opal pulled out her cell phone.

"Who are you calling?"

"I don't know. Maybe David. I'm just doing it to do something. I need to hear his voice."

"Want to go with me to Janie's?"

"I have to get to work. My cell will be with me all night. No, better yet, I'll ask David to come on the cruise tonight. That way he can be sure I don't miss a call from you saying they found Nick." She put her phone away. "Being bad isn't that much fun when something like this is going on. Damn, I hope he's all right."

* * *

On the walk back to Waited4You for my car, I texted Caroline Pak at the library and asked her to keep everything said in this morning's meeting confidential. On the drive home to take Stickley and Morris out, I called Paul and told him everything that had been said in the conference room about Nick's tires and a possible connection to the Labor Day break-in. "Have you said anything about the authenticity of the letter to anyone?"

"I'm still trying to get over the letdown," he said, half joking. "It was the way you told me. No sugarcoating from my own dear mom."

I had said that I was right and he was wrong, and he needed to get over it. "Tough love, my own dear boy."

"Ha-ha. It's going to be worse for Doc Branch. I haven't had a chance to call him, and he should be told right away."

"Good, then don't tell anyone else. And be sure he doesn't tell anyone. The caller knows the letter is a fake, so maybe she's seen it."

"Or maybe she created it," Paul suggested.

"Chief Harrod wants to flush out other people who have inside information on the letter."

"If you mean he intends to round up people who know it's fake though they haven't seen it, you better watch out, *dear* Mom."

* * *

I was happy to see that Janie had remembered to call the Watergate security guard. She let me onto the grounds of what was almost a small village. Rizzoli licked my face all over when I let her out of her crate. I put her leash on, and we went out. We walked around for ten or fifteen minutes, then went back inside to get warm.

I gave her water and poured a scoop of puppy food in her bowl. Then I sat on the floor and watched her eat. She ate a few bites and looked at me, then a few more bites. "I'm still here." Since I didn't have the energy to get up, I checked my phone again for any word from Janie. Nothing at all. I was so far gone that not even music could help me.

When I got up from the floor, Rizzoli thought something exciting was happening and came and pressed her head against the side of my leg. Puppies love routine and this wasn't part of hers, which made her suspicious. When were Mom and Dad coming back, and why was I there? I ran my fingers over the top of her head.

"Good question. Why am I here? I wish I could do something to help. I have an idea." I looked around the kitchen, dining room, and living room for Nick's phone. Then I went to the bedrooms. As self-contained as Janie was, she might not appreciate this intrusion, but if it were Paul who was missing, I would want heaven and earth moved to find him.

I had helped her decorate this one room. The walls were painted peach, and her crumpled bedding was in the oat hue she'd used in the living room. Dramatic black-and-white wall art cut the softness, keeping the room from being cutesy or sweet.

There it was on the bedside table, still plugged into a charger. Rizzoli stood up with her front paws on the bed, wanting a sniff of the phone. I held it out to her and let her smell it to her heart's content.

"Let's go, okay?" Her crate was on the other side of the room, against the wall. The plan was to have her go back in, but now I wasn't so sure. My own phone rang with "I'm Sending Out an S.O.S."

"Any news?" Opal asked.

"I haven't heard anything. You?"

She said she hadn't and asked where I was. "I'm still at Janie's. I have Nick's phone. Guess I'll take it to her."

"Are you bringing the puppy home with you?"

"Yeah. I didn't want to, because it sounds like I'm jinxing the search for him if I admit they aren't coming home any minute."

"What is this going to do to Janie? I can't think about it," Opal said.

"I've never heard you like this! What happened to not borrowing trouble?"

"He's been missing for three hours. Someone who killed one but more likely two people is out there. Only an idiot wouldn't be scared right now."

Chapter Thirty-Seven

A glassed-in porch connected the contemporary ranch house to Ritchie's work studio, which was a warehouse building. Metal panel walls on a concrete pad. There was a gravel parking area in front of it, and I parked my Range Rover behind Ritchie's van. Hadn't there been a sign on its doors advertising Custom Quality the last time I saw it? I opened the sunroof a few inches and told my passenger I wouldn't be long. "Try to take a nap. Please."

Instead of getting out of the car, I leaned back against the headrest. I needed a minute before I went inside and tried to carry on a conversation. I hadn't taken a full breath since Janie's phone call. I was here because the town had forgotten about Roberto Fratelli's murder and even Gil Harris's—and that one had been committed just last night. Hard to believe, but it had been less than twenty-four hours ago. I was at Ritchie's studio to look for his computer desk and chair. It certainly seemed as if he'd stolen Roberto's design, but until I saw the bottom, I wouldn't know.

Did that have anything to do with the murder? If Ritchie had stolen his design, wouldn't that be a motive for Roberto to kill him, not the other way around? I couldn't think anymore.

Or had the mysterious rare-book thief, who was also the forger of the letter, come back? I was having a hard time thinking about anything other than Nick. Where was he? Was he still alive? Was he being tortured?

Rizzoli let out a shrill, loud yelp.

"Whaaaat?" I yelled. It had been a mistake to bring the puppy with me. She was agitated and on my last nerve. Maybe she was car sick, or maybe she had to go out? Both options meant I needed to get her off the beautiful upholstery in my car, and soon.

Her leash was navy blue with little orange 1960s-style television screens dancing along the length of it. I didn't know if this was a reference to the *Rizzoli & Isles* series or to how she looked like Lassie as a puppy. I hooked her up and opened the car door. "I'll help you—"

Young puppies shouldn't jump from heights, since not all their bones have fused, but not being old enough to read a science book, this one leapt across my lap and jumped down to the ground. She headed to Ritchie's van, and I tightened my grip on the leash. Those dew claws might scratch his paint job.

My phone pinged with a text, and when I saw it was from Janie, I jumped for it. The dog pulled in the direction of the van, so we had a tug-of-war, which I won, at least temporarily.

When I tried to swipe my phone to read the important text, she yanked me back. Finally, I stood on the leash to stop that from happening again. "Please, please," I said.

Is Rizzoli ok? No news here.

In this case, no news was bad news.

None? I typed. My screen didn't show that she was typing, so I sent another text. **She's good. See you soon.**

Good? The puppy was acting like a possessed maniac, pulling the leash and whining. I picked up the squirming mass of hair and muscles and walked to a patch of grass. "Spot," I commanded, though that probably wasn't the cue word Janie and Nick used with her. I shortened the leash by wrapping it around my fingers. She pulled once more and then looked at me. To make me happy or to get her way later, she squatted. As soon as she was finished, the whining started up again.

I picked her up and unceremoniously put her back in my car.

Janie had sent another text. **Ransom demand. Richmond field office is coordinating. Email sent from I-64.**

Nick was alive. I leaned my forehead against my car. The hope I felt made Rizzoli slightly easier to handle.

"I'll be right back, and I'll take you to play with Stickley and Morris. I promise! Maybe they can teach you some manners."

* * *

The roll-up warehouse doors were down, but the entry door was unlocked. I heard Ella's voice in the back: "Why tonight? Okay, okaaay."

"Hello? Anyone here?" I called out, not exactly having made an appointment.

"In the back." Ella sounded more breathless than her norm, which was breathy. I also heard one voice over another, like when someone is chipper to cover up a big fight she's just had with her spouse. Or gruff threats to cover fear. Ella's top voice was intended to convey friendly professionalism, but the bottom note was something else altogether. "Coming," she trilled.

This was quite an operation Ritchie and Ella had. I had imagined him working by himself in a small workshop, not an enterprise on this scale. The main part of the warehouse was about the size of half a football field. Aisles were actually grids made by the rows and rows of no-nonsense wooden work tables. Some held power tools—I recognized wood lathes and a sander—while other tables were for bolts of upholstery fabric. Clipboards and pencils sat on still others.

I headed in the direction of the voice. The concrete floor was coated with sawdust and grit and who knew what else. Walking was awkward: Take a step. Slide a little. Repeat. I decided I would let Ella come to me. She appeared from a back room and let the ceiling-to-floor panels of the industrial flap door fall back into place before she walked forward.

"Oh, hello. I thought I heard someone pull up, but then I didn't hear a car." No need to mention I'd been in the parking lot a good five or maybe ten minutes fighting with a demon dog.

When she recognized the visitor as me, she blinked, then narrowed her eyes. The smile on her face held fast, even though she broke eye contact to look at the door again. Despite her efforts, the strips still swayed from when she'd parted them to walk through. She was checking for something, but what? More of the fake Victorian tables? The vertical panels were made of gray vinyl, so it wasn't possible to see into the room, but something was wrong.

"It's because of the kind of car I drive." I laughed. She smiled back, because that was how the game was played. "I'd like to talk to Ritchie about some carpentry work. Or should

I talk to you instead?" Again the smile was batted: me to her, her to me.

"No, you would need to talk to him, but he's not here now." Under the harsh industrial light, she looked about a decade older than Ritchie. Maybe a decade younger than Roberto, but still closer to her first husband's age than I'd thought the other two times I'd seen her.

"Do you know when he'll be back?"

She hesitated. "I'm not sure." This time there was no smile, not so much as an attempt at baring her teeth. She spoke slowly and came to stand in front of me. Too close. "I'll have him call you." With each word, the volume went down and the subtext went up. *Leave*, it read. So I did.

"Thanks." I retraced my last few steps, then turned. "Ella?"

"Wh . . . yes?" Her tone wasn't that far off from how I spoke to Rizzoli. I didn't care. I had come here to compare Ritchie's award-winning design to Roberto's "new workplace furniture for a new millennium" computer desk.

"Could I see the famous desk your husband designed?"

She slowly closed her eyes and pressed her lips into a tight line. "We don't have one here."

"Oh well, that's too bad." I gave a regretful shrug and left, but instead of walking straight back through the warehouse the way I'd come in, I turned toward the side with the adjoining sun-room. A poster with the photos from Ritchie's web page announcing the German Emerging Furniture Designer of the Year Award hung, framed, on the wall next to the door leading to the sun-room. I wanted a better look. *Winner!*—in a six-inch, overexcited font—spanned the top. Other squares of text, drawings, and images bordered the whole collage. Did that mean the actual chair was in that room? Or maybe one image showed the footrest. It was worth a shot. Confusion sapped my energy. I craved order.

Granted, Roberto Fratelli was known as the meanest man in Marthasville, but he was a local *character*. Someone you talked about and said, *Guess what he said to so-and-so?* about. Not someone targeted for killing. What about the thefts and the throwing away of the books? And the letter? Had his string of bad luck started last Labor Day? The three things had to be connected. I felt it in my bones. Why hadn't I believed in myself enough to tell that to the police, or anyone else who would listen?

Couldn't at least one part of this week's hell be tied up with a bow? Yes, it could, if I saw that chair. Then there was how badly I wanted to delay getting back in the car with Rizzoli.

"Uh, Camille? The door's that way!"

*   *   *

Metal shelving lined the wall. Some held tubs of finishing wax and bottles of mineral oil safe for use on cutting boards and wooden salad bowls. The website for Custom Quality also said Ritchie Potts made cutting boards. This was why my feet kept walking when I should have gotten the hell out of there. Three or four were lined up, finished, ready to sell.

I became aware of the symptoms of a rise in adrenaline before my brain told me what I needed to fear. A cutting board. Those heavy objects with a flat surface and mineral oil residue.

Roberto Fratelli's head had been bashed in with a cutting board.

My fingers and lips tingled. My breathing had changed. The design was squares set at forty-five degree angles, making a diamond pattern. *Do something. Get out.* Ella and I were the only people there. *You're fine.* I would walk around her and leave.

When I heard her footsteps on the grit on the concrete floor, I took a deep breath and turned around. Ella had come a couple of steps closer. "I heard about this award," I ad-libbed. "You don't have even one of the chairs here that I can take a look at?"

"No," she said, walking to me.

"Hmm, too bad. It's beautiful." That part wasn't a lie.

I walked back along the makeshift aisle between two rows of tables. She was headed in my direction but one aisle over. We had to pass one another, but I wouldn't be next to her. I exhaled when her phone rang and she moved to the side. She was going to let me leave. Whoever the customer was, I silently thanked him.

Ella swiped the screen and held it up to her ear but didn't say anything. That wasn't a customer on the phone. Her eyes darted to the room at the back of the warehouse, the room she'd come out of. It was what gamblers and bridge players called a *tell*. What was in there? Maybe the computer desk? Why didn't she want me to see it?

I'd come to see the chair, or at least that's what I'd thought a few minutes ago when I was sitting in my car. A lifetime ago. Before I'd breathed the toxic air in this warehouse. There were secrets here. So big a woman could choke on them. That was obvious. But what was being protected? A Marthasville police detective, someone I considered a friend, was missing, and I didn't want to be sitting at home doing nothing.

Ella was walking toward me again. The distance between us was almost nothing now. When we passed, our eyes locked.

I was determined she would look away first, and she did. She walked to the sun-room, and I went to the front door.

I pushed it open but didn't go out. After she walked into the next room, the rubber flap on the bottom edge of the door slowed its closing long enough for me to get to a worktable and crouch down. I took a quick peek and saw Ella sitting behind a desk in the glass-walled room. She opened and closed drawers—or rather slammed them shut.

I stepped out of my slides, tucked them under my arm, and put my handbag over my shoulder. I would see what was in that back room, then I would get the hell out. There had to be a back door, and I was going to take it. I wasn't returning this way.

I took a step. Beautiful silence all the way to the vinyl curtain. The air rustled the panels, and the smell of citrus came at me all aggressive.

I pushed the flaps apart, but at the same moment I was pulled back by my left arm.

"Wait!" Ella yelled.

I looked at her hands, both of them, on my sleeve. I'd seen this movie before. For a split second I thought about getting out of it by saying I wanted to work with Ritchie, passing off his newly made merchandise as antiques the way Roberto had. My eyes met Ella's, and I could have sworn she wanted me to make something up. She would see through any lie I told her, would know something was off, and she wouldn't care.

We both knew it was too late for all that.

The smell was stronger, and for a split second, I wondered if Nick was back there. If he was, what did it mean?

I stopped pulling away and looked at Ella. "This is what you did to stop Roberto from going into Waited4You on Saturday night." She let go of my arm. "Ritchie was inside, and you tried to warn him that Roberto was about to come in."

"Lotta good it did."

I turned from her and parted the vinyl panels. Ritchie Potts stood near the back of the room, behind a worktable covered with blocks of different types of wood. Cherry, walnut, maple, all smoothly carved and in beautiful hues. At the end of the table was his half-completed project, a cutting board with the square blocks, placed at forty-five degrees, making a diagonal or diamond pattern. The way my boxes had been left.

The smell was stronger now. Maybe it just seemed like that because I knew what it was. Pure tung oil had an odor that was unpleasant to some people. It was often mixed half and half with a citrus solvent to cover the scent and also for better absorption. That blend was what I smelled now. It had gotten on Nick's hands from the money in Gil Harris's wallet. Money from Ritchie. Roberto's murder, the theft of the practically worthless books, the defacing of the library's rare books, the forged letter, the killing of the photographer without a moustache—they all touched in a pattern, just like the blocks in the cutting board.

The man in front of me had committed all of them.

There was a row of tables between us, but Ritchie's deep voice carried. It sounded like he was inches from my face, but that could have just been my fear.

"The award-winning computer desk was Roberto's creation, not yours," I said. I was ready for answers. For order. Or I hoped I was. Maybe I wasn't. "You didn't design it."

"That didn't do me much good." Funny, but he didn't look like a man with nothing to lose, though that's what he was. He looked like a man with a plan. "Nobody wanted it. I always thought it was weird, but I entered it in the competition. It won, so somebody must have liked it." He shrugged.

I made a show of looking around. "Looks like it helped you start a successful furniture-making business."

"This is all me. Me and my hands." He held them out, palms up.

"You stole, what, the plans? The prototype?" I asked.

"I found his drawings in some of Ella's old boxes and used those. You know, I can make anything if someone gives me a picture, or even just tells me what they want."

"Was Roberto blackmailing you for claiming it was your design? Is that why I couldn't find record of any payments to you? You made the tables. He sold them and kept the money. Was that how it worked?"

He nodded, but it looked more like he let his head fall forward, then lifted it. "I tried everything to get him off my back. I thought if I gave him something a lot more valuable to sell, we'd be square."

"That was the letter?"

"Yeah," he mumbled. "Instead, he used that against me too."

Had he known Roberto planned to stay in Marthasville and would probably blackmail him forever? Had the second round of blackmail, over the letter, been the deciding factor in his retiring? Or had it been the fact that his health was failing fast?

"If you hadn't moved to Marthasville, would anyone have known it wasn't your design?"

"Probably not. I mean, it was a German award no one outside the business ever heard of."

"Must have been horrible to find him here. Who figured this business out first? You or him?" How long would we go on like that, with me asking questions and him answering? Surely he knew I would call the police as soon as I got out of there.

"Him. He saw that." He pointed in the general direction of the poster on the wall. "Never let me forget it." He blew out a puff of air, deflated but far from defeated. Then he turned around to the worktable behind him. When he turned back again, he had a gun in his hand. A revolver.

"Nothing is going to stop us from getting out of here," he said. He motioned to the door with his head.

I chuckled. "Well, I'm certainly not trying to keep you."

He inhaled and exhaled in exasperation, obviously not appreciating my humor. I hadn't really thought it would be over as easy as that. We'd all come too far for me to get in my car and drive off and let the two of them go to, well, anywhere. "I have to wait a little while longer before we can go," he said.

The guy was crazy, so I didn't bother trying to figure out what that meant.

He snickered and made a face, glaring at me wide-eyed and intentionally bulging his eyes. *I'm not going to carry crafts. Happy holidays and bye for now.* His voice sounded funny, like he was mimicking someone. Roberto? Was that the significance of the protruding eyes? "That's what Fratelli said to me."

No, it wasn't. That was what I'd said to the woman from the makers' co-op on the phone the day he came by for the table. I'd thought I was frightened when I saw the gun, never having been held at gunpoint—ever. That was nothing compared to how I felt watching this guy unravel before my eyes.

There was still a table between us, but that gave me virtually no protection. I needed to think. "Ella, would you come in here?" I called.

Ritchie opened the chamber and checked to be sure the gun was loaded. He seemed pleased when he snapped it closed. I took that as a yes.

"Ella?" Still no sign of her. "Ritchie, so you wrote the letter? I know you stole the books from the store. Was that what they were for? To get paper to write the letter on?"

"Nah, that was just to scare him. I thought I could get him to leave town. How did you know it was me that broke in?"

"The date of your accident proves you were in the area. And what Roberto said to someone made me think he knew whoever did it." I stopped myself from saying Helen's name. I heard Ella's footsteps behind me. He raised the gun and looked through the sight at my face. If I ran now, she might be able to slow me down long enough for her husband to shoot me. Maybe I would go back to the questions and answers. That had worked before. "You tried to give him one big payoff with the letter?" I kept my voice soft. Gentle. I didn't want to die.

"Yeah. He saw through it. I had to keep making the tables plus give him cash. Every month. He said if I didn't, he would let everyone know that I wrote the letter. I would be ruined." He looked at Ella. "And embarrassed. I was fine with the tables because I wasn't the one saying they were mid-nineteenth century. He was. If anyone tried to pin that on me, I'd say I didn't know he was going to claim that. Don't you see? I had to get that letter back. What if he took it with him and I had to keep paying? That night I looked everywhere for the letter. I went through every box. I even looked in the ceiling."

He lowered the gun to the table but kept it in his hand, like it was getting heavy. He inhaled and then exhaled. It looked to me like this nightmare was winding down. It was about to be over, one way or the other.

"How did you know you were in the photograph Gil Harris took Saturday night?" I prayed he wouldn't point the gun at me again. I had come up with a plan.

"I looked right at the kid when he took it. All those cops in there and they never saw me. Then when I saw the morning paper and only you were in the photo, I thought everything was okay. Then Ella told me the original of it was out there somewhere. She made up something to talk to Amby Jones. He used to know her family. We wanted to know if he gave it to the cops. It didn't seem like he had. Then that punk tried to blackmail me! How did you know about that?"

I couldn't think of a good lie, because I was trying to imagine the emaciated boy-man making demands on this dumb-as-a-post pretty boy. "He really tried to blackmail you?"

"Yeah, he asked if I wanted to buy the photograph." That was what Gil did for a living. Did he even know what he had photographed?

Ritchie started talking again. "I gave him the money to get rid of him, but when he said he wanted more, I lost it. I wasn't going through that again. I snapped his scrawny neck."

Involuntarily, I gulped. I had to get out of there. I only knew of one way to do that. He raised the gun again and looked at me. His head dropped to the side for a beat, like *Sorry I gotta do this. No hard feelings.*

I had one final chance to get Ella to stand near her husband if I was going to get out of there alive. He cocked the gun. "Did you kill Roberto because he wouldn't give you the letter, or because of the photograph?"

"What photograph are you talking about? He was dead before Gil took it." Ella's voice shook. She came forward, but she stopped next to me, not Ritchie.

"Not that one." *Silly.* "I have it in my handbag." I looked at Ritchie, not her. "You'll want to see this. Sorry, but it implicates both of you." I kept my eyes on her husband, as if to say I would only deal with him.

"What photo?" she screeched. With every minute that passed, Ritchie was getting colder, more resigned to doing what he felt he needed to do, but Ella sounded like she was close to hysterics.

I rummaged in my satchel. "Ritchie, here it is." That brought her around the table to stand by her husband. She scurried on the gritty floor to get a look at what I handed him.

I walked to the end of the table and held out what was actually Opal's tour schedule brochure to him with my left hand. They studied it, hunched over. While they were looking down, I overturned the five-gallon can of tung oil. I tipped it and then shoved it hard to flood the floor more quickly. I wanted it under their feet before they had time to run away from its flow.

Then I ran for my life. On my way out of the room I grabbed a can of upholstery tacks off a shelf and tossed them in their direction, for good measure. Even if none of the tiny nails hit them, they might land in the oil.

In seconds the two were sliding and falling on the oil and the sharp tacks. Both Ella and Ritchie shouted, screamed, cussed, and made threats as I ran back through the warehouse. The gun went off, but I didn't slow down. A lost lonely bullet pinged off a metal wall somewhere. I was still alive.

I pushed the door open and didn't slow down until I got to my car. In one move I opened my car door, and when my foot was on the brake, ready for me to press the start button, I placed a call.

"911. What's your emergency?"

Before I could close the door behind me and start the engine, Rizzoli soared across my lap and out of the car. I jumped out and ran after her. "You idiot mangy mutt. Ridiculous excuse for a dog. Get back in here. I will leave you! I swear I will, and if he shoots you dead with that gun, I'll laugh my ass off."

"What is your emergency?"

I tossed the phone onto the passenger seat and jumped out and ran for the dog, leaving the door open so we could hurry back in. The puppy stood with her front paws on the back bumper of Ritchie's van and barked even louder. I reached for her, and she snarled, threatening to bite.

"Dammit, get in the car. You're not worthy of the title *dog*."

"Camille?" A voice, weak but steady, called to me from the van.

Chapter
Thirty-Eight

"Nick!" I screamed.

"Don't open the door. It'll decapitate me. The wire wrapped around my neck is tied to the door handle."

"I have to get you out of there, and we have to get out of here! Ritchie has a gun."

"Leave me here. Call 911 when you are safe." His words were measured. Almost staccato.

I could have done that, but instead I tried the driver's side door. It was open, and I jumped in and looked in the back. Nick's arms were tied behind his back. A line of steel cable ran from the side of the van, wrapped three-sixty around his neck, and ended at the rear door handle. A trickle of blood had dried in a fold of skin on his neck.

Mm, mm. Rizzoli whimpered.

"Hurry up and get in."

The van reeked of the same citrus smell. It had a keyless ignition, which wasn't really keyless, since the keys or fob or something had to be nearby for the car to start. I scooted up in the seat to reach the brake pedal. I prayed Ritchie was one of those people who kept their keys in an ashtray or some niche. I pushed the engine start button.

Nothing.

I heard Nick fidgeting on the van floor.

"Please, please don't move," I begged. "You'll bleed more."

I jabbed the ignition again and again, like that might get me a different outcome. It did not. I stopped when I heard the door of the warehouse burst open. Ritchie was in front, still holding the gun, only now with both hands. Ella came out after her husband and limped to his side. I reached over to the buttons by my side and locked the doors.

"Get out of the van!" he ordered.

I shook my head.

"Yes, you will. Ella, take this." Ritchie handed her the gun. "Just a little longer," he told her.

Maybe she hadn't wanted it, maybe it had oil on it. He pressed it to her hand. It was limp, so he had to press the gun against her palm, then take her other hand and put it on the other side.

Whatever the reason for the delay was, it gave me time to notice the red-and-black tool bag on the floorboard. I opened it up and glanced at my pursuers one more time before I rummaged through the jumble of tools, searching for something, anything, to cut the wire that made up Nick's lasso. I raised my head and looked out the window again. Ella was there, but where had Ritchie gone?

Rizzoli was quiet and out of my way. She was afraid of me, and for good reason. I was a dog person, but I'd be damned if that man was going to die because of an excited and untrained puppy.

Ouch. My hand rubbed against something sharp. It was a pair of wire cutters. A steel tape measure was wedged inside the handles. The end of one handle was stuck inside a loop to some other tool. It took both of my shaking hands to extricate it.

I twisted to get one of my arms and then the other through the space between the two front seats.

I saw Ritchie through the rear window. He tried to open the van's back doors. When he figured out it was locked, he hit the door with the meaty edge of his fist. "Aagh," he yelled out as he pushed, then pulled the van door latch, making us sway. I was on my knees in the front seat, reaching back, and the motion of the van made me rock.

"No." The word escaped from somewhere in my throat when I saw the rivulet of blood from Nick's neck drip onto the floor of the van.

Suddenly Ritchie stopped and glared in the window, snorting like a racehorse. He had become an animal. He had killed two people and was ready to kill again. The ransom he'd been willing to wait for earlier seemed to be forgotten. His eyes widened, and he slapped his khakis and then his shirt pockets. He was searching for his car key. If the fob was on him, would the car start with him the length of the van away? If I tried and the car started, I could drive away from him. If it didn't work, I'd have wasted precious seconds.

Finally, I made contact with the wire and squeezed and squeezed. I could tell from how Nick's shoulders moved that he was still working to free his hands. His neck bled in a second spot, and the look on his face showed the pain the sawing wire caused. Thankfully the dog was still and quiet.

Ritchie pulled the key out of his pocket and aimed it at the door, grinning like a kid holding a lightsaber. I used both hands and all my strength to cut through the cable. The doors around the van unlocked with four pops. The handles of the back door turned the same second that the wire snapped apart. Nick kicked both doors open, and one of them knocked Ritchie to the ground as it flew back. His ankles were bound, but not his hands. He torqued up and out of the van, on top of Ritchie. He pounded him with his fist. Once. Twice. Both connected. Suddenly, Ritchie came to life and fought back. He rolled Nick over in the gravel. He might not have been able to get the upper hand the way he did if Nick's ankles hadn't been strapped together. He got one punch in that was painful to watch.

"Stop or lose an ear," I said. I had the lobe of his ear in the grip of the wire cutter.

Ritchie froze. "Don't," he said. How vain was this guy?

I kept the side of the wire cutters pressed against Ritchie's neck, his earlobe between the blades, until Nick rolled out from under him and tried to get up.

"Get down on the ground, hands behind your back," Nick told him. He still wasn't able to stand, but he sat up.

Ritchie lowered himself like he was in the middle of doing his morning push-ups. He moved slowly because the wire cutters and I were still there. I backed away, half expecting Ritchie to *do* something. After all, neither his feet nor his hands were tied. Was he waiting for Ella to save him with the gun?

I reached down and cut through the vinyl tape on Nick's legs and helped him stand. Though Ritchie was on the ground, he didn't put his hands behind his back. He rested them under his cheek. His eyes flitted around. He didn't find what he was looking for.

"Ritchie . . . what's his last name?" Nick asked me.

"Potts," I said, over the sirens drawing near us, beautiful music emanating from who knew how many police cars.

"I'm arresting you for . . . well, everything." Nick was calming down, coming down from his high, but I wasn't. Ella was still out there with the gun. I looked over at the warehouse door. She was nowhere to be found.

Chapter
Thirty-Nine

Friday

"Ella Coleman couldn't make a deal fast enough. She's going to testify against her husband." Nick smiled ear to ear.

Janie, Nick, Paul, Pepper, and I sat on the lower deck of Opal's boat. Stickley and Morris had fallen hard for Pepper, and it looked like Paul had too. The two dogs sat at her feet. I wasn't too terribly jealous. I knew they would be coming home with me.

Rizzoli hadn't been invited. Opal had been at the helm with David but came to the stern to sit with us.

Nick and Janie had told Paul, who'd texted me, that Ella was arrested before she got on the Beltway. She denied everything at first, as Ritchie had when he was arrested. I'd texted back, asking if her hands smelled like oranges. That was the first brick that fell in their denial of everything Ritchie had said when he'd thought I wouldn't live to tell anyone. Ella's hands smelled like the gun she'd tossed into the shrubbery. Confession had not been good for either of their souls.

The waves lapped on the sides of the boat and the *Admiral Joshua Barry* jostled side to side. Masts on the sailboats around us clanged as the boats rocked. One of the large tour boats, or maybe even the water taxi to National Harbor, had sailed past. I hadn't noticed it go by. A lone biker rode along the pier in the direction of the marina. I watched until I could no longer see the bike's flashing back light.

"Ready to set sail?" David called out.

"Aye, aye," Opal answered, holding up a margarita.

We weren't really sailing—we were cruising—but why split hairs? The Potomac River ran from West Virginia to the Chesapeake Bay. Being on it made me feel like a part of something larger than myself. George Washington was born along that river. History had always made me feel as if the best was yet to come. Looking at Paul with his arm over Pepper's shoulder made me feel like a part of the future. They'd cleared up their miscommunication, and it looked like smooth sailing ahead for them.

Nick took a call but held out his phone to me right after he answered it. "It's Dad. He wants to talk to you."

"Let me guess, he wants a word," I said.

"Huh?" The absolute incomprehension on Nick's face cracked us all up.

"You say that too. All the time," Janie said, swatting his leg.

"I'm sure he wants to thank you again for saving his only son's life," Opal said. She put her hand on her heart and smiled up at the night sky.

I took the phone. What was this *again* business? He hadn't thanked me the first time. I'd seen him when he pulled up at the scene, and he had nodded at me. Maybe that was the gratitude she meant. Stomping up to his son and the man on the ground, he'd looked like a bulldog—and like I wasn't his favorite toy.

"A word, Ms. Benson." *Of course, a word.* "You may know that since you did not hang up on your call to the emergency operator, we followed and recorded everything that was said."

"Of course." The whole town knew the story. Or at least everyone who read the *Marthasville Daily News* knew. The phone call had provided a way to locate us, and my mention of a gun had started the response. When they heard me scream Nick's name, the full-scale rollout began.

"I was listening to the tape of the 911 call again to be sure I hadn't missed anything. At one or two points, you express your affection for Janie and my son's dog in rather strong language. Now, I want you to know that I don't intend to mention to them how much you care about their dog. I wouldn't want them to think you were covetous of the little fella."

"Rizzoli?" I offered, since he obviously didn't know the name of his grand-dog.

"Whatever. All you must do for our agreement to continue is to run your little antique store and not try to solve any more crimes. Do we understand one another?"

I smiled at the others and returned the phone to Nick. Of course, the recording might be played in court. Oh well, I had no intention of trying to solve a murder ever again. What were the odds there would ever be another murder to solve? This was Marthasville, and other than the two this week, we didn't do murder. Then there was the reality that I had a business to run, with no free time for crime solving. But the main reason I wouldn't be involved in another murder was that I didn't want to live in an ugly world.

"That was it, wasn't it?" Opal asked. "He wanted to tell you how indebted he is."

"He was his usual gracious self," I lied.

"That was so nice of him," Pepper agreed.

Janie leaned forward. "Want to hear some gossip?"

"From you? I want to know what you did with the real Janie!" I said.

"Huh?"

"Babe, she has you nailed," Nick said.

"Anyway," Janie said, rolling her eyes at us, "Ella called Amby Jones and asked for his help when she was trying to make her getaway."

"Then he called Dad," Nick added.

"Were there other calls between the two of them?" I asked.

"Yeah, one earlier the same day. He called her and asked her to lunch," Nick answered. "What made you suspect that there was?"

"Just a guess." I looked out at the night and smiled to myself. One question had bothered me all day: How had Ritchie known Nick was going to Charlottesville? Now I had the answer. Dr. Harold, disgruntled and disappointed, was the person from UVA who, in Amby's words, had him on speed dial. He'd told the newspaper editor that Nick was coming to get the letter, and Amby had told Ella to try to get her to go to lunch with him. I decided to keep all that to myself. Oh, of course I would tell Opal. I had put Amby through enough, and he'd done the right thing in the end by calling Chief Harrod. That had to count for something. At least, it did with me. And Opal and I had made him a promise that his wife wouldn't find out about his flirtation with Ella from us.

"Camille, are you okay with Ella making a plea deal?" Janie asked.

I mentally rejoined the group and shrugged. "She'll serve some time. Just not as much as Ritchie." Paul had told me Ritchie was trying to make a deal too.

Nick looked down, and Janie squeezed her eyes shut. The terror of his kidnapping was too fresh to talk about. He looked at the river to cleanse his mind and took a drink of his margarita. "According to her, she wanted to keep Roberto from going in because Ritchie was waiting inside to kill him. She was trying to save his life. Do you think that's true?"

"I don't think Ritchie went in with the intention of killing him. He didn't have a weapon on him. He must have taken the cutting board from the kitchen out of spite." Since it wasn't merch, it hadn't been inventoried, and I hadn't known it was missing. "I think he was looking for the letter to stop Roberto's second round of blackmail. It's more likely that Ella was trying to warn Ritchie so he wouldn't get caught rather than trying to save Roberto. I think he demanded the letter, but since it wasn't there any longer, Roberto couldn't give it to him. Ritchie had the cutting board in his hand, so that's what he hit him with." In my imagination, I saw the two men standing there in the semidarkness. Talking. Arguing. Then the violence.

Opal leaned out and gulped the night air. "Yeah, Roberto didn't have the letter because Brennan had taken it—trying to help you. I wonder how he feels about that now?"

I didn't want to go there, so I changed the subject. "She had to make that scene outside the store. Remember, Ritchie's phone was at home that night."

"And it made us think he was there too," Nick said. "I was sloppy." He wore a brown polo shirt under an olive-green wool sweater, and occasionally he pulled the collar away from his neck.

"Well, the way they alibied each other was another reason they weren't suspects," I reassured him. "Anyway, she had to try to keep Roberto from going in because she couldn't call Ritchie to tell him to get out of Waited4You." I looked out over the water to the lights on the Woodrow Wilson Bridge, the only one in the country to go through three state-level jurisdictions—Virginia, Maryland, and the District of Columbia. "Maybe she was trying to save my life yesterday," I said. "She didn't need to buy Ritchie time at the warehouse. She didn't fire the gun, and it seemed she didn't want to hold it for him." I had made a statement covering all of this.

Janie motioned to Nick with her thumb. "The fight between them could have had a very different outcome if she had decided to use the firearm." *Different outcome* was a stand-in phrase, because no one wanted to say that Nick could have been killed, though everyone was thinking exactly that.

"Nah, Camille would have cut off her ear if she'd tried." Nick squeezed her shoulders.

"Don't laugh. That's what I did to Ritchie van Gogh," I said.

Opal tried to mimic protecting her ears from me with her hands, but her heart wasn't in it.

Everyone was quiet, and we enjoyed being on the water. Or we maybe we enjoyed just being. Then Paul got up and came over to hug me, despite being jostled by the motion of the boat. Pepper was next. Then each of the others came over.

Nick said, "I think Ella was the one who called in that tip to Barrett Library."

"Ritchie told me her mother had been a librarian in Marthasville," I said. It felt right that books were important to Ella, because they had been a part of her mother's life. "Nick, where is the letter now?"

"The police found it in the van. It was in the glove compartment. It'll be returned to the library when the trials are over."

"I wonder what Ella and Ritchie thought when they saw all those articles in the *Daily News* about it and its possible worth," Paul said with a chuckle.

"They probably had a good laugh at Amby's expense," Opal said, after taking a swig of her margarita.

"They're not laughing now," Nick said.

"You're both safe. That's what counts," Paul added.

Opal raised her glass. "To Handsy Amby!"

"What's this?" David asked, suddenly all ears.

Opal stood and walked to the wheel at the bow of the boat to kiss her husband. "You know the effect The Car has on men! Drives 'em wild."

"Handsy Amby!" we toasted.

"Were you all waiting to find something redeeming about Roberto Fratelli?" I asked the group. "I was. All week. I only gave up hoping for some good quality yesterday when I figured out the blackmail scheme. He really was as bad as everyone thought. I was such an idiot."

"Oh no, you weren't," Opal said. "As bad as he was, you never gave up trying to get justice for his murder. That deserves another toast."

We motored past boats docked at the City Marina. The biker I'd seen minutes before was there. Paul caught me watching as the man lifted his bike and put it on board. "That's Brennan Adler's boat."

Nick whistled. "Beneteau, huh? Nice."

"How big is it?" Pepper asked.

"Has to be less than forty feet to be moored here," Paul told her.

"Big enough to *cruise the ditch*," Nick said. "That's what they call the Intercoastal Waterway."

I looked at Janie. I had another question, but I didn't know if I could trust myself to speak. "Why did you suspect him? Really."

She shook her head. "I'm embarrassed to say. It was unprofessional."

Opal leaned toward her. "I get it. You knew Nick wasn't guilty, so it made him a more likely suspect?"

Janie shook her head. "It had nothing to do with Nick. Or at least I don't think it did."

"Well, how do ya like that?" he said, pulling her closer and kissing her temple.

"It's because no one is good enough for Camille or Opal."

David leaned out of the cockpit. "Yeah! How do ya like that!"

"Except you, David," Janie called up to him. "I don't want anyone to steal Camille away."

"Sweetie, that's not going to happen." I looked at the lights around us. "You said he could leave as soon as the case was solved, and I guess he took that literally. I'm surprised he didn't leave today."

"He's leaving tomorrow morning," she said.

I caught David looking back and studying my face when that bit of news hit me. "This calls for a Melville quote," he said.

"Nothing calls for that!" Opal said.

"This does."

"Then I need another drink." Opal got up and went to the cooler.

He cleared his throat and acted like he was offended. "*In the cold courts of justice the dull head demands oaths, and holy writ proofs; but in the warm halls of the heart one single, untestified memory's spark shall suffice to enkindle such a blaze of evidence, that all the corners of conviction are as suddenly lighted up as a midnight city by a burning building, which on every side whirls its reddened brands.*"

"Perfect," I said.

Chapter Forty

Saturday

Opal stomped the spider with the heel of her boot. "I hate spiders. With maybe one exception. Isn't there one kind that has sex and then dies?"

"No, that's my son." I took Pepper's arm. "Wait, I shouldn't say that in front of you." She was laughing too hard to care. We were celebrating her first day of work at Waited4You by starting the day with breakfast together.

Waited4You would have a soft opening on Monday, Tuesday, and Wednesday. The real opening day would be Black Friday. The store looked beautiful and inviting, and I was so ready to see how customers would respond to my modern antiques theme.

We were at the Royals Restaurant for the good food—and because they had their own parking lot. Trucks delivering fruits and vegetables to restaurants in Old Town made their deliveries at this time of the morning, and free spaces for street parking were hard to come by. The original restaurant on North Royal Street had been torn down in 1964, and this location at North

St. Asaph Street and Madison Street had served delish dishes since 1965. The clanging of cargo doors and the blocked lanes because of double-parked vehicles felt like blessed normalcy for Marthasville, and that extended to Waited4You. We walked through the lot on the side of the restaurant.

"Do I need to bring anything besides rolls and pumpkin pie?" Pepper asked.

"That's all." This year I was hosting Thanksgiving for Opal, David, Pepper, and Paul.

"You have me down for creamed corn and broccoli casserole, right?" Opal asked.

"Yep. I invited Caroline Pak. Did you know she's married and has a son? She's cooking their Thanksgiving dinner, but they may stop by for dessert. Wouldn't that be nice?" They agreed it would. I looked around to be sure no one was listening. "Pepper, did Amby Jones talk to Gil's parents?"

She nodded. "I didn't even have to use the password."

"What password?" I asked. That was news to me.

"Opal told me to say *brunch* if Amby put up a fuss. Paul and I listened in when he called them. He did very well. He knew exactly what parts to leave out."

"That does seem to be Handsy's particular gift, doesn't it?" Opal announced.

Pepper whispered, "He didn't mention that their son tried to blackmail someone. Or that he wanted to sell the photograph to the murderer instead of turning it over to the police to help solve the case."

"That will probably come out during Ritchie's trial, if he doesn't plead guilty." Ritchie had killed two people and abducted a police detective. I shook my head at the enormity of what he had done. "Those crimes dwarf what their son did."

"Was Nick's attempted murder added to Ritchie's charges?" Opal asked.

"No, but defacing the two rare books was. Caroline Pak got the library board to write a letter to Janie."

"You don't want to mess with her," Opal said.

We stopped to finish our conversation outside the crowded restaurant. "The Harrises were offered front-row seats to tonight's fireworks show for Common Good for the Commonwealth's kickoff, but they're not staying for it," Pepper said. "Since their son's body has been released, they're going to follow it back home to Suffolk later this morning. Paul and Dr. Branch are going to stand with them when his coffin is put in the hearse. I'm sure that will mean a lot to them." The softness in her voice when she said my son's name meant a lot to me.

Opal opened the restaurant door and gasped. "Camille, there he is. There's Brennan Adler. Is he staring at us?" If he hadn't seen us before, he did now, because she was motioning excitedly. He wore khakis and a navy sailing jacket and carried a to-go bag. "He's headed our way," she stage-whispered.

"He has to if he wants to get out of the restaurant." I elbowed her. "Stop it."

"Hmm? What? I didn't say anything."

"I know that song you're humming," I whispered, because he was getting closer.

"Louder. I can't tell what it is," Pepper said.

"It's 'Baby, I Love Your Way' by Peter Frampton. And it's not funny."

When Brennan got to the door, we stumbled around and laughed as we tried to figure out who should step to the side and who should go through the double glass doors first.

Manners told Brennan to let us come in first, but the same rules had him holding the door open, which was hard for him to do holding his food and coffee. Finally, he was outside and we were on our way in.

"Camille?"

The others got us a table, and I went back outside to talk to him. "I thought you had left."

"I wouldn't leave without saying good-bye." He waited, I guess for my reaction. I didn't know what to say to that, so I just looked off into the distance. "Good work getting to the bottom of the murders. Chief Harrod told me what happened at that house on Thursday."

"He gave *me* credit?"

"Yes, he did. He also told me he was friends with your mother." What an odd way to phrase that. A friend of my "mother" rather than my "parents."

"He's not my father, if that's what you're implying."

"Ha!" He yelled out one of his no-holds-barred laughs. "That's not what I was saying. He didn't have words to express his gratitude for you saving his son's life. He ended up saying you remind him of your mother."

"Thank you for telling me that."

Brennan looked down at his deck shoes. "This morning's edition of the *Daily News* finally walked back their speculation on the validity of the letter. The article made a lot of sense. It got the facts right. Did you write it for Amby Jones?"

"Marthasville's local historian, Caroline Pak, helped one of his staff writers with it. All I did was encourage him to run something, anything, to get the correct information out there. They stopped running their hourly updates, with their wishful thinking, but that didn't go far enough. I don't call stopping spreading rumors a correction."

He looked at me, and I looked around. There was nothing else to say.

"I, uh, I'm sorry things didn't work out. Uh, you know," he said.

I took a deep breath. "What are you apologizing for?" I would count to ten. *One, two, three . . . too late.* "Are you apologizing for not giving me the great honor of having dinner with you? I'm sorry too. I'm sorry you have the maturity level of a toddler. I'm sorry you think absolutely everything is about you."

"Uh . . . uh . . ." he stuttered. He tried to motion with his hands, but he held the bag with his breakfast and his coffee thermos.

"If you're about to say I have a trust issue, then don't. It smacks of gaslighting. You had the letter in your office."

"You are mad at me? You reported me to the police."

"I had no choice but to tell the police the letter was there. And if there had been options, I would have done exactly what I did! If you want an Ella, I hear she'll be single again soon."

"Ella? What?" he sputtered.

"I have no regrets!" I said.

"I have nothing but regrets."

He stared at me for a moment before, well, I went inside . . . and he went away.

But not for long.

Acknowledgments

I finished my first pass edits on *Dead Men Don't Decorate* about ten minutes ago. Now I'm topping off my caffeine buzz with more iced tea and trying to get my head around just how many people I have to thank for their help with this book. Wow!

I'll start with my agent and friend, Dawn Dowdle of Blue Ridge Literary Agency. The best agent on the planet—no, wait, in the universe. The folks at Crooked Lane Books are amazing, professional, and just downright nice. I'm talking about you, Tara Gavin, Rebecca Nelson, Madeline Rathle, and Melissa Rechter. Thank you!

A couple of real-life experts helped me with research and then found themselves in the book. One is author and retired crime scene supervisor John L. French. Thanks! And the other is Patricia Walker, local history/special collections branch manager at the Alexandria Library. Tricia taught me about red rot and other interesting facts about rare, old books that I loved including in the manuscript. I gave her the name of Alexandria's Burke Branch manager, Caroline Pak. The moral of the story is if you're friends with an author and you have a great name, watch out. We are kleptomaniacs and we will steal your name.

Speaking of friends, I'm a member of the Royal Writers Secret Society. We meet at the Royal Restaurant, and there's absolutely nothing secret about us. If you see us at a book fair or conference, please do come up and introduce yourself. (Just remember the caveat above.)

I hope you enjoyed the book,
Cordy Abbott